QUENTIN & Toi

A Legendary Hood Tale

A NOVEL BY

MOLLYSHA JOHNSON

Royalty Publishing House is now accepting manuscripts from aspiring or experienced urban romance authors!

WHAT MAY PLACE YOU ABOVE THE REST:

Heroes who are the ultimate book bae: strong-willed, maybe a little rough around the edges but willing to risk it all for the woman he loves.

Heroines who are the ultimate match: the girl next door type, not perfect - has her faults but is still a decent person. One who is willing to risk it all for the man she loves.

The rest is up to you! Just be creative, think out of the box, keep it sexy and intriguing!

If you'd like to join the Royal family, send us the first 15K words (60 pages) of your completed manuscript to submissions@royaltypublish-inghouse.com

SYNOPSIS

For La'Toia "Toi" Henderson, money is the motive. With a family to take care of, she turned to setting up men and taking what she wanted by any means necessary. After meeting Quentin "Legend" Santana, Toi begins to question the hustle that's allowed her to make sure her family never struggles.

Quentin Santana is a street king who's used to having any and everything he wants. When he meets Toi, he sees a strong young woman unselfishly doing what she needs to for her family and their connection is immediate.

Family drama and secrets have Toi wondering if she can really handle a legend's love.

NOTE FROM THE AUTHOR

To everybody that supported my first series *Let a Real Boss Treat You Right*, thank you. I appreciate it. I hope you guys continue to enjoy and support me with my future projects. For any questions or concerns about me, feel free to hit me up on social media.

La'Toia "Toi" Henderson

I pulled my black sweatshirt over my head before putting on the pair of black sweat pants that were on the floor. I had just taken off a red, skin tight dress that I wore when this Rick Ross look alike picked me up. Once I finished changing, I put my hair into a low bun and added a black skully on my head. I put on a pair of white gloves then walked over to the bed, so I could get a closer look. I screwed my face up before turning my attention to my best friend and partner in crime Mickey. Something wasn't sitting right with me about the way this man looked, and it was freaking me out.

"Mickey," I called her name, but she didn't answer because she was too busy trying to open his safe. "Mickey." When she didn't answer me the second time, I grabbed a pillow off the bed and threw it at her. When the pillow hit her head, she looked at me with an annoyed expression on her face.

"I know you hear me Michelle." I walked over to where she was, so I wouldn't have to yell across the room and wake that nigga up.

"First of all, calm down with saying my damn name! Fuck is wrong with you and what do you want?" she whispered.

"I think that nigga is dead. Look at him, his chest isn't moving or anything. I think I gave him too much of that mystery powder."

"It's not mystery powder, it's just crushed up sleeping pills."

4

"What? Giving somebody too many sleeping pills will put them into an eternal sleep. Are you stupid?"

"I'm far from stupid, but you're kind of close to it. I gave you two crushed pills. We've been doing this for a year and you always act scary. Get it together."

"This nigga looks dead to me."

"You're getting on my nerves. He's not dead he's just asleep and I want to get in this damn safe before his fat ass wakes up."

I looked at the dark skinned, fat nigga that was lying on the bed in just his draws. I almost wanted to throw up at the sight of his big ass belly poking out. I didn't have to have sex with him, but just the thought of him touching me was disgusting.

"What the fuck is taking you so long?"

"If you would shut up, I could get this done."

I rolled my eyes but stayed quiet, so she could finish working on the safe.

"That's what I thought," she smirked at me before turning around and giving her complete attention to the safe.

Looking at her, you would never think she was into this type of shit. Mickey is a five-foot-nine, light honey colored beauty. Her slim but curvy body was an attention grabber, but it was her choice of wardrobe, hairstyles, and makeup that really made her stand out.

Mickey was in no way, shape, or form afraid of experimenting with unusual colors. She would sport blonde hair, gold lipstick and a green jumpsuit on Monday, but by Friday she'd switch it up to black hair, blue lipstick, and a matching one-piece. She pulled it off though, every nigga that meets her wants to lock her down, but she's not for that shit. She's all about her money and she doesn't plan to stop getting it any time soon.

"Whatever inspector gadget."

"Inspector gadget these nuts bitch," she said back making me chuckle. It was another two minutes before this bitch finally made another noise. "I got it, I told you just be easy sometimes." She pulled the door open and my mouth dropped when I saw all the money that was in there.

"Holy shit! Damn you were right!"

"When am I not right? This must be at least fifty thousand Toi. Do you know how set we'll be after this shit?"

I wanted to jump up and down and scream at the top of my lungs, but that nigga was still sleep and I didn't want to wake his ass up.

This was the best lick we've hit so far. Usually we would end up with a little over five thousand dollars each after a job, if that. It sounded like a lot of money, but that shit went straight on bills, so it was gone before long anyway. The quicker the money went, the more we had to do this robbing shit.

About a year ago, Mickey came to me telling me how this nigga that was trying to spit game at her left his safe open one night when she was there. That night she didn't take anything, but the next time she went she hit that nigga up for three stacks. That's when she got the bright idea to start using a man's thirst and weakness for pussy against them. I was nervous as hell, but the shit was lucrative and with the money we got tonight, we wouldn't have to do this shit for a good couple of months.

"I know we're excited as fuck but let's get this shit and get the hell out of here before one of his boys pops over here or something."

"You're right, let's go."

We bagged up all the money and made sure we had everything including his car keys before finally leaving out of the house. Mickey hopped in his all black Mercedes S500 while I got in the black infinity truck we used for the night. I waited for her to pull out, then I followed right behind her all the way to Vin's chop shop.

Vin was somebody we knew from around my block. Mickey and I work with him a lot, anytime we target a nigga we take one of his cars and sell that shit to Vin. That's more money in our pocket.

"Damn who y'all hit this time?" Vin asked us when we hopped out of the cars and walked up to him.

"Don't worry your handsome little face about that. Just give us the money so we can go," Mickey told him.

"Alright ma, it's best to keep me out of it anyway. I'll give y'all fifteen stacks."

"Each?"

"Each? Come on now Mick, you're stretching it now."

"I look stupid to you Vin? That's a brand-new Benz, damn near worth a hundred grand. I'm trying to give it to you for thirty. What the fuck I look like taking less than that for it?" Mickey snapped at him. "Don't play with me, I can take this right down to those white boys and get way more for it easy, I'm trying to help you out."

Vin shook his head, then sucked his teeth. "Fine, I'll give y'all fifteen each. You're a tough ass bitch Mick."

"I know this, don't forget it either. Just get my money." He went to his office, then came out a few minutes later with two black book bags.

"It's all there. Get the fuck outta here man." We both grabbed a book bag from him with smiles on our faces.

"Thank you, we'll see you in a few months," Mickey told him.

"Bye Vin," I winked at him tossing the keys to the black infinity truck he let us use to him then walked out with Mickey right next to me. "So, we have fifteen grand plus whatever we got out of that safe. This shit doesn't seem too easy to you?" I asked Mickey.

"It was kind of easy, but fuck it, we're good. Trust me. Now let's go to my house so we can count this shit."

We walked a couple of blocks away from Vin's shop and hopped into the black Range Rover Mickey said she borrowed from some nigga she talks to. We never use our own cars on a job. Even something as simple as going to and from Vin's shop had to be done in another vehicle. We weren't taking any chances at all.

Michelle "Mickey" Whitfield

*S*itting my blunt down, I smiled looking at the money that was on my bed. Tonight, was a great night if I do say so myself. We've never made this much money and from now on we'll just keep moving up. Tonight, was proof that we could go after a big-time nigga and get away with it. It turns out ole boy had a little over twenty bands in that safe.

We just made damn near thirty thousand each in one night and we hadn't gotten rid of his jewelry yet. I was proud of myself to be honest. This was just showing me I needed to keep going for the big fish. I was tired of dealing with these *little pissy, only had ten stacks in the cut if that much* ass niggas. I was ready to keep going after any and every nigga with a big bank.

Unlike myself, Toi thought about things more. I'm not going to call her scared, she's careful if anything. She's always saying taking down bigger hustlers may bring in more money, but it comes with a bigger risk. I know she's right, but who gives a fuck? These niggas have their hustle and we have to ours. Money makes the world go round and I'll be damned if I'm sitting on pause because somebody might be a little more dangerous. Nope, I'm good.

"Toi, this right here is all the proof you need. We can do this, get these niggas for all they're worth if not more."

"It's not that easy, I had to be around this nigga for a good minute before getting invited to his place. Don't you think it's going to be weird that the night his ass gets robbed his *supposed new girlfriend* goes missing?"

"That's why we wear disguises," I said while snatching the long, blond, curly wig out the bag with her clothes from tonight. "That nigga has no idea what you look like for real. Shit, I was so heavy on that foundation you're damn near my complexion," I joked.

"I just love my life, alright? I don't want to risk it or somebody I love for a few dollars."

"I hear you, but you just need to think about it some. In the meantime, take the money, find your own place and go shopping."

"I'm fine where I am," she chuckled.

"That's what you say, but how much longer do you want to live with your grandmother and those bad ass twins? Girl, you're better than me because I swear to God, I couldn't do it."

"I love my grandmother, besides with me being there all the bills get paid. As far as the twins go, you're right they're bad as fuck which is more of a reason for me to be there. My grandmother is seventy-two years old, she can't look after them like she did me and I'll be damned if I leave those disrespectful ass girls in the house with her alone. In fact, I need to go home now just so I can make sure they're in the house and not on the block this late."

"It's only 11:45, it's not even late."

"To you it's not late. You're twenty-three they're fifteen I'm not having that shit. They know they have to be in the house by ten o'clock."

"You sure you're not their mother?" I asked making her laughed. Toi treated her little cousins like they were her kids. She did everything for them as if they were hers, sometimes I had to remind myself that she was only twenty-two years old.

"I'm the closest thing they got to it, shit I might as well be," she said. Toi bagged up all her money, then stood up straight. "I'll call you tomorrow. Maybe we can go out and do something."

"Aight just let me know what time."

"I got you, see you later."

I walked her to the front door, then locked it behind her once she left. After locking my shit down, I went into my bathroom and took a long, hot shower. I always needed one after a long night of taking a nigga for all he had.

Toi

"Good morning grandma," I kissed her cheek when I walked in the kitchen. Lucky for me she was in here cooking breakfast, so I didn't have to.

Mickey thinks I'm crazy for still living at home with my grandmother but fuck that. I would rather be here than somewhere else. My grandmother owns this house, she and my grandad worked their asses off to maintain this place and they have. It's just that now with my grandmother being too old to work, all the bills are on me. Luckily, the house is paid for, so a mortgage isn't an issue. It was every other bill we had that was drowning me. My grandmother gets social security, but I make her keep her money. I didn't want her dipping in it for anything other than the things she wanted.

"Morning baby, how did you sleep?" she asked once I sat down at the table.

"I slept fine, what about you?"

"Not too good. Those little girls are going to be the death of me one of these days."

"Don't talk like that. What happened now?"

"I wake up from my nap last night and Kayla had some nasty little boy in my house, Jayla was outside with a skirt so short you could almost see her ass hanging out. I can't take too much more of those two."

"I'll talk to them. Is that all that happened?"

"No, when I told her to come in the house and change into something more appropriate, she cussed at me."

"Who cursed at you?" I hopped up out of my chair and pulled my hair into a tight bun. I didn't tolerate disrespect, especially not towards my grandmother. Those two dummies had me fucked up if they thought they were just going to do whatever the fuck they wanted with no consequences.

"Jayla, then she came in and pushed past me. The little heffa almost knocked me down."

"I'll be right back."

Turning around I walked out of the kitchen and ran upstairs to the twins' bedroom and banged on the door until it opened. When I saw black hair swinging, I grabbed a handful and pulled her out of the room.

"OW! Get off me Toi!" Jayla screamed in pain. She tried to snatch away from me, but I grabbed her neck slamming her against the wall.

"What the fuck is wrong with you?"

"What are you talking about?"

"You cursed at grandma then had the nerve to push past her like you're fucking stupid? Have you lost your fucking mind?"

"I didn't push her!"

"So, she's lying on you? I don't fucking think so. Go downstairs and apologize to her!" I pushed her towards the stairs then went in the room and looked at her twin sister Kayla. They were identical, same light complexion, naturally long curly hair, big gray eyes, and deep dimples. They even had the same size six frame. The only way to tell them apart was their hair color. I let Kayla dye her hair light brown while Jayla chose to keep her hair black.

"I didn't do anything to grandma, so you don't have a reason to come yelling at me," Kayla said while holding her arms up like I was the cops or something.

"You did, you had somebody in this house yesterday." When she didn't say anything, I knew it was true. "I told y'all little fast asses about being around these stupid ass boys and bringing them in this house! You don't bring anybody in this bitch, and you don't go up in nobody's house! Y'all really take me for a fucking joke! When one of y'all ends up pregnant, I'm not saying a fucking thing! You're just going to pack your shit and get the fuck out. You got me?"

"Yeah I got it."

"Good, now you can go downstairs and apologize to her too because that shit was disrespectful."

I walked downstairs and watched as they both gave her sincere apologies. When they finished, I took them in the living room and made them sit down.

"Look, I know y'all think I'm mean as hell to y'all for no reason but trust me when I say I do shit for a reason. I don't want you two to end up like our mothers, alright? I want y'all to go to school, go to college and make your money in a legit way. These streets are nothing nice, and it's nothing out here for y'all."

"You're out here though," Jayla said. She always had something smart coming out of her mouth.

"I am, but I do what I do for all of us."

Jayla and Kayla didn't know I was out here robbing niggas, but I paid all the bills by myself without a job. They are a lot of things, but stupid isn't one of them, so they knew I was doing something out here, they just didn't know what.

"Grandma is seventy-two years old, she can't work and pay these bills, so I have to. You two don't have jobs, so I buy all your stuff. The least you could do is act like you have some sense and respect her. She won't be here forever, then when she's gone what are you going to do? You're going to feel like shit for taking her for granted. That disrespectful shit is out. The next time she tells me about something one of you did, I'm beating your ass like you're a bitch on the street and that's real shit."

"Ok, we get it Toi. We're sorry we shouldn't do stuff like we do," Kayla told me.

"Mhm, get out of my face. I was going to take you little bitches shopping but now I should keep my money to myself."

"No!" they both screamed at the same time.

"Please? Come on! We'll clean the whole house when we get back. Please can we go?" Jayla begged.

Raising an eyebrow, I looked at both.

"Fine, go get dressed."

As soon as I told them that, they ran upstairs. Making my way back into the kitchen, my grandmother smiled at me.

"Thank you."

"It's no problem grandma. I'm taking them shopping. Do you wanna go?"

"I am not about to be out here running behind y'all. I'm fine."

"Alright, but I don't want you stuck in the house. How about I take you to a spa? They'll give you a massage, do your nails, your hair all of that. Do you want to go?"

"That would be lovely, but you don't have to spend your money on me baby."

"Yes, I do, you've taken care of me since I was what? Four years old? It's my turn to take care of you now. Get dressed so you can have a good day." I kissed her cheek then went upstairs so I could get dressed.

My grandmother is the most important person in my life. It's been me and her since I was four years old. My mother, Geneva, and her sister Grace, who is the twin's mother, got caught up in the street life. My father was the one who got her hooked-on drugs then he dipped out. My mother never got her shit together or adjusted to be a good mother. She was too into her freedom, so I was raised by my grandparents.

When my Aunt Grace got pregnant with the twins, she stayed away her entire pregnancy but came back once she had them. She was here with them for two years until she passed away from a heroin overdose. My mother is still alive, but I have no idea where she is and to be honest, I really don't give a damn. She chose her life and I'm not in it so oh well.

As soon as I got old enough to make some money and help, I did. I had a couple of part time jobs while I was in high school. When I graduated, I moved up into a full-time job and worked that until Mickey came to me about robbing niggas.

I didn't want to do it at first. I love my damn life too much and I know how niggas get about their money. She wouldn't leave me alone about it and we needed the money, so I said fuck it and started helping her. After we did it a few times, I got more comfortable, but I know I'm not about to do this shit forever. I don't know about Mickey, but I'm giving this shit up the first chance I get. This isn't a career and I'm not going to convince myself it is. Shit, the way I'm feeling, last night might've been my last job period.

⚜

"Put that down, I wouldn't even wear that bullshit and I'm grown. Go look for some jeans, something that actually covers your ass," I told Kayla shaking my head at the little black booty shorts she was holding up.

I dropped my grandmother off at the spa thirty minutes ago and now I was at Jersey Gardens Mall, in Neiman Marcus with the double mint twins. They were in here picking clothes out like they had video auditions to go on.

"Come on Toi, these are cute," Kayla tried to convince me, but it was not happening at all.

"No, I can look at them and tell they're too damn short. Go pick out clothes that are appropriate for your age or you're not getting a damn thing. I'm not playing." She sucked her teeth and walked away but she knew to put that shit down.

Shaking my head, I walked over to the jewelry section and looked in the display cases. Nothing really caught my eye until I spotted this silver toggle bracelet with a diamond heart charm on it that made my mouth drop. Looking up, I waved over the sales person, who just so happened to be an older black woman. She reminded me of the actress Monica Calhoun a little bit.

"How may I help you?" she asked with a smile on her face.

"I would like to see that bracelet right there," I pointed to it and she pulled it from the case.

"This is one of my favorites too, do you want to try it on?"

"Can I?"

"Sure," she put it around my arm, and I was in complete awe by it. It wasn't anything outrageous, but it was beautiful, and I loved it.

"This is gorgeous."

"It really is. Do you want to purchase it?" Before I could open my mouth to say yes, something else caught my eye. It was a pair of Avenue Diamond and pearl earrings that I knew my grandmother would love.

"Hold on, how much are those earrings right there?" I pointed to them.

"Those are six thousand, six hundred and sixty dollars."

"Damn, okay and this bracelet is how much?"

"Two thousand, three hundred and fifty dollars."

"Wow, okay. I can't get both right now." There was no way I was going to bring attention to myself in this store by dropping this much on jewelry, then spending however much on clothes when the twins and I finished shopping.

"Well I think this bracelet suits you very well."

"I do too, but I know my grandmother would love those earrings."

I bit the corner of my lip while I thought about it. I rarely spent money on myself. Usually my money goes to the bills and making sure the twins and my grandmother have everything they need. At the same time, I do have a couple of bracelets already and I would love to the see the smile on my grandmother's face when she sees these earrings.

Fuck it. I'll just get the bracelet later. "I'll take the earrings," I took the bracelet off my wrist and handed it back to her.

"Are you sure?"

"Yes, my grandmother would be so happy with those earrings. I can get the bracelet another time." I pulled out some money and counted out six thousand, seven hundred dollars then handed it to her.

"This is too much miss."

"No, it's fine, just keep the change. Can you put those earrings in a gift box for me please?" I smiled at her and she smiled back nodding her head.

"Sure, just give me one moment." She walked off to wrap the earrings up, leaving me standing there.

"That was a nice thing to do," a deep voice said from behind me. "Your grandmother would be proud."

Not even turning around I shrugged my shoulders. "Thank you, what can I say? I love my grandma," I chuckled.

"Here you go miss," the woman said when came back. I took the bag from her and was about to walk only for whoever the man behind me was to cut me off.

"Wait a minute, she'll take that bracelet she was looking at." Confused I turned and looked at the guy who was doing this and I got stuck for a second, he was so damn fine.

He was taller than me, had to be at least 6'3", skin the color of peanut butter, and from what I could see his arms were covered in tattoos. His hair was cut low, waves spinning like crazy and he had a perfectly line low cut beard. I didn't know who he was but damn, God took time with him.

"Um, I'm fine without the bracelet I'll just wait until another time," I said once I finally got off creep mode.

"Or you can just take it this time," he spoke in a tone that said don't even say anything else just take it. He pulled out a wad of cash, counted some out then placed it on the counter. "Keep the change and wrap that up for her," he told the lady behind the counter who nodded and did what he said.

Looking me up a down a small smile came across his face I smiled back him while moving a piece of my hair out of my face. "Thank you," I spoke softly.

"No problem ma, what's your name?"

"Toi."

"Toi? As in Toys you play with?" He chuckled.

"I guess you can say that. It's short for La'Toia."

"So, everybody calls you Toi?"

"Yeah, that's me. So, what's your name?"

"Quentin."

"Quentin? I like that it fits you."

"Appreciate it ma. Look, tonight I'm having a party. You should come through." He went in his pocket and pulled out in invitation. I looked at the flyer than back at him.

"An all-white party at The Mansion? I've heard of that place it's down South Jersey, right?"

"Yeah that's the one."

"I wanted to have my birthday party there, but they wanted a grip for it."

"I could've made that happen for you."

"How were you going to do that? You're friends with the owner or something?"

"Something like that," he smirked. "I am the owner." He grabbed the bag from the sales lady then handed it to me. "Make sure you come through tonight."

"Can I bring a friend?"

"Boyfriend?" he looked at me suspiciously.

Laughing I shook my head no. "Nah, it's a girl."

"Oh, yeah bring her with you. I'll be looking forward to seeing you ma. I'll see you later Toi," he smiled at me again then walked off.

"You definitely want to go to that party tonight young lady," the woman behind the counter said to me before walking off to help another customer. Smiling I tucked the invite into my purse then went on to find an outfit for tonight.

Quentin 'Legend' Santana

*W*alking out of Neiman Marcus I hopped right into the black Mercedes sprinter van that was waiting for me. "Nigga what the fuck you went in there to do that couldn't wait?" My nigga Yung asked me.

"Don't worry about that nigga you just worry about you. The fuck is you in a rush for anyway?"

"I gotta go drop some fuckin money off to KeKe's sickening ass, that bitch is about to make me take my daughter and just blow her damn head off."

"She's that damn bad?"

"Bruh yes, I'm telling you right now don't have kids by a bitch you don't plan on being with, the shit will drive you fuckin' crazy."

"Why the fuck would I do some stupid shit like that? I'm not you nigga," I laughed at his stupid ass. I don't feel bad for this nigga he's the one that tried to turn an obvious temporary bitch into a wife and got her ass pregnant. Now he's stuck with her, dumb ass nigga. "I just want to know how you're sitting here complaining about shorty but you're still fucking her."

"Fuck you man, if I'm going to get bitched at, I might as well get my dick wet. That doesn't even matter I'm ready for the party later. I'm getting at least three bitches to go home with me tonight. Fuck with me."

"Nah I'm not trying to catch some shit, that's how niggas dicks start falling off. Besides somebody I want to see is coming through tonight so you can have those broads," I told him as my mind went back to Toi.

From what I could see of shorty she was perfect, she stood at a good five foot seven inches, nice dark caramel complexion, long wavy black hair, and she a nice pair of lips and teeth on her. She put me in the mind of a slightly darker skinned Zaria from that ninety's show *The Parent Hood* with Pocahontas like hair that cascaded down her back and a body like the model Draya Michele. She has a slim build but enough hips, ass, and titties for a nigga to grip.

On top of the fact that she's beautiful, she's clearly not selfish. How many bitches out here willing to give up some jewelry for themselves to get a gift for their grandmother?

"Aww shit, who you done invited out tonight nigga?"

"Don't worry about that."

"Oh, now you wanna be all secretive? I got you, act like that if you want to. I will be finding out who shorty is."

"The fuck ever man, what's going on with that nigga Nolan though? I heard his fat ass got robbed."

Laughing Yung nodded his head. "He did, by his bitch. Shorty got him for at least twenty stacks then took his car and jewelry. I told that nigga about trusting bitches, he thought because he dated shorty for a while, she was good enough to bring to the crib. Fuckin' dummy."

"That's fucked up, it's on him though. You can't play too many of these bitches close. He better start watching everybody around his ass."

"I tried to tell him that he wouldn't listen. Not my problem it ain't me, I'll fuck around and kill a bitch." He shook his head. As crazy as he sounded, I couldn't agree with him more. As much as I bust my ass to make my money you think I'm going to let somebody let alone a bitch steal from me and nothing happens to her? Fuck that

"BRUH THIS SHIT IS POPPIN, you did a good job this time my nigga." Yung came over and gave me some dap.

He was right, my party was poppin' just like I knew it would be. This was the most successful club I owned. I named it The Mansion because that's what it was. Any nigga could buy a club and make that work, but how many could really buy a mansion and turn it into a hot spot? Only me, that's why they call me Legend, I do shit nobody else can. What's funny is my house is just as big as this club and it's only twenty minutes away from here.

My name rings bells all over Jersey, at first it was because of my uncle Saint. He had the streets on lock for as long as I could remember. My father left right after I was born so my mom got help raising me from my uncle. He taught me the game and everything I needed to know. He's the one that started calling me Legend.

Growing up I had a bit of an anger problem, and I used to get into a lot of fights. Most of those fights were with niggas older and bigger than me, that shit didn't matter because I took them down with no issue. Saint saw how I was and said once he taught me everything, I needed to know I would be a Legend in the making. He started referring to me as Legend and when it came down to introducing me to people, he would say that was my name, so it stuck.

I moved weight for a couple of years, I got started in that shit when I was fifteen and now eleven years later, I'm about done with that. Even though I had money coming in like crazy, I was cleaning and quadrupling the shit through my legit business endeavors. Investing is a very lucrative business venture for me. Along with that I own four gas stations, three laundromats, a couple of retail stores, two luxury car detailing shops and my most popular business is my night club The Mansion. With everything I have going on, money will never be an issue. I'm sitting on millions and I plan to keep building that shit up even after I'm done with this street shit.

"I told you it was going to be like this, next time don't doubt me muthafucka." Laughing I looked around at the crowd of people here. Everybody was having a good time which I was happy about, if it stayed like this and nobody got out of line, I'm cool. Turning my head towards the bar I smirked when I saw shorty from earlier standing there talking to some girl who looked to be just as bad as she is.

"Aye bruh I'll be back alright." Before his nosey ass could question me, I walked down towards the bar and tapped her on the shoulder. When she turned around a big smile came on her face.

"Hi Quentin," I gave her a small side hug then looked her up and down.

"You look good as fuck ma, for real." I wasn't lying at all. As if she isn't already gorgeous enough, she had her shape on display wearing a white quarter sleeve mini dress that was cinched at the waist with a gold belt. Her hair was on some wild curly shit and it looked like she had no makeup on but that didn't dumb her beauty down at all.

Blushing she moved a piece of her hair behind her ear. "Thank you." Looking up she pointed in front of her. "This is my friend Taj, Taj this is Quentin."

"Hi," her friend smiled.

"It's nice to meet you ma. Well both of you look gorgeous and it's a little bit crowded right here how about we go up to my section?"

"Okay, come on Taj." They both grabbed their drinks off the bar then I led them to where I was sitting at with my people.

"Aye y'all!" I shouted at them getting their attention. "These are my dumb ass homies, that's Barry, Tone, and that nigga over there drooling is Yung." I pointed them out one by one. "This is Toi and her friend Taj."

I could tell by the look on Yung's face he was already feelin' her friend. The funny thing is she took the seat right next to him when she sat down. I'm not even shocked he was on her, she was just as bad as Toi. Taj had a light brown complexion and long black hair that was straightened with a part down the middle. She was on the petite side but the short white dress she had on showed that she still had a nice frame. Her left arm was fully covered in tattoos, while she only had a few on her lower right one, and she had a big piece going across her chest. Knowing Yung, he was going to fall for that shit. It's something about a bitch with tatts that weakens that nigga.

22

"I'm glad you could make it out here, it wasn't hard for you to find it right?" I asked Toi after I had her attention again.

"Nah, I've been here before, so I knew where I was going. Nice little drive from Jersey City but it was worth it, I guess. I didn't know about this party though, I feel a way about that."

"Why?"

"Nobody told me shit and I see half my damn city in here," she chuckled. "So, what is this party for?"

"Celebrating."

"Celebrating what? Is it your birthday or something? I would've bought you a gift."

"Nah ma, I'm just celebrating life. You have to do that sometimes."

Shrugging her shoulders, she took a sip of her drink. "Maybe you're right. Life isn't perfect but I'm alive, that's a good enough reason to be happy.

"Exactly, now you're getting it. Come with me."

"Where?" She raised her eyebrow at me.

"Outside it's too loud in here. Don't worry about your friend trust me she's good with them."

"Okay, let's go." Grabbing her hand, I led her outside to the backyard which was like a whole other party. "Wow, last time I was here I didn't come back here. This is really nice, you're doing big things with this."

"I'm glad you like it." I sat down on a chair and pulled her down so that she was sitting on my lap. "So, tell me something."

"What do you wanna know?"

"Where is your boyfriend at?"

She laughed. "What makes you think I have a boyfriend?"

"Look at you, you're bad as fuck. How could you not have a boyfriend?"

"I just don't, besides if I did, I wouldn't be here let alone be sitting on your lap."

"Why not?"

"That would be disrespectful. When I get a man, respect has to be first on both ends."

"So, if you had a man and he said you couldn't come you wouldn't have come to my party?"

"No, would you want your girl going somewhere you didn't want her to go?"

"See nah, the difference is my girl would know better so I wouldn't even be worried. Asking me wouldn't have happened period."

"Oh, so you're just the boss in your relationships huh?"

"I just know what I want, and I know how to treat a woman. If she wants me to respect and take care of her, she must be able to understand how I am. You feel me?"

She gave me a slow head nod. "Yeah, I got it, you like to be in charge. That's good, it's attractive."

"So, you find me attractive?"

"I didn't say that," Toi shook her head laughing.

"Um I think you just did."

"No, I didn't, I mean you aight, but you don't look better than me." She flipped her hair dramatically making us both bust out laughing.

"I see how you do me ma." We sat there talking about random stuff until she got hyped up, they put on an old ass Mya song on.

"Ya lips are telling me yes, while you're kissing on my neck. Making me feel so…Should I stay, should I go. I don't know. Your hot boy style drives me wild, but in the back of my head. Even though I wanna see, how you put that thang on me I can't let you, best of me," she sang along with the song and moved around on my lap with her eyes closed.

"Why I feel like you trying to tell me something by singing this song?" I asked her. Opening her eyes, she raised an eyebrow and looked at me.

"Don't blow my shit," she laughed.

"I'm just saying, listen to the words."

"I know what the song is about but no I'm not trying to tell you anything."

"Oh, so you wouldn't care if I kissed you right now?"

Shaking her head, she chuckled. "I'm not going to say I wouldn't care, I might slap you for it. Just a risk you'll be taking."

"So, I can't have a kiss?"

"Nope," she replied quickly.

"Why not?"

"When you deserve a good one, you'll get it." She winked at me then stood up and walked back inside with a smile on her face.

I could already tell she's about to make me chase her, and to be honest I like that. Most of these bitches will throw the pussy at me just because of who I am. Easy pussy is convenient, but that shit gets boring after a while. Toi was really piqued my interest. I'll be keeping a close eye on shorty for sure.

Mickey

"**Y**o what's up Mick?" I heard a nigga shout from across the street while I walked to my car. I looked over and gave him a head nod.

"What's up Perry? Come here I need something really quick!" I shouted back. When he came across the street, he looked me up and down basically fucking me with his eyes. Nasty ass nigga.

"What's up ma, what you need? A good fuck because if so, I definitely got you," he cheesed.

"Nigga, you will die and be brought back to life by Casper the friendly ghost before you ever touch me. I need an eighth how much for it?"

"Mean ass bitch man," he shook his head. "It'll be thirty dollars. Where are you about to go?"

"I gotta run Bia somewhere really quick but I'm coming right back. I got you on the money when I come back too so make sure you have my shit please."

"You'll have it, oh yeah that bitch Maria was out here looking for you earlier."

"For fucking what?"

"I heard it was about you fucking her nigga or something." He shrugged and I couldn't help but crack the fuck up.

"Oh my God aight, I'll see you later." I got in my car and drove off towards my cousin Bia's house. As soon as I pulled up in front of her door she hopped in since she was standing there waiting. "What's good bitch?"

"Nothing, the fuck was up you the other night? The Mansion was straight poppin' you should've come down there."

"Toi hit me up about that shit, she wanted me to go but I was chillin' with Case that night."

"I did see her there with Taj, I wanted to slap her ass," Bia shook her head.

"The fuck? Why?" From what I know Bia and Toi never had a problem and were cool so what the fuck is she talking about?

"I had a plan that night. I was going to go there and finally snag Legend's fine ass, but she was in the way."

"What do you mean she was in the way?"

"He was all in her face that night, you would think she was his date or something. She really killed my fucking plans bruh."

Laughing I shook my head at this bitch. "Maybe she was, wait you said Legend, right?"

"Yeah he's fine as fuck and his money longer than a muthafucka."

"Doesn't he own that shit?"

"Yes! Another reason I was mad. She's a lucky ass bitch."

"Mhm she sure is." I'm going to go off on this bitch, I wanna know why she didn't tell me she bagged that nigga out of all people.

Legend is just that, a hood legend. His name is the equivalent to a celebrity out here. That nigga was moving more weight than Scarface and everybody knew it, but he was smart and low-key about how his operation was ran. Plus, he was cleaning his money so the FEDS would have a tough time catching him in anything anyway. Word is he has ties to multiple lucrative businesses all around New Jersey. Legend is just that nigga so if Toi bagged that, she was about to get introduced to a whole different world.

"So, you said you were with Case? I thought he was with that bitch Maria, I just saw them together last week," Bia said like I was supposed to care.

"Alright," I shrugged.

"Don't tell me you're fuckin' that girls' man."

"I'm not telling you shit, all I said was I was with him last night. That's all you need to know."

"He has a whole damn family, why are you fucking with him? I know Maria, she's cool as shit."

"What's your point? What are you going to do? Call her or something? Y'all friends now or some shit?"

"No but damn Mick. Why are you always fuckin with some other woman's man?"

"You act like it's your nigga I'm fuckin and we both know that nigga has a better chance at swallowing glass and living than fucking me. I'm going to do whatever the fuck I want. You know what? We're not about to have this conversation."

"Yes, we are, you have your own nigga yet and still you fuck with the next bitch man. When Brick gets out, he's going to fuck you up."

"Brick ain't fucking shit up, he's in jail the fuck does that have to do with me?"

"You're supposed to hold him down, yes or no?"

"Hell no, I'm not. We were not together when he got arrested. I left his ass. He was dogging me and beating my ass like I was a nigga in the street, the fuck would I hold him down for? You sound stupid!" I snapped on her quick. "He's the reason my son is with my mother now, so miss me with that."

Bryson aka Brick to the streets is my baby father and ex, emphasis on the ex-part. Fuck him, fuck his life. I give not one single fuck about him. He and I were over before his stupid ass got locked up two years ago and it's going to keep being that way even when he gets out. Bia likes bringing his ass up because for whatever reason the nigga still thinks it's alright to claim me.

He tells his homies and anybody that will listen that I'm still his. Those bitch boys go back and tell everything they could about what I'm doing out here. He's obviously pressed about it because he's made it known that when he gets out, he's supposed to be fucking me up.

If he didn't have a hand problem before he went in, I would think it was bullshit, but I know Bryson and the nigga is dead serious. That's exactly why his ass was getting shot as soon as he came near me. I've made trips to the range just for that nigga.

Not only was he putting his hands on me, he was cheating on me like crazy. The nigga fucked any bitch I've ever called my friend except Toi and Taj. He especially can't stand Toi and that's because she wouldn't and won't ever fuck him. They hate each other and he hates that I ride for Toi so hard but she does the same for me so he can continue to be mad.

"I'm just saying you know how crazy that nigga is, he's in there steaming like a muthafucka over you."

"So? What am I supposed to do? Stay with his ass and deal with his bullshit like you and Kareem?" I shot back at her.

Kareem is Bia's bum ass boyfriend and coincidentally he is Brick's cousin. The apple really doesn't fall to far from the tree in their family because they both have temper and hand problems. I was smart enough to get the fuck away from Brick, unfortunately Bia is still stuck on her nigga. He would beat her ass for the smallest shit, and she made excuses for him every time. Kareem's head could've been blown off a long time ago because a lot of people fuck with Bia the long way, but she protects his ass.

"The fuck is that supposed to mean?" She asked, sounding as if she was offended.

"Exactly what it sounds like, I know he knocked you the fuck out at that basketball game last week." I glanced at her just in time to see her roll those damn eyes of hers. "What you thought I wasn't going to hear about it?"

"I'm not saying that, but why people always gotta be in my business."

"You're my cousin Bi and you damn near got your head knocked off in front of a park full of people. You thought that shit wasn't going to get back to me?" I shook my head at her simple ass. Not tooting my own horn but I'm well known around my city. I'm cool with a lot of niggas and a lot of bitches hate me, so my name was forever coming up "What happened? You bought his soda back and it wasn't cold enough?"

"Fuck you bitch, he didn't knock me out, we got into it because he irritated me. Don't talk like I don't provoke him sometimes. My mouth is reckless."

"Do you think before you speak, or do you just let bullshit flow out of your mouth? Who gives a shit about how reckless your mouth is? You think that gives him the right or a reason to beat on you? Fuck is wrong with your brain?"

"I didn't say that."

"That's what it sounds like you're saying but hey you do you Bia. Don't call me when he's beating your ass again."

"So, you're just going to let it happen? You're my cousin you're supposed to have my back."

"I do have your back, I love you to death, but I can't keep jumping in that shit only for you to take his bum ass back. The last time I broke up some shit between you two I got Roc and them to beat his ass and what did you do? You came at my neck like I was the one who slapped you in public."

"They were about to kill him!"

"So, the fuck what? He was about to kill you and you got over that shit quick. Like I said Bia, don't call me about that shit when he beats your ass again."

"That's fucked up," she shook her head.

"Nah it's the truth I'm tired of being the middle of the bullshit. I left Bryson for that stupid shit, I'll be damned if my ass ends up in a body bag because he doesn't want to or can't control his fuckin' temper. Keep thinking it's nothing big it's going to happen to you. I'm not trying to bury my cousin so please get it together."

"Whatever man," she waved me off. Bia knows I'm right so why she's acting like that, I don't know. If she wants to be stuck on stupid behind Kareem that's on her, I'm over that shit. I'm not holding down a nigga that couldn't even treat me right. His ass can die there for all I give a fuck.

SITTING on my porch I took one last pull from my blunt while I waited for Toi to pull up. Since I didn't get to go to that all white party at the mansion, she was supposed to come tell me all about it. Just as I was putting my blunt out a bunch of yapping caught my attention from up the street. I could tell it was some angry hood rats, I knew the tone of that shit.

Looking down the street I laughed when I saw this girl Fatima walking towards my house. I smiled from ear to ear as she and her little crew approached me.

"I don't know what the fuck you are smiling for bitch. I should punch you in the fucking face," she called herself snapping at me, that shit only made me laugh.

"You ain't about to punch nobody in the face, so calm all that shit down. The fuck you coming over here so stupid for?"

"What the fuck were you doing with Bugg the other night? People told me they saw you with him, you're always fucking with somebody else's nigga! Hop off my man's dick and get your own."

Seeing Toi's white Hyundai Genesis pull up in front of my house I got up off my steps and looked at Fatima. "First of all, I'm not fucking Bugg. I don't want your punk ass man, he can't even afford to get a hug from me. Now, I was with him because I bought some weed from him trying to put money in your fucking house bitch. Don't ever approach me on some foolish ass shit. You're acting like somebody really wants that nigga. He's damn near broke and ugly as fuck just like them wombat looking ass kids you had with his ass." Pushing past all of them I walked over to Toi's car and got in the front seat.

"The fuck is going on around here?" Toi looked at the group of dummies in front of my door then at me.

"She was coming at me about her nigga, nobody wants that dust bucket." Looking over at the group of girls I rolled the window down. "FUCK AWAY FROM MY PORCH!"

I shouted at them and they all went walking away. "Fuck was they about to do? Jump you or something?"

"Those bitches ain't that dumb, shit would've been real around this muthafucka if they even thought about that shit. Fuck those broke bitches. I want to know what happened at that party."

"Oh, it was poppin' you really should've come."

"Bia told me, she was there."

"I thought I saw her, but I wasn't sure. She was right, I had a good fucking time."

"I'm sure you did, especially with Legend in your face all night."

"What was in my face?" She asked looking confused.

"Legend, you were with him, right?"

"Who is Legend?"

"You don't know the nigga's name? Tall as fuck, tatted up, looks good as hell. Who were you damn near attached to all night?"

"Oh, you're talking about Que. Well his real name is Quentin or at least that's the name he gave me."

"Quentin? Oh, shit he gave you his real name."

"I would hope so," she laughed. "Why are you so excited about this?"

"No reason, I'm just happy you like someone. How did you meet him?"

"I was in Neiman Marcus looking at jewelry. I wanted a bracelet, but I saw some earrings my grandmother would love so I got that instead. Getting both would've been too much. So, as I'm walking away, he gets it for me."

"Gets what?"

"The bracelet." She held her arm up showing off the diamond charm bracelet she was wearing.

"Oh shit, homie must really be feelin' you. So, he invited you to the party?"

"Yeah and we spent time together a little bit and exchanged numbers. He's nice," she shrugged.

"Yeah and he's paid, I'm talking millions in his account type paid."

"Ok, what does that have to do with me?"

"Toi, if we get him, we'll really be set for life. Not for a couple of months either, I mean for life. We won't have to do shit anymore."

"Hold up Mickey, I know you're not talking about robbing this nigga." She looked at me like I just said something crazy. The shit sounded good to me.

"Hell yes, what part of he's paid didn't you get? This is too big of a catch for us to turn down."

"Besides the fact that I'm just not here for it there are more reasons why we can't."

"What? You only spent a couple of hours with his ass, it's not like you're in love."

"I'm not saying it like that. What I'm saying is he knows my name, he knows exactly what I look like and where I'm from. How are we supposed to rob him if he knows about me already?"

"Don't tell him anymore about you. Let the shit build into a mystery or just lie, damn what's so hard about that?"

"You're saying that because your ass isn't on the line. Everybody knows me just like they know you. All he must do is drive around my area say my name, then boom everything he's ever needed to know about me will be known. Besides just like you said he's paid right? If that man has millions, then he has a million-dollar army and I'm not losing my life over some dollars."

"So, you don't want to go after this nigga because you're scared?"

"I'm not scared of shit, I'm just not dumb. There is no way we would be able to pull the shit off so why even try it?"

"I thought you wanted some real money to take care of your family. This can do that easily."

"What good is that money if my ass isn't alive to spend it? He's too big of a target, we can't do it Mick."

Shaking my head, I sucked my teeth, I hated when she made sense. "Fine, fuck man. We could be good for life if we got this nigga though."

"Money is all well and fine, but your ass is trying to die getting it? It's not that deep for me I will work part time again before inviting bullets to my chest. No, pick another target and his boys are out of the question too Mickey so don't even ask me."

"What the fuck are you a psychic?"

"No, I just know how you are, I'm sorry but I'm not going after this nigga."

"Aight man, you get on my nerves sometimes Ms. Goodie Goodie."

"I love you too, what are you about to do?"

"Not a damn thing, I need a fucking hobby or some shit. You wanna hit the nail salon or whatever?"

"Yeah, you don't need anything from your house?"

"Oh, shit yeah hold up," I ran in my house and got my purse along with my phone and keys, locked up then got back into her car. "Let's go," nodding she hurried and pulled off.

Toi

$\mathcal{A}$fter spending most of my day shopping and getting my nails done with Mickey, I drove to the store and picked up a few things to eat for the house then headed home. Mickey really had the nerve to bring up robbing Quentin three more times while we were out, and it took all of me not to curse her ass the fuck out. It's like she doesn't understand the word no. I wasn't going after him, it's too big of a risk. Money isn't worth my life so it's a hell to the no for me.

As soon as I walked in the house, I could smell food cooking. Being that neither of the twins can cook, I already knew it was my grandmother. I sat my purse on the couch then rushed into the kitchen with a smile on my face to see my grandmother bent over going the refrigerator.

"Looks like I came home just in time, what are you cooking?" I asked.

"All of your favorites," a vaguely familiar voice responded. Confused I sat the bags on the table and waited for whoever that was to stand up straight because it damn sure wasn't my grandma.

"Okay, who are you?" Standing up straight and turning around, she smiled at me while my mouth damn near dropped to the floor. Why the fuck is my mother in my kitchen right now?

"I know it's been a long time but how do you not recognize your own mother? You're so beautiful look at you." She closed the fridge door then came over to me and tried to pull me in for a hug, but I backed up.

"What are you doing here? Where is grandma?" I asked her with a disgusted look on my face. I wasn't happy about seeing her at all and the fact that she thinks I should be is irritating.

"She's upstairs taking a nap, she didn't want me to wake her until I was done cooking."

"Ok that doesn't tell me why you're here."

"I'm living here now."

"Living where?" I know I heard her wrong, she's not living in this house.

"Living here as in my mother's house. Look Toi, there are some things you don't know ok."

"You mean like who the fuck you are exactly?"

"I'm your mother that's who I am."

"Oh, now you're my mother? I haven't seen you in years and the last time I did you stole from me so please don't start with that mother shit it's really not going to get you anywhere."

"I don't care, you can be mad, and I don't blame you but you're not going to disrespect me. My mother has welcomed me back so that's all that matters."

"Well I pay the bills here, and unless you're putting money in my hand when the first rolls around you won't be here too long."

"I know you're grown but you're not going to talk to me like this. I'm here. You might as well get over it La'Toia, I'm not going anywhere."

"For how long? You're going to be clean for a week or two then what? Find some stuff you can sale then go out and get high again? We've been through this bullshit too many times and I'm not here for it. So, if you plan to play games with my grandmother you can just go. She doesn't need you breaking her heart all over again."

"I'm not going to do that, I've been clean for the last year."

"Yeah right."

"I'm serious, I was in rehab. Mama knows I went, she didn't tell you because whenever I come up you act like you don't have a mother."

"I don't, you've never done a fucking thing for me so why would I respect you as a parent? Parents take care of their children they don't leave a four-year-old with their grandparents then go out sucking glass dicks all night." Before I could blink her hand went across my face.

"That's enough! You don't have to like me Toi, you may even hate me, but you will not disrespect me! I brought you into this world, you're here because I had you. I am your mother!"

Shaking my head, I wiped the tears that came down my face. I wasn't crying because her hit hurt, I was crying because I was pissed off. If my grandmother wasn't upstairs asleep, we would've been boxing all over this damn kitchen. My grandmother was protecting her right now and she didn't even know it.

"You're not my mother, you don't know what the fuck a mother is! You want respect from me? That's something you're going to have to earn. I'm not going to just up and give it to you, why should I? Fuck you as far as I'm concerned and that little slap you just gave me. That one you get for free, the next one your ass will be paying for it and I don't take credit cards, or IOU's I'll just be whoopin yo ass all over this fuckin' house." I walked out of the kitchen and went straight upstairs to my room closing and locking the door behind me.

Here I was thinking I was going to have a good peaceful day and boom it just got ruined by her being here. My grandmother knows how I feel about her, and she not only let her ass come here she's okay with her moving in. What the fuck is that even about and why didn't I know about it? So many questions were running through my mind and I couldn't wait for my grandmother to wake up so she could answer them.

Even though she looks it I don't believe this whole I'm clean for good this time bullshit. She's done it before, a couple of times actually and every time she relapsed. She'll be clean for a week, even go with my grandmother to church like she's a changed woman then turn around and do the same bullshit. The last time she was here she took the light bill money I had in my grandmother's room then left. If it wasn't for Mickey loaning me some money, we would've been in the dark.

I refuse to be lied to again. I'm not dealing with it this time, if my grandmother wants to believe her sob story and forgive her that's completely her choice but I'm not here for that. She's going to have to prove to me how much she's changed if she has. One thing I did know is I really have to buy and hide a safe now. I'll be damned if my shit goes missing again.

Toi

*W*alking into the Beautii's Hair Spa I waved at a few of the girls I knew in there before sitting down in Taj's chair. She probably had a gang of people before me but right now I didn't give too much of a fuck. If anybody had a problem they can wait until I'm done to express their feelings.

"What's wrong with you? You look like somebody just pissed you off," Taj asked.

"My mother is at my grandmother's house right now, talking about she's moving back in."

"Oh, hell no, when did that happen?" Taj, just like Mickey knows the relationship I have with my mother. I met her a couple of years ago when she first started working for Beautii. One day Beautii wasn't here to do my hair and Taj was the only person open so she did it, killed it, and we've been friends ever since.

"I don't know, I didn't even get a chance to talk to my grandmother about it, yet she was still asleep when I left. I don't have time to have some thieving ass bitch around me for real."

"Is she still getting high?"

"She claims she's clean, but I don't believe that bullshit, all she does is lie. Why would this time be any different?"

"All you can do is pay attention to what she does and keep eyes on her. Calm down alright. What do you want done to your hair since you just came in here going off?"

"I washed it last night, you can just straighten it for me though."

"Aight, I got you."

"Thank you."

After she got me all settled in the chair, she began to straighten my hair. Taj is the only person I trusted to touch my hair besides myself and Beautii. I take a lot of pride in my mane and I'll be damned if a hating ass bitch cut my shit off or damaged it on purpose.

"Can I cut your hair and turn it into a wig?" Taj asked me and I turned my head to look at her like she was crazy.

"Bitch what? Hell no, the fuck type of question is that?"

"Your hair is what weave dreams are made of okay. Bitches pay hundreds for bundles of hair that feel and look like this, but you have it growing out of your head. The fuck is you for real?"

"I'm black bitch, what do you think?" Taj does the same thing every time I sit my ass in her chair.

My hair is long, and I mean it goes past the middle of my back long and whenever it gets wet it waves up. I'm sure way down in my gene pool it's some white or Native American in there because of slavery but as far as my immediate family goes, we're all black. People see my hair and assume I'm some Hispanic, like dark skin black girls can't have naturally long hair without being mixed with something.

"Looking at you I can't tell. It must be something else up in there, like some Indian or something. I've seen black girls with long hair don't get me wrong but this texture? Your hair feels like Brazilian bundles."

"Well my grandparents are black, my mama is black, and my daddy was black so boom I'm black. Now shut up."

"Man, your mother is light as fuck, I'm just saying."

"That's because my grandfather was her complexion, so she looks like him. I look like my damn grandma if you haven't noticed. Can we stop talking about my bloodline? I'm black bitch."

"Taj don't pump her head up, that's nothing but a perm doing its job," this hating ass bitch that was in the chair across from me named

Angela said. This bitch has been a pain in my ass since high school, you would think hating would get old.

"Angela, hop off my dick alright. I don't have a perm not that it's any of your business," I told her.

"Nobody is on your dick I'm just saying, all you do is walk around like you're the shit when you're not. I can't stand wanna be perfect ass bitches."

"First of all, I'm not perfect and I know I'm not. You think I'm perfect that's why you're so damn bothered by me. It breaks your heart that you can't point out my flaws. Shut the fuck up and get those crunchy ass tracks of yours taken care of."

"Y'all need to cut it down, nobody is about to be fighting in my shop. We've already had this discussion too many times," Beautii turned her chair around and said. Beautii was the top bitch around here, I'm not even mad at her. She had her shit together and she was self-made. You can't help but respect her hustle. "Angela, quit hating for real that's what you were just doing."

"Beautii you're forever taking her side like she's your family or something." Angela rolled her eyes. See why did she have to throw that little dig in about family in? Hating ass bitch.

"She's not my blood but she is my niece, that doesn't have shit to do with it though. You started with her, cut the little girl shit out. It's unnecessary. Sit there, get your hair done and be quiet."

Laughing I looked at Beautii and waved. "What's up lady?"

"Not a damn thing, we have to talk later so when you're done come to the back alright."

"Pause, am I in trouble?"

"No, you're not in trouble," Beautii laughed. "Just come to the back like I said."

"Alright I'll be back there."

"I'm going to the back, but I can hear everything, don't play with me in here," Beautii warned everybody before heading back to her office.

After an hour Taj was done with my hair. I got up out of the chair and paid her before looking in the mirror at myself. "Okay Taj, my shit is laid I love it."

"You're welcome Pocahontas."

"Cut that shit out." I cut eyes at her.

"Tell me you don't look like a damn extra from that movie with your hair straight like that." I looked in the mirror and saw exactly what she meant. I looked what most people would call exotic with my hair pressed but she was still annoying with that Pocahontas shit.

"Shut the fuck up Taj."

"Just saying, what are you about to do after you talk to Beautii?"

"Nothing, I don't feel like going back home with Cruella there. Why what's up?"

"Remember that nigga from The Mansion."

"Which one that bitch was crowded."

"The one your nigga introduced me too, Yung," she said with a smile on her face.

"Oh yeah, okay I remember him. Y'all exchanged information?"

"Yeah, he's supposed to be coming by here in like ten minutes to pick me up."

"Alright what does that have to do with me? You want me to tell Darrell we're together or something?" I asked talking about her dog ass boyfriend Darrell. The nigga is straight community dick, but he keeps her pockets fat, and pays her bills even though she doesn't need him to, so she keeps him around. I personally can't stand the nigga but that's just me.

"Nah, he's not coming alone. Your boy is with him, they ride around in this Mercedes van sometimes and when I spoke to him that's who he was with. They're on their way here."

"Let me guess, you told him I was here so you wouldn't be alone?"

Laughing she nodded. "Yes, I couldn't chill with him by myself. Too much temptation, can you come? You drove here?"

"Lucky for you I didn't, I walked. I'll go but let me see what this lady wants. Tell me when they get here."

"Aight thank you boo."

"Mhm, you owe me." Walking to the back I knocked on Beautii's door when I approached it.

"Come in," I heard her say so I opened the door and went inside. "Sit down Toi," I sat in one of the chairs that was in front of her desk then looked at her.

"What's up?"

"Nothing I just heard some shit."

"Like what?"

"You know Saint still keeps his ear in the streets, so you know he knows everything that goes on. "She said talking about her husband Saint was a big-time hustler before he retired. I heard he still dabbles here and there but he's not in it like he was a few years ago.

"Okay, what happened?"

"I heard that nigga Nolan got robbed a few days back." That name caught my attention. "The thing is he and his homies think he got robbed by a bitch. That's different right?"

"Yeah, how did he let that happen?" I asked playing dumb.

"He got caught slippin' somehow," she chuckled. "Listen Toi, I know what you're about and it's not this street shit."

"I'm not sure I know what you mean."

"You don't? So, you and Mickey didn't rob him?" I didn't even bother answering, I'm not going to tell on myself and I'm not going to lie either. "I'll take that as a yes. I'm not going to lie I didn't think of you two at first until Saint said it was his girl. I had to go back to my mental rolodex and remember I saw you out with him a few times in that horrible ass blonde wig with the fucked-up curls in it. Then I knew you wouldn't do it by yourself and you two are besties, so it made sense after that."

"Beautii I- "

"No wait let me finish. I get that you're hustling and you're making it happen for your family since you do have people to take care of, but robbing niggas is not the way to do it. The one thing these niggas don't play with is their money Toi. One slip up and your whole family can be gone. You think they care about taking the life of an elderly woman? When it comes to money niggas don't give a fuck, they will kill anybody."

"I know that."

"I hope you do. Know and remember it Toi. That wasn't just some average ass nigga you hit up. Do you know what they will do to you? The only reason he's not even digging deep into it is because I had Saint talk him out of it. The money is not worth your life, so I need you to tell me right now that Nolan was your last job."

Raising an eyebrow, I looked at her. "I have bills."

"So, handle that then flip the money you have to make more. From what I understand you have enough to start something of your own. Whatever you do, just do it quick. What are you going to do when that money runs out? Go out and rob someone else? That's stupid ma, I'm telling you."

"So, what am I supposed to do?"

"Get a job, go to school, I don't know do something productive. Use your brain instead of relying on your body to distract these niggas. You're better than that."

"Does Saint know?"

"No," she shook her head and I let out a sigh of relief. I was not trying to hear shit from him out of all people. "I made sure I didn't let him know I knew I was you. That's all I wanted to speak to you about, don't keep doing that dumb shit Toi, it's not worth it alright."

"Alright, I hear you. Right now, I can't promise you I won't ever do it again, but I will promise you I'm really going to think about it."

"You better." We both stood up and hugged. "Alright go ahead and go about your business lil mama." Nodding I walked out of her office.

If that wasn't a sign for me to quit what we have going on I don't know what was. If Beautii can figure us out anybody can. I pulled my phone out and sent Mickey a text about the conversation I had with Beautii.

I put my phone away then went back out to the front where Taj was getting her stuff together. "They're outside Toi come on." Moving my hair out of my face I walked outside with her to see Yung and Quentin both standing outside of the van Taj was talking about.

When I got close enough to Quentin, he pulled me close to him for a hug. When we separated, he smiled at me. "How have you been ma?"

"I've been good for the most part. What about you?"

"I'm doing alright, I'm not going to lie though I feel some type of way."

"About?"

"You couldn't hit me up? What's up with that?"

Chuckling I shook my head. "Nothing I've just been dealing with some things. You could've hit me up. You do have my number."

"I know that now since you like forgetting about me and shit. So, you do hair too?"

"No, I just got mine done actually. You can't tell it looks all nice and fresh? That's messed up, you need to pay attention more," I joked.

"Yeah aight, get in the car ma." He helped me in the van and sat next to me with Yung and Taj coming in right after us. "Aye Kev, take us to BBQ's!" Quentin shouted to the guy that was driving the car then looked at me. "You like barbeque, right? I don't need a chick that doesn't eat."

"Oh, I eat trust me, that place is fine. You sure you want to go all the way to New York though?"

"Yeah it's nothing, I'm not the one driving." He shrugged his shoulders. The whole ride to the restaurant we were talking and laughing.

He seemed like a genuinely nice guy which is crazy because from what I heard from Mickey he was ruthless out here in the streets. He did not play when it came to his business and his money. He wasn't showing me that side of him though and it was kind of refreshing. Usually guys who make moves out here are so thirsty to prove who they are and show that they have a name. He was just being himself and I like it so far.

Legend

"So, tell me something about you that nobody else knows," Toi said to me while walked down the boardwalk.

Yung had this bright ass idea to go to come down to the waterfront in Jersey City after we ate, so here we were. He and Taj walked off in a different direction having their own conversation.

"I did."

"No, you didn't."

"What's my name?"

"Quentin."

"Alright then," I chuckled. "A lot of people don't know my real name. Besides my family, you, and some of my homies, nobody knows my government."

"I don't know your full name though, just the first one."

"Santana."

"Quentin Santana," she nodded then looked at me with her eyebrow raised. "Wait did you say Santana? Are you related to Saint?"

I paused and looked at her. Only a few people knew my uncle the fact that she said his name like she was so familiar freaked me out. "You know him?"

"Hell yeah, he and Beautii are like my adopted uncle and auntie. So, are you related to him?"

"He's my uncle actually," I chuckled.

"Seriously? Wow, small world. I should've figured, y'all kind of look alike. The same complexion, same box heads and everything. Yeah I see the resemblance."

"You got jokes I got you ma, I got you. How long have you known them?"

"I've known Beautii since I was old enough to get my hair done by myself so since I was thirteen. I started going to her hair salon and I got close to her, then Saint used to be in there to check on her all the time, so he took me under his wing too. They're good people, they don't play but they're good."

"Believe me I know, they helped raise me."

"They did?"

"Yeah, I mean I have my mother, but my father was nowhere around so Saint kind of stepped up and helped my mother raise me. Beautii is like a second mother to me."

"That's understandable."

"What about your family?"

"What about them?" We stopped then took a seat on a bench facing the night view of the Hudson River.

"Is it just you and your grandmother?"

"No, I have two fifteen-year-old cousins. They're twins and a handful."

"What about your mother?"

Sighing she shrugged her shoulders. "She's been on drugs since I was four, or at least that's when I can remember."

"Damn, is she still getting high?"

"She says she's not but who knows if that's true or not. I just have to wait and see." Nodding my head, I could tell by the look on her face this wasn't something she wanted to keep talking about, so I changed the subject.

"So, when are you going to let me take you out?"

"We're out now," she laughed.

"No, I mean just us two, don't try and act like you don't know what I'm trying to do."

"I don't, what are you trying to do exactly?"

"See what you're about, from what I know so far you could be my girl, but I have some more observing to do."

"How do you know if that's what I want?"

"Oh, it's just a matter of time I'm not worried about it," I smiled at her.

"I'm not worried at all. I do need you to understand that I don't have time for the bullshit. So, if you're not ready to monogamous you better stay in the friend zone."

"I take it you've been done wrong before."

"Mhm," she nodded. "My ex had me going through the motions like crazy."

"Like what?"

"Lying, cheating, just being a fuck boy all around. I know he cheated on me more than once with more than one chick, but this one bitch in particular, was damn near stalking me over him. She would pop up at my house, when I did have a regular job at Rainbow, she popped up there doing the most. I had to beat her ass one too many times for my liking. I don't feel like dealing with the bitter ex bullshit, do you have that going on?"

"Nah, the only ex I have is dead to me. The bitch was scandalous."

"What did she do?"

"Cheated."

"Did you?"

"Cheat? Hell yeah, but that's not the point."

"What do you mean," Toi laughed. "Niggas love sticking their dicks in different bitches but let your girl give her pussy away, all hell gotta break loose."

"Hell yeah, she did it on some get back shit and it was niggas I knew. I understand I wasn't perfect, but she took the shit to a whole new level fucking one of my boys."

"What happened to them?"

"I don't know what's going on and I don't give a fuck. As far as him, he's not even breathing anymore so," I shrugged my shoulders. "He should've shot that shit down and told me that she hit on him. He decided to fuck with her like that and violate me, so he dealt with the consequences."

"You said that with too straight of a face. Now I'm wondering if I should be scared of your ass."

"Nah you're good. Don't be scared of me, I'm not about to do anything to hurt you. I learned my lesson with that shit. I'm not fucking up another relationship on some dumb shit."

"You're so sure we're going to be in a relationship," she noted and we both laughed.

"The fact that you doubt me is cute ma. Just know I always get what I want," I looked down at her with a smile.

"You need to stop being so cocky," she smiled back showing off her pretty white teeth.

"Nah I like the way I am, and I'm confident don't get it twisted ma."

"Yeah sure."

"You work?" I asked. I heard her loud and clear when she said the bitch stalking her showed up to her 'regular' job. That shit didn't fly over my head at all.

"I do something like that," she looked away from me and out onto the water.

"What do you mean something like that?"

"Let's put it like this, I do what I have to do and that's all you need to know," Toi said then turned her face back towards mine. "Before you ask no I am not a prostitute, or an escort. I don't fuck anybody for money, and I don't sell or move drugs."

"So, what do you do?"

"You'll find out when I'm ready to tell you."

"I don't know how I feel about that." Looking up at me she smirked slightly.

"Listen, we all have to have a hustle. I'm not going to ask you about yours and mine doesn't affect you, so you don't need to know about it until I'm ready to talk to you. Besides I'm done with it anyway, I'm ready for something different."

"Like what?"

"I want something I can call my own. You're a business owner you know how it feels to start something and see it prosper. I want that for myself."

"So, do it."

"I don't know where to start, I wouldn't even know what to do."

"What would you want to own? What peaks your interest?"

"Nothing I can make money in, I just want something I can pass on to my kids when I have some."

"I feel you. You just must figure out what it is you want to do then go for it. Hell, I'll help you with it if it's makes sense."

"What do you mean?"

"If the idea makes sense and I feel like it could be big I'll help you get it started. I can't have my shorty out here not working."

"Pause, who said I was yours?"

"I did, it's just a matter of time I keep telling you that."

"Why? Jersey is full of bitches dying to be with you."

"True, but that's why I don't want them. It's all about the chase, as soon as bitches start throwing pussy for no fuckin' reason that shit is nothing but a nut."

"That's crazy, well you don't have to worry about that because I'm not fucking you or offering it anytime soon."

"No, what's crazy is what you just said. I'll bet you I'll have you begging me to fuck you."

"Yeah okay you wait on that. So, what do you do? I mean I have an idea but it's more to it than just one thing, right?"

"What are you asking me Toi?"

"Well I don't think everything you do is exactly legal. I know Saint, and I know his background in the streets. If he's the reason you're the business man you are then you must've followed in his footsteps. Am I wrong?"

"Nah you're not wrong at all, I picked up where he left off. You are right, it's more to me than that business wise, way more."

"Alright so let me know, what else do you do?"

"Well as soon as I turned eighteen, Saint got me involved in rental properties. That was making me a lot of money, so I expanded on

QUENTIN & TOI: A LEGENDARY HOOD TALE

that. I own quite a few properties, affordable and luxury. Then I got into investing and that really got my shit rolling."

"Like?"

"Franchise spots, I started buying properties and opening different things all over Jersey. I own five Burger Kings, two Footlockers, and some more shit. I even got money tied up in a couple AMC theatres."

"Oh, so you're just out here doing it big huh?"

"I wouldn't say I'm doing it big I'm just doing me."

Investing is my biggest source of income outside of the street shit I have going on. My uncle always said it's harder for the FEDS to pin some shit on you when your legit money doubles or triples anything they try to find illegally. It's not too much you can do with dirty money so cleaning it is my only option and I'm doing a damn good job of it.

"Well I need to do me, I have people to take care of."

"I hear you. Stick with me and I got you baby girl."

"Yeah aight we'll see." We both laughed and kept talking until my phone started to ring. Pulling it out my pocket I was about to ignore it until I saw it was Tone hitting me up, he doesn't hit me up for bullshit, so I know it's something.

"Hold up really quick," I told Toi who nodded her head and went over to get a closer look at the water while I answered my phone. "What's up?"

"We got it."

"Got what?"

"That dog you told us to pick up. We're at the spot waiting for you nigga," he answered. Clenching my jaw, I nodded as if he could see me.

"Aight I'll be there in a minute." I hung up the phone then went over to Toi wrapping my arms around her waist and placing my head on her shoulder. "Would you be mad if I dropped you off at home? I gotta go handle something."

"As long as it's not another bitch I'm good. You have work to do?"

"Yeah, so I'm about to call this nigga so we can drop you and your girl off. I'm going to call you tomorrow so we can go out alright?"

"That's fine with me, handle your business." I couldn't help but smile at that shit. Most bitches would throw a fucking temper tantrum or act all mad and upset. In my line of business, I don't need a woman who's going to act up every time I gotta go handle some business so it's refreshing to know she isn't on that bullshit.

"Aight come on ma," I grabbed her hand and we walked off to find Yung and Taj.

WALKING into the warehouse I removed the shirt I had on leaving me topless. I reached into my back pocket and put the black leather gloves I had, on my hands.

I really had no plans to get my hands dirty today but when I got the call about this nigga, I had to come handle it. Scrappy, was a loyal runner of mine for a good minute. He always brought his money in on time, picked up on time, he was doing everything right, and then he had to go and steal twenty bands from me. Bad fucking idea.

"Where did y'all find this nigga at?" I asked Tone as he handed me the long machete.

"Hiding out at his baby mama crib, luckily his kids weren't there. I wouldn't feel right fucking a bitch up in front of her children and shit."

"I wouldn't have given a single fuck." I looked down at this punk ass nigga Scrappy who was tied to the chair with his hands facing forward. "What's up playboy? You thought you could steal from me and I wouldn't find your stupid ass?"

"Fuck you man!" He said after spitting out a mouth full of blood. They did a number on his ass before I got here. His eyes were swollen shut and his face was covered in so much blood I couldn't tell where the shit was coming from.

"Fuck me?" I laughed. "Bruh this nigga said fuck me." I nudged Tone as we all laughed. "Fuck you too bitch." I swung the machete down slicing both his hands off making his punk ass scream like the bitch he was.

"AHH FUCK!"

"The fuck is you screaming for? You said fuck me remember? Nigga you forgot who the fuck you dealing with? Take this shit like a man and quit being a bitch. Yo ass wasn't screaming when you were stealing my shit!"

"I-I'm sorr-sorry man," he cried.

"Oh, now you're sorry? A minute ago, it was fuck me. Aye bruh this nigga is sorry now. What should I say to that?" I looked at Yung and asked.

"Man, fuck him, turn this scrappy doo ass nigga into dog food."

"You know what? I like that idea, aye bruh dump it." I nodded at a worker and he along with another one grabbed a big bucket they had filled up with ground beef and poured it all over that nigga after knocking the chair he was in over.

"It's sad that all of this shit could've been avoided if your ass just stayed smart and not stolen from me my nigga. You really thought that shit was a good idea to steal from me? Me? Muthafucka nobody takes from me and lives to tell about that shit." I kicked him in mouth breaking his jaw before I backed up. "Let them out!" I shouted and just like I said they opened the gates for both bull mastiffs I had starving for two days to come out. Both dogs ran directly to that nigga and chowed down.

Screams filled the warehouse while I sat down in a chair and lit up a blunt smiling. I couldn't help but smile, I love seeing niggas who are dumb enough to cross me get what the fuck they deserve. I don't play that sneaky bullshit. I don't like being lied to and I don't like mutha-fuckas withholding information. If you're going to be around me, you better be a hundred or your ass will end up like little ole Scrappy here.

Toi

*A*fter a week of avoiding my grandmother about the situation with my mother, she finally made me sit down and listen to her. I thought I was about to leave but she caught me right before I went out the door. I really didn't want to talk about this shit because I still wasn't here for it. I don't even understand why my grandma is so forgiving. I know I'm not perfect and I've done some fucked up shit too, but it's certain things you can't just come back from.

"La'Toia, you need to learn how to let things go," my grandmother said to me.

"I do know how to let things go but I'm not going to be taken for a fool. She's been gone for how many years? Now she wants to pop back up with her little sob story about being clean and I'm supposed to just believe it. She's lied about it so many times before what's different this time around?"

"Your mother isn't perfect, she's far from it but she went to get help. Toi, she was a teenager when she got hooked on that stuff. Hell, she was a teenager when she had you. She messed up and now she's taking the necessary steps to fix it."

"After the first time it's no longer a mistake grandma, she knew exactly what she was doing. I'm not about to sit here and have compassion for some bullshit."

She put her hand up while looking at me like I lost my mind. "Hold on now, I don't care how upset you are. You need to watch your mouth when you're speaking to me."

"I'm sorry, it slipped out. That was wrong of me, but I meant what I said. If you want to deal with her, then fine grandma do that, but she can't expect hugs and kisses from me right now. I'm not at that point."

"That's your decision, hopefully you'll change it before you don't have the chance to."

"What does that mean?"

"Exactly what it sounds like." Getting up off the couch, she walked out of the living room leaving me there to feel like shit. I knew she was disappointed, and I hated that she felt that way, but my feelings are my feelings. I can't fake like I'm alright with her being around when I'm not.

"You know I love your grandmother, but I understand how you feel. I would be pissed off too," Mickey told me while handing me the blunt she just lit. "Shit, you know I understand the mommy issues thing."

"I don't want her unhappy but just because she forgives her doesn't mean I have to. It's just annoying, I don't need this shit on my plate. I got enough to worry about." I took a long pull from the blunt letting the smoke settle in my lungs before blowing it back out. I wasn't that big of a smoker, that was more of Mickey's thing, but I needed something to relax my nerves right now and it was too hot to get drunk.

"Like what?" She looked at me confused.

"What the fuck I'm going to do when my money runs out."

"Get some more, duh." Mickey looked at me like I was stupid.

"Not that damn easy, did you forget about what Beautii said? If she can recognize me it's nothing for somebody else to."

"That's why they won't, we just have to branch out a little farther. I have a nigga tonight that I planned on hitting up."

"Without me?"

"Yeah, you said you were pausing for a minute and I respect that,

55

so I didn't tell you. I don't give a fuck about what Beautii said. The day she pays my bills is when I'll care about her knowing some shit."

"What about Saint though?"

"If it's not him he shouldn't give a fuck. I don't want to hear his mouth, but he can kiss my ass too. I have shit I have to pay for and last time I checked neither of them were funding the bank of Mickey so fuck it. I gotta live out here."

"They're trying to help us stay alive, you know how niggas are out here. She made a good point."

"She did, but I took it as I just have to step my game up."

"Well you do you I'll just bow out this time."

"I'm fine with that but come on Toi you're dealing with Legend. He's paid as fuck."

"He's paid, that's his money not mine."

"Same thing, the nigga is basically claiming you."

"He is not, where did you hear that from?" I shook my head. I heard people talking about Legend and I around the way but niggas are nosey so it wasn't a surprise. This news about him claiming me was something I had yet to hear about though.

"The streets talk Toi, and the streets are saying you are his girl. I've never heard about him sporting any bitch like he does you. Well, at least not recently. Weren't you with him all weekend?"

"Yeah so what?" I chuckled.

"So how does the dick work?"

"Well, being that I've never had it I wouldn't know. I didn't spend the night. He came and got me on Friday, we went to the state fair then he took me back home. Saturday, we went out to eat and to the movies, then Sunday we just chilled at his condo watching TV."

"How does that shit look?"

"His condo? Sick as fuck, you can see the entire New York skyline from his window. He lives out in Edgewater you know how they live. Fuck all of that though back to what I was talking about. I need to do something to make some money."

"Start a business, come on now bitch we live in the hood. Think of something these bitches need, make it then charge them for it."

"I don't know," I whined falling back on her couch.

"Oh my God Toi," she snatched the blunt from me before taking a pull. "What about a spa?"

"Beautii has a spa."

"Beautii has a hair salon and calls it a hair spa. All she does is hair, you can have people doing nails, waxes, massages, facials, full spa treatments."

"Do you know how many spas it is in the city?"

"Okay and? How many are black owned? You're a well-known person Toi, if you open some shit people will come to it."

"Bitches can't afford spa treatments and shit."

"Oh, please they'll find a way to be in there just like they find a way to spend hundreds on bundles then another couple hundred to get it installed."

I thought about what Mickey was saying and she made a lot of sense. That would be a pretty good business to tap into. The only problem with doing it would be finding the money. "You may have a point, but I don't have that much. After paying everything off, getting those demon twins, me, and my grandmother some new clothes, I have about twenty thousand dollars left, and we still have to survive."

"First you have to get a business plan in order then once that's done you can get a loan or find an investor."

"I'll look into it, it does sound like a good idea. I'm done talking about me, what's going on with you? I heard you and Case were fuckin' around again."

"Is Bia running her mouth?" She asked. I couldn't help but laugh because I did hear it from Bia one day when I ran into her.

"Of course, she is. Don't be surprised if his bitch comes for you."

"Fuck that ho I don't care. She can come for me and get beat the fuck up if she wants to. I'm slapping Bia for spreading my business. That bitch can't hold water for nothing."

"You know how she is. When did you and Case start fucking around again?"

"About two months ago, I ran into him when I was at Perfections and we exchanged numbers. We chilled one night and boom, it just started but I don't give a damn about that boy."

"Well you know I don't agree with what it is you're doing," I told her, and she rolled her eyes.

Mickey is a gorgeous girl who is smart and will be down for you if she chooses to be. She could have any nigga she wants so why she goes after a nigga who's already taken baffles me a little bit but, then again, I understand why she is the way she is. After everything she went through with Brick's bitch ass, I don't blame her for having a guard up and not wanting to be serious with anybody. Hopefully, she'll find somebody to make her want to change that.

"I know you don't but it's my life, I'm going to do what I want. Sure, his girl well be hurt but so what? I've been hurt before too. She'll get over it, nobody gave a fuck about my feelings when they were fucking and sucking my nigga all the time so why should I care?"

"You're better than those bitches but do you Mick. Just be careful, don't catch feelings."

"The fuck is feelings?" She shrugged making me laugh.

"You're a cold bitch."

"Oh well. You love me anyway. So, what are you doing tonight?"

"I should be at this block party Que invited me to, but I wanted to chill with you first."

"Are you talking about the block party they always have at that motorcycle spot every year?"

"Yeah that's the one, you've heard of it?"

"A little bit here and there but I never went before. Let's go."

"You wanna go?" I asked.

"Yeah, from what I've heard that shit is always poppin when they throw any type of party. Besides, I want to meet this nigga that has you open."

"I'm not open."

"Oh please, you like that nigga. Admit it."

"I do but it hasn't been long, I still have more learning to do about this nigga. Are you going to change clothes or nah?"

She looked down at her clothes then back at me. She had on some black sweat pants and a beater. This is the most regular I've seen her look in a minute, plus her Mohawk was all black too. "Yeah but I'm not going all out like I usually would. Besides where those parties at I might end up slapping a bitch and I don't need to do that in my really cute stuff."

"Don't come out here starting shit Mickey, I don't feel like fighting."

"I won't start but I will respond if someone gets dumb." Mickey got off the couch and walked towards her bedroom. "Give me ten minutes."

Shaking my head, I couldn't help but laugh. Mickey is always fighting, bitches can't stand her ass at all. She's not the type to start some shit but if you approach her talking tough you better be ready to back it up because she doesn't go easy on anybody.

Why they decided to keep going after her is unknown to me. Maybe it's because of the way she carries herself or because they know she could have their nigga if she really wanted to. Either way they need to get over it. I've seen Mickey fight I don't know how many times and I have yet to see her lose one.

Mickey

*H*opping out of my Nissan Armada I chuckled while people took it upon themselves to stare at Toi and me. This wasn't anything new, anytime we went somewhere we commanded attention. Why wouldn't we? Who's badder than us? No fucking body.

"You know why they're staring at us right?" Toi asked me when I walked over to her.

"Because we look bomb as fuck."

"That, and you look like a superhero," she teased.

"Fuck you bitch I look good," I waved her off while she laughed. I was wearing a multi-color spandex two-piece, long sleeve crop top and leggings Adidas set with the matching shell toes. I know I looked good as fuck and I didn't give too much of a fuck about what anybody thought. If I wanted to wear a bright ass, tight ass outfit then that was my business. Nobody could dress like me or say I copied somebody else, this is one hundred percent all Mickey right here.

Toi kept it simple in some fitted ripped jeans, a white fitted t-shirt and nude dust low top Adidas on her feet. Her long hair was pulled back in a side swept ponytail and gold hoop earrings hung from her ears. Both of us had oversized Gucci sunglasses over our eyes with gold bangles and rings on our wrist and fingers. Neither one of us put any real effort into getting dressed today yet we shut down every bitch around us. The envious looks on their faces had me ready to point and laugh at their asses, but I kept it cute. I just hit them with a smile and kept it moving.

"You know I'm playing, you do look good. I wouldn't have let you leave the house if you didn't."

"Exactly why I wasn't worried, come on let's find your little boyfriend."

"He's not my boyfriend so stop it, you just remember to be nice."

"Mhm we'll see if I can." I gave her a sneaky smile. Toi is always trying to tell me to behave, when she knows damn well it's never me who starts. I just react.

"Come on I see him over there." She pointed ahead before grabbing my hand and leading me over. When she got close enough to him, he spotted her came over, so she let my hand go and hugged him.

She wrapped her arms around his neck while he pulled her body close to his with arms gripped around her waist. As they started to let each other go he kissed her on the forehead while his hands roamed her body a little bit. Not her man my ass.

"Well damn bruh, you tryna fuck her out here or something? Cool down," one of his boys said making his whole crew laugh.

"Shut the fuck up, hating ass nigga," Legend countered back.

"He's right though let me go," Toi laughed. Once he finally let her go, she waved to his friends before giving each of them small hugs. "What's up y'all?"

"Nothing much, what's good with you? Who's your friend?" The light skin one on the side asked. I didn't know who he was, but I've seen him around before and I knew he had money.

"This lady right here is my bestie Mickey, Mickey this baby face nigga is Yung."

"Aye watch that shit girl," he playfully checked her then looked at me. "What's up baby girl? Damn you fine, ass fat and all."

Chuckling I shook my head looking him up and down after. "Don't get too excited for what you're not blessed enough to have shorty," I told him. "This is the one Taj talks to, right?" I asked Toi.

Taj told me all about this nigga Yung and her description of him was right. He was tall as hell, had a light brown complexion, tattooed like crazy just like she likes them, and his hair was braided at the top and tapered on the side. He was cute, I could see them together.

"Yeah that's him. Anyway, moving on, that right there is Barry." She pointed to a dark skin muscular dude. I could tell he was used as the muscle. "Tone is next to him and this big rock head nigga is Qu-Legend," Toi said, correcting herself at the end. I guess she was about to say his real name, I don't know why she's acting like she never said his real shit before.

I waved at all of them then looked up at Legend who is just as fine as his reputation let's on. Toi damn sure picked a good one right here. "So, you're the one who's getting my bestie all sprung and what not. That's cute."

"You sprung on me already?" Legend questioned her with a smile on his face.

"No nigga, she's playing with you and she needs to quit it," Toi answered him lying like hell. She was feelin' this nigga but for some reason she doesn't want to admit it.

"You don't have to lie I already know what it is," he joked with her again before speaking to me. "It's nice to meet you ma, she's speaks about you a lot. Listen, since you're her homie, you're mine too aight. Nobody is going to fuck with you out here. Just do me a favor and tell your girl to stop playin' with me."

"Nah I think she's catching on, it's not too much for me to say, you got her already," I assured him.

"Don't make his head big Mickey. Come on though I want something to drink," Toi said, and I shrugged my shoulders.

"What does that have to do with me? The liquor store is across the street."

"I know that, you're not going to go over there with me?"

"I don't want a drink, I'm good right now."

"Come on ma I'll go with you," Legend gabbed her hand and they walked off leaving me with his boys. I didn't mind though, it was time for me to be a little bit nosey.

"So how long have y'all known each other?" Tone asked me.

"Too many years to count, what about y'all?"

"I watched that lil nigga grow up."

"I figured you were older than the rest of these niggas," I told him. It wasn't because he looked old, he looked damn good. He just had a different aura around him. Tone stood a little over six feet even, muscular build, a light complexion close to mine, and a short beard that was lined to perfection. His hair was cut low with waves spinning. He had on a fitted black t-shirt, dark Robbin jeans and black Retro twelves on his feet. A Rolex on his wrist, a gold cross chain around his neck, and diamond stud earrings, was the only jewelry had on. Tone is what I like to call grown ass man fine.

"Only by like four years but it's enough."

"How old are you?"

"I'm thirty baby girl, what about yourself?"

"I'm twenty-three, but I'm not a baby so don't call me baby girl," I smiled at him.

I don't usually smile at niggas genuinely unless it was on some homie shit but the way this nigga was eyeing me, I could tell the last thing he wanted to be was just a homie. I think I'm going to have a little fun being around this crew. I made a mental note to tell Toi good job later.

After five minutes of talking to Legend's friends, he and Toi finally came back. She pulled out two ice cups then filled them with a mixture of Grey Goose, pineapple, and cranberry juice. She gave one to me and we sipped on that while Legend and his boys drank Hennessey.

We sat around with Legend and his friends for a little while before I saw that it was starting to get dark. I went to tell Toi that I was about to head out but stopped when I saw her lighting a blunt. I figured I could leave after I got a good high going.

Before Toi could even pull from the blunt Legend snatched it out of her hand. "What the hell are you doing?" She asked looking at him like he was crazy.

"You good, you don't need to smoke. Pour something to drink and chill out."

"I already had a drink and now I want to smoke. Bruh we're not about to do this because I am not that girl." She removed herself from his lap then took the blunt back from his hands. "If I want to smoke, I'll smoke. You're not going to dictate what I do. Comprende?"

Chuckling Legend stood up grabbed the blunt from her then gave it to me. "We'll be right back." He grabbed her hand and they walked off leaving me confused.

"I'm feeling nice so I'm not so quick right now but what the hell is he about to do? Tell me something so I know if I need to swing or not," I looked at his friends and said.

"Nah they're just about to talk, he's not going to do anything to shorty. He actually likes her, he's not going to fuck up trust me," Tone answered me.

"Oh alright, just making sure. I like y'all and shit, but I'll kill for that one."

Legend and his boys were cool from what I could see. None of them had been disrespectful yet which is a record in my books. Usually niggas get around some women and don't know how to fucking act. These niggas were chill, they could joke without getting all up in their feelings like a bunch of bitches and I appreciated that. I didn't want to deal with any drama, I've had a couple of drinks, smoking will only enhance my shit I'm trying to stay this way. If someone blows my shit, they're getting slapped.

"There that bitch is right there!" I heard some bitch screaming. "Nah fuck that get off me Case!" As soon as I heard that name I laughed. This isn't what I wanted to happen here, but I should've known it would. I'm me, bitches hate my fuckin' guts.

Getting up I turned around to see where the noise was coming from and got a better laugh. Case had his bitch around the waist while she faked like a wild banshee for the crowd. This bitch couldn't bust a grape in a fruit fight in a Welch's backyard, her hands are lighter than a Listerine strip. I know this because I've had run-ins with this hoe before and she got her ass beat every time. The only reason I'm not running up on her is because I know I can sleep this bitch easily. Besides, her looking so angry was amusing to me.

"The fuck is you laughing at ho?" she shouted at me.

"Your simple ass, you're doing too much ma calm the fuck down," I answered her.

"Fuck you! You fucked my nigga!"

"I sure did and so? So what? You're mad and trying to fight me for fucking him but you're going to go right back to sucking his dick tonight so cut the dramatics." I can't stand bitches that do this shit. Do all this barking about your man cheating but still go home with his ass at the end of the night. Get the fuck outta here.

"You a ho ass bitch! Stop chasing my nigga, he not leaving me for you."

"Well, can you tell him that because I don't think he knows, or maybe he just doesn't give a damn. This nigga has offered to leave your ass multiple times ma. I'm not trying to hurt your feelings but you're yelling at the wrong one, so handle that nigga. Don't come trying to handle me."

"It's bitches like you that have these niggas doing loyal women like me wrong." I passed the blunt to Tone before giving shorty my undivided attention.

"You sound stupid. Let me tell you something, if your nigga isn't loyal to you it's not my fault boo. I don't owe your stupid ass a damn thing. It's up to your nigga to be faithful to you, I couldn't give a fuck about you. Talk to the nigga holding you instead of coming at my neck." I guess the truth was getting to this bitch because she broke loose from Case then came rushing over to me.

As soon as I saw this bitch coming forward, I got ready to tag her ass, but she stopped before getting close and bruh, this nasty, broke down, big back having ass bitch spit at me. It's like everything happened in slow motion because I watched her spit come towards my way and it landed on my shirt.

I closed my eyes looked down at my shirt again because I thought I was seeing shit; this bitch did not just spit on me. When I reopened and looked at the spit stain on my shirt, I started to walk over to this bitch, but somebody grabbed me from behind.

"Let me go! That bitch spit on me!" I shouted at whoever was holding me. "BITCH IMMA KILL YO ASS I PUT THAT ON MY

OWN GRAVE IM KILLIN YOU BITCH! IF I DON'T DO IT MYSELF KNOW YOUR ASS IS GETTING TOUCHED TONIGHT!"

"Chill out!" I recognized Tone's voice in my ear. He turned me around and started walking me backwards, but I could hear Toi's voice behind us.

"The fuck is going on?" Toi questioned. "Where that bitch at?" I heard her shout. Out of nowhere I heard damn near the whole crowd go "Ooh!" I don't know what the fuck that was about but knowing Toi the way I know her, Legend was about to have a challenge on his hands.

I couldn't help but laugh because I just warned this bitch. If I didn't get to you, somebody was going to get to you for me and that person is Toi. When you're fucking with one of us you better be on the lookout for the other because it's always going to be some shit when we're around.

Legend

"*N*ah I heard Mickey yelling," Toi walked past me and back over to where everybody was. Here we were talking and vibing when this loud ass commotion caught our attention. I was going to ignore it, but Toi wasn't even trying to hear that because she felt like Mickey was involved. By the time we got over there I saw Tone walking Mickey off. Shorty really knows her friend because she was right about her being mixed in.

"The fuck is going on?" Toi questioned.

"That bitch spit on her man," Yung answered her, and it was like a flash went off on Toi's eyes.

"Where that bitch at?" She was about to go over to whoever this bitch was that was going off was, but I grabbed her waist.

"Chill out, don't go over there," I told her, but she wasn't trying to hear that.

"Nah fuck that!" Before I could get a real grip around her waist her little ass broke loose from and ran over to this bitch and punched her straight in the face so hard the whole damn crowd reacted.

Out of nowhere they were in a full-blown fight on the ground. At first, I wasn't going to break it up basically because not only was she fucking shorty up the bitch deserved it. The fuck spits on somebody? Nasty ass broad.

When Toi grabbed two fistfuls of her hair and started banging her head against the street, I pushed everybody out the way and picked her up, but she wouldn't let the girl's hair go and was still throwing punches. At least I know she can fight, and she goes real street with it.

"LET HER FUCKING HAIR GO MAN!" I yelled in her ear, but she wouldn't listen. It took Yung and Barry to get her hands off the girl's hair. Once she did, I lifted her off her feet and started walking the opposite direction away from the crowd.

"Weak nasty ass bitches!" Toi screamed as I was pulling her away.

"Watch your mouth and chill the fuck out bruh," I told her while we walked.

"I'm good now, let me go."

"Hell nah."

"I'm serious Que I'm good let me go."

"If I let you go and you wild out again it's going to be a problem," I warned her.

"Mhm okay, just let me go. I already fucked her up. I'm done." I let her go and she started to walk over to where Mickey was with Tone. Mickey came out her shirt and everything. All she had on was her pants and a black sports bra. "Where is your shirt?"

"I took it off that bitch spit on it, the fuck would I look like still wearing it."

"Wash that shit."

"Fuck no," Mickey said before throwing her shirt in the street. "I'm about to go home so I can calm the fuck down. If I stay here, I'll kill a bitch for real."

"Well I rode with you, so I'll leave with you," Toi offered but Mickey shook her head no.

"Nah girl, you stay here with your boo or whatever. No need for both of our shit to be blown. I'm going to take a shower then I'm out to do that shit we were talking about earlier."

"Oh alright, be careful. Call me when you in the house for the night."

"I got you. I'll see y'all another time or something man," Mickey told us before walking off.

Once she was gone, I shook my head. "Y'all on some other shit," I said aloud.

"Man, shorty doesn't play games. I'm feelin' her," Tone smirked.

"Oh lord," Toi laughed looking up at me. "Listen I don't know if you're ready to go or whatever, but I need to get the fuck away from here before one of her little flunkies try to say some bullshit. Then it'll really get bad."

"Aight come on man," I put my arm over her shoulder then told Tone I was leaving. "You know you're too pretty to be fighting like the rest of these bitches, right? You and Mickey both," I said to her as we walked to my car.

"We do know that but if they start what are we supposed to do? She spit on her, the only reason I got involved was because I could tell Mickey didn't get a chance to touch her ass. I'm sorry if I fucked up your good time but that couldn't slide."

"You good, I understand why you did it. You had to have your homies back. Just know this much, when I say that's enough, that's enough. You could've killed that bitch."

"I got you. So where are we going? I really don't wanna go home but I can't stick around here either."

"You're still not fucking with your mother?"

"No, and I don't feel like talking about it."

"Fine, we don't have to talk about it right now, but we will at some point. Why don't you find your own place?"

"There's no way for me to afford my own spot then still pay the bills at my grandmother's house. She can't work, the twins don't work yet and even if they could they wouldn't make enough."

Nodding my head, I leaned against my car once we got to it and pulled her in front of me. "Alright look I might be able to help you out."

"How?"

"You've been to my condo remember."

"Yeah, what about it."

"Move in there."

"Wait," she looked at me confused. "You want me to move in with you?"

"No, I said move in there, I'm barely there."

"Why?"

"I'm always working man; besides, you really think that's my only spot? You can move in there, and still take care of your grandmother's house, but I have some conditions."

"What kind of conditions? Ass better not be on the list."

I chuckled. "Nah it's not. I don't want niggas up there, don't bring anybody I don't know to my spot aight."

"Oh, that's already understood."

"I'm not playing, nobody better not be in my shit. You need to get some legit business going on. I don't know what the fuck you do to get money and at this point I'm not caring. You just need to find something permanent."

"I was talking to Mickey about that earlier, she suggested I do a spa."

"A spa?"

"Yeah, a full-service spa where you can get facials, nails, waxes. All the stuff women love, I just need to know where to begin with it."

"My sister might be able to help you out with a business plan."

"You have a sister? You didn't tell me that."

"You didn't ask. I do have a sister, a little sister but that's not who I'm talking about."

"So, who are you talking about?"

"We're not blood we just go way back, I can hook you up with her or you can just talk to Beautii about a business plan."

"Nah I rather have someone fresh on this, give me her information."

"I got you. I need something first."

"That would be?" Smirking I leaned in closer to her face before pressing my lips against hers. Pulling her body closer to me, I parted her lips with mine before sliding my tongue into her mouth while her hands found their way around my neck. My hands went down her backside before I gripped her ass in my hands

Smiling she pulled away from me then looked to her right like she was trying to avoid eye contact. "Why you looking away? Don't go getting shy on me," I joked.

"I'm not getting shy, shut up," she laughed. "Come on, let's go." She grabbed my hand and we walked over to the passenger side of the car. I opened the door for her then helped her sit down. After closing her door, I went over to the driver's side and got in.

"Seat belt ma," I told her. Once we were both buckled up, I pulled off. "You hungry?"

I don't know what it is about this girl but I'm feelin' her. The shit is scary.

Legend

"So, you're giving shorty your condo? Okay when is the wedding because I'm trying to be in there with a camera for proof," Yung joked while I drove down the street.

"Shut the fuck up ain't nobody getting married. I'm helping her out for a reason."

"You're feelin' her, it's simple as hell to understand bruh. I don't blame you she's cool as fuck and she keeps people like that around her."

"Talking about Taj?"

"Hell yeah, she's bad as fuck in many ways. I mean come on you see her she sexy as hell but it's more than that. She's not sweating my ass when I need to be somewhere, she's just chill."

"Toi is the same way, but I don't know it's making me wonder if it's just a cover up for some crazy shit. She's probably waiting to show that crazy psycho side."

"Man, that's women in general, there all cool in the beginning but then once they get comfortable, they start buggin'. I don't mind it from Taj though, that's the funny part."

"Sounds to me like you trying to lock her ass down."

"You damn skippy, she got a nigga though and that shit is killing me."

"So, you're trying to steal someone else's girl?"

72

"Yeah pretty much, do you think I give a damn? Fuck nah, I'm good. Toi moved in your shit yet?"

"She has some of her stuff over there, she said she was going to slowly put more stuff into it. It's not like she needs to go shopping for furniture or something so she's good. I told her to hook up with Dutch to get her business plan together."

"You sent her to Dutch? I bet you she hit on her."

"She better not, besides Toi doesn't go that way."

"None of the girls' Dutch fuck with go that way, you think that stops her? All I'm saying is watch your girl bruh, she's going to snatched from your ass."

I looked over at this nigga before grabbing my phone and calling Toi then I put it on speaker only for her to answer on the second ring.

"Hello biscuit head, what's up?" She said when she answered.

"I told you about that shit," I chuckled. "What are you doing?"

"Going over some things for my spa with Dutch."

"Where y'all at?"

"Condo, she's your sister it's not a problem, right?"

"Nah let me speak to her real fast though."

"Okay hold on, here it's Que," I guess Toi passed her the phone because the next voice I heard was Dutch's.

"What's up nigga?"

"Nothing, the fuck is you doing with her? Better be business and that's it," I said making her bust out laughing.

"Bruh nobody is going to hit on her I can tell you like this one. I'm not going to go after your girl calm your ass down."

"I'm just making sure we're on the same page. What's up with her business plan though?"

"It's done, all she needs is the money."

"Is it worth my investment?"

"From what I see it is, you'll be dumb as fuck not to invest in this shit. It's going to make a lot of money."

"You're sound so sure."

"Man, bitches will spend the money to come here and everybody knows who she is, so they'll be there off the strength of her too. Then on top of that she's your girl so people will come because of your name too. If you're serious about helping her out, do you."

"Aight good lookin' out. Get off her phone now nigga." Dutch laughed then gave Toi her phone back.

"Are you coming over here tonight?" Toi asked when she got on the phone.

"I don't know yet, I gotta see how shit is out here I might have to handle some shit. Why? You miss me already?" I laughed.

"Not really I just wanted to know if you could pick me up some pizza or something. All you have in this bitch is liquor, I need to go food shopping. Nigga don't you eat?"

"I told you I'm barely there and when I am, I just order shit."

"That's a damn shame, you know too much takeout is bad for you right?"

"Well I don't have anybody to cook for me, so it is what it is."

"Sucks to be you," she laughed hard as hell at that like it was funny. Corny ass.

"If I don't have too much to do, I'll be over there so you need to cook."

"I need to cook? Hmm you know what? That didn't sound much like a question."

"That's because it wasn't one, it was a statement."

"Well you need reword that and turn into a question. I don't take orders boo."

I chuckled, she's lucky she's cute. "Aight ma, can you cook tonight?"

"Yes, I can, what time are you coming over here?"

"I'll let you know, it'll be late I know that much. I got my keys, so I'll just let myself in."

"Mhm about that, those keys need to be given up. I live here now, you can't be up in my space anytime you feel like it. You don't have it like that sir."

"Like hell I don't, don't play with me La'Toia."

"I'm dead ass serious Quentin," she shot back then laughed. "I can say government names too. I don't want to go back and forth with your big head ass I gotta go. Get up off my line and go to work or something."

"Oh, now you're telling me what to do?"

"Sure am, bye Que. I'll see or talk to you later. Whichever one comes first."

"Aight ma." After hanging my phone up Yung started laughing.

"Nigga y'all act like y'all been together for years. If I didn't know anybody, I would think that shit."

"Good thing you don't get paid to think nigga, shut up."

Toi

"You ou should just come out, it's like eleven and he hasn't called. He's working, damnit Toi you're not even in a relationship yet and you already sitting in the house waiting up for the nigga. Dick must be awesome. I wanna be like you when I grow up real shit," Mickey teased.

"Bitch shut up," I laughed. "I want to go out too, but this couch is too damn comfortable."

"So what? Just come out girl damn, I'm picking you up in twenty minutes. I have to get Bia and Taj afterwards so you can't be taking forever."

"I got you damn, I'll be ready."

"Aight I'll see you then." I hung up the phone before hooking it up to the charger then turned the stereo system all the way up making my way into the bathroom after.

Hopping in the shower I cleansed my body using my Victoria's Secret's Secret Craving body wash. Once my shower was over, I got out, dried off then moisturized my body in my bedroom before picking getting dressed. I was wearing a simple army green sleeveless body suit, slightly ripped blue jeans and thigh high army green peep toe boots. My hair was still straight so I had it pulled back into a tight sleek ponytail. My makeup was super light and the only jewelry I wore was some diamond stud earrings and the bracelet Que bought me.

Just as I was finishing my makeup Mickey sent me a text letting me know she was outside. I grabbed my things then went rushing downstairs and hopped into the front seat of her car.

"You look cute ma," Mickey smiled at me then pulled off.

"Thanks, I'm surprised to see you toned down tonight. Growing up some?" Mickey was wearing a tan spaghetti mini dress and some gold ankle strap heels. Her makeup was light, and her Mohawk was curled to perfection.

"Bitch I been grown I just felt like keeping it simple. Don't try and play me."

"I'm not you look good. So, Bia is coming out huh? I was surprised to see her ass at that all-white party. Kareem doesn't usually let her ass go anywhere."

Kareem is a controlling ass nigga when it comes down to Bia and the shit she's allowed to do. He doesn't like her out unless his ass is there to watch her, and usually that ends up in a damn fight because he can't control his fucking liquor.

"I know, but she wanted to come so I gotta pick her ass up. She better not blows my shit talking about leaving early. Her ass will be walking home or something. I'm not here for that shit tonight bruh."

"I feel you, we haven't been out together in a minute. Usually it's work if we do go."

"I know which is why I'm turning the fuck up and anybody with a problem can kiss my ass." We both laughed while she made her way to pick Bia and Taj up. I haven't been out with all my girls in a long time, so I was looking forward to just having a couple drinks and turning up.

Club Envy was packed as usual. It was like the street was filled with any and everybody it was so many people out. Envy always pulled in this type of crowd, so it wasn't surprising, I just knew it was going to be one interesting night. It's never a dull moment in this bitch.

All eyes were on us as we walked across the street and to the entrance of the club. I wasn't about to stand on line, that shit was around the damn corner, who was about to deal with that shit? Not I said the duck.

"Jay!" Mickey shouted just as we approached the bouncer that was in the front.

"What's up Mick?" He asked while giving her a small hug. "How many you got with you?"

"Three, you know them nigga don't act new."

"Aight go in, no fighting though Mickey."

"I know I got you. Come on y'all."

Beyoncé's" Drunk in Love" blasted through the club as we walked in. If outside looked crazy packed the inside was just as insane. Club Envy is usually packed, but this was like it was a special occasion or something.

"It looks like we got here on the right night!" Mickey shouted over the music.

"Come on." We made our way to the dance floor and at once got it poppin'. I would've loved to get a drink first but fuck it, might as well work up a little bit of a sweat.

After dancing through five songs straight we all made our way to the bar where Mickey ordered a round of shots. After downing the shot of liquor, I waved my hand at the bartender and ordered a drink for myself. I wasn't about to take shots all damn night and pass out, nope it will not be one of those nights.

We walked around the club for a few minutes until we finally found an open table so and sat down.

"It's mad niggas in here, and they fine as fuck!" Bia exclaimed making us all look at her like she was crazy.

"Now you know damn well Kareem will try to kill your ass if you even think about approaching one of these niggas. I saw a couple of his homies when we came in here, and they will tell on your ass if you do anything stupid. Bia if you blow my shit I swear to God," Mickey got on her.

"I'm not going to do anything I'm just saying; damn can I look?"

"Fuck no, I don't need drama tonight bruh. I got enough of that shit to fucking worry about with Case's stupid ass in here."

"You saw him?" I questioned Mickey. I knew she wasn't looking forward to talking to that nigga especially since she stopped fucking with him when his bitch got stupid with her now, he was damn near stalking her ass. The nigga will not leave her alone.

"Why do you think I got the fuck away from the bar? It's like he doesn't know what leave me the fuck alone means."

"Just keep ignoring him Mick, he'll get the hint eventually," Taj told her.

"He better I will fuck him up if he's on some bullshit."

"Just calm down alright, we came here to have a good time and we will. Now I need to go to the bathroom really fast I'll be right back. Watch my damn drink." I got up from my seat before making my way to the restroom.

After using it I washed my hands, I retouched my makeup before exiting the bathroom. Before I could make my way back to the table, I felt my arm being grabbed. Turning around ready to swing I stopped when I saw one of Quentin's boys. I didn't know his name, but I saw him around before.

"Legend wants you ma," he said in my ear.

"He's here?"

"Yeah come on," I followed him over to the VIP section and there he was with all his people. I walked over to where he was sitting and bent down to speak to him.

"Now I see why you couldn't come over," I said with a smile on my face. When he looked up, he smiled then pulled down to his lap.

"What's up ma?"

"Nothing, what are you doing here?"

"I should be asking you that and with this shit on? Who are you trying to pick up?"

"You're funny, I don't pick niggas up you know that. I just like looking good. These are just jeans Que."

"Damn the jeans I'm talking about the top. I can see your bra." I looked at down at my black bra that was visible because of the sheer material the body suit was made of.

"Be lucky I wore a damn bra. I look just fine, be happy about it and hush."

"Yeah aight man, keep these niggas away from you is all I'm going to say," he said before kissing me. "Who are you here with?"

"I came with Mickey, Taj and Mickey's cousin Bia."

"Word?" He looked over at Yung who had a bitch on his lap and threw something at him to get his attention.

"The fuck bruh?" Yung looked over with a frown on his face.

"Your girl downstairs nigga! You see how this one is dressed, you know she on the same shit. Go handle that!"

"Oh, shit for real?" Yung pushed the girl off his lap and walked off.

"You still didn't tell me what you were doing here," I said to Quentin when he turned his attention back to me.

"I'm working actually."

"Working? In here?"

"Yeah, you don't need to know the details. What you do need to know is you need to get out of here."

"Why?"

"It's not safe, some shit is going to go down in here tonight and you don't need to be anywhere around."

Raising my eyebrow, I looked at him. "What are you up to?"

"I'm not up to anything but I know what I'm talking about. Get your girls and go somewhere, anywhere out of this area."

"Quentin what's going on?"

"We'll talk about that shit later, just go. I'll see you in the morning aight." He kissed me again then tapped my leg for me to get up, so I did.

"You better not do something stupid, be careful." I pecked his lips one more time before leaving his section and going back to where Mickey was still sitting.

"Where did they go?"

"Taj walked off with Yung and Bia went out to the dancefloor. I didn't feel like going back out yet."

"Well we need to find them so we can go."

"Go? Why?"

"Que was up in his section and sent some nigga to come get me."

"Let me guess, you need to go home?"

"Home no, the fuck up out of here yeah. He said something was supposed to pop off tonight."

"Aww shit, I know what that means. Come on get your stuff and grab theirs too." We both grabbed everything and went to find Taj and Bia.

Taj wasn't too hard to find she was by the bar talking to Yung. "Aye nigga call her later so we can go," Mickey told him.

"Oh yeah y'all need to go. I'm going to call you aight. Go with your girls." He kissed her on the cheek then walked off.

"What's going on?" Taj asked me.

"You don't want to know, we just need to go before some shit goes down. The fuck is Bia."

"She's over there on the dance floor." Taj pointed and we all looked over at this fool backing her ass up on some random nigga.

"This bitch does not like her life, she's doing that bullshit like Kareem can't walk his ass up in here." Mickey shook her head.

"Speaking of Kareem," I said just as I saw him walking through the crowd. The only reason I saw his black ass was because the crowd split as he walked through.

Hood infamous is the best way to describe Kareem. He knows a lot of people and vice versa. Don't get it twisted he wasn't known for anything good. The nigga is a complete maniac, he's known for busting up the party with some bullshit. Everywhere he goes ends up in a big brawl or a complete shootout. Right now, I'm wondering which one it'll be tonight.

"Oh fuck, come on." Mickey moved past me and started walking ahead. I could tell she was trying to make it to Bia before Kareem could but that was dead as soon as he grabbed her by her hair and dragged her outside of the club.

"Oh shit!" Taj shouted and we all rushed outside to find them.

When we figured out which way, they went we made our way

over. The closer we got to them we could hear him yelling like he was stupid while she sat there with the dumb face crying. Mickey was about to step in front of Bia when Kareem swung his fist hitting Bia straight in her face making the whole crowd gasp when she hit the floor.

"Get the fuck up!" He shouted at her.

"I'm sorry Kareem!" Bia cried making herself look even more foolish. This nigga just knocked the fuck out of you and you're the one apologizing?

He started to grab her again, but Mickey pushed him back. "You on some other shit, leave her the fuck alone!" Mickey shouted at him.

"Shut the fuck up bitch. You probably the one making her do this stupid shit. You want her to be a hoe just like you."

"I'll bust you in your shit just like I did the last time. Don't fuck with me. I got your bitch!" Mickey started to get in his face, but I grabbed her dress from behind and pulled her back.

"Chill Mickey, we're just going to get her and get the fuck out of here. Bia come on," I helped her off the floor and she started screaming at him.

"You always do this bullshit to me!"

"Bitch I'll slap the shit out of you, the fuck you think you talking to? I told your stupid ass not to come out tonight and you leave anyway. Then you got the nerve to be shaking yo ass on another nigga trying to make me look stupid!"

"You can run the streets with your niggas, but I can't go out with my friends?" she screamed back at him.

"Bia chill," Taj told her.

"Friends? These hoes ain't your fucking friends! I told your stupid ass they don't give a fuck about you and I didn't want you around these gold diggin' ass bitches!"

"Hold the fuck up!" I shouted. Now he was pissing me off. "All of that extra shit ain't even called for. Watch who the fuck your black ass is calling names I'll get yo ass fucked up!"

"Shut the fuck up and mind your business! Bia let's fucking go before I really get mad out here man," Bia stood there like she really didn't know which way to go and before I knew it his ass punched her dead in the face again.

"Nah man," Mickey who was already unbuckling her shoes while Kareem was talking, kicked them off and was about to rush this nigga. I grabbed her waist pulling her back again.

"Kareem," I tried to keep my voice calm while I talked to his dumb ass. If Mickey got to swinging on him, we would all be out this bitch boxing. "You really need to fucking chill right now! You disrespectful as fuck and this supposed to be your woman? The fuck raised you to treat anybody like this?"

"Not a crackhead like your mother that's for damn sure," he shot back.

"Alright, Mickey you get him first and I'll follow up, he on some other shit." I gave my shit to Taj ready to fuck this nigga up. Bia can take that disrespectful shit if she wants to but I'm not going for it. Now it's about to go down out here, he has me completely fucked up.

Before I could even get to the nigga, I felt a strong pair of arms go around my waist. Looking behind me, I sighed when I saw it was Que holding me. Looking over I saw Tone pull Mickey back then Barry stopped her when she tried to get past him.

"Aye man, you out here buggin'. You need to go home and sober up," Que said to Kareem.

"The fuck, is you? Her keeper?" Kareem looked at him with his face all screwed up. Clearly, he didn't know who the fuck he was talking to.

"I'm Legend and your talking to my woman crazy isn't sitting too right with me. Just move the fuck on before it gets real out here," as soon as those words left his mouth all of his boys stepped up with their guns drawn.

Kareem, who was standing there by his damn self, shook his head and walked off. "Bitch ass nigga," I mumbled.

"You good?" Que asked me.

"Yeah I'm fine, thank you I guess."

"No problem ma, I knew I told your ass to go home or something though."

"We were about to leave when his ass popped up, blowing my shit."

"You'll get your shit back up, just get out of here before something else pops off. I'm calling you later." He kissed me on the cheek before walking off and going back in the club. When he was gone, I walked over to Mickey, Bia, and Taj.

"You okay Bia?"

"No but I will be," she sniffled. "I need to go home I'm not even feeling this shit anymore."

"You're not going home, as soon as you step in the door, he's going to be on you and I'm not letting that shit happen. You're coming with me," Mickey told her.

I didn't bother saying anything while she and Mickey went back and forth about her going home. This shit always happened, why the fuck she would even want to go be in the same house with that nigga I don't know. I don't know why she dealt with it period, he treats her like she doesn't mean shit to him. It's obvious she doesn't if he can do her like that and not give a fuck about it. It's like everybody sees this shit but her.

Looking at her I shook my head in disgust. Her eye was swelling shut and her lip looked like it was busted. He just fucked her face up in a matter of minutes and she wants to go back. I'm completely confused.

"Going back and forth makes no sense right now. Bia your ass is going home with Mickey and that's it. Can we get in the fucking car and go now? Damn," Taj said. I could tell she was frustrated, and I don't blame her, I was too. A good night ruined by a fuck boy.

We all got into Mickey's car and left. I'm ready for this night to be completely over.

Mickey

y phone ringing woke me out of the deep sleep I was trying to stay in. The damn thing rung at least twice but I ignored it. Whoever is calling me, interrupting my sleep is about to get cursed the fuck out.

Reaching over I picked the phone up and sucked my teeth when I saw it was Case calling me. That shit just sent me on level ten in five seconds. I wanted to ignore it again but from what I could see it was after five in the damn morning, so he had to calling for a reason, or at least he better be.

"I know you see it's early as fuck, the hell is you calling me at the butt crack of dawn for?" I asked him with my voice drenched in attitude when I answered his call.

"Mickey calm down, this shit is important."

"It damn well better be the fuck is going on bruh?"

"You heard about Bia?"

"Did I hear about Bia? That's my fucking cousin of course I heard I was there with her last night when Kareem started spazzing out."

"Nah ma, that's different I'm talking about earlier. From what I heard they got into it at their house now the cops and shit all up in their spot. They got damn near the whole block locked down."

"How would they get into a fight when she came home with me

last night?" I got up out of my bed and walked out of my room to go down the hall.

The streets are saying something different so go check on your cousin ma. You know that nigga Kareem crazy. I'll holla at you later." Before I could tell his ass not to, he hung up.

Once I got to my guest bedroom door I knocked twice then walked straight in when I got no answer. The bed was completely made up and Bia's stuff was gone. "Fuck!" I ran to my room throwing on a pair of basketball shorts and grabbing a hoodie from my closet before leaving.

I was about to grab my car keys, but Kareem just said they had the street blocked off which means it's probably traffic out the ass. Bia only lives four blocks over so grabbed my keys and my phone and ran all four blocks down to her house.

I don't know what the fuck done went and happened this time, but I do know I was going to fuck Kareem up as soon as I saw his ass. I'm tired of this shit between them two and I want Bia to leave his ass alone, but she doesn't know how to do that shit on her own.

Her situation with Kareem isn't even shocking, she's always been attracted to the wrong niggas. For whatever reason she finds it ok for a nigga to put his hands on her ass. I was dumb like that too at one point, but I grew out of it, plus I fight back. Bia is nowhere near a fighter. She's never had to fight since she's the baby of the damn family everybody always fought her battles for her. Maybe that's why her mouth is so damn reckless.

All I know I know is this is the last time, I'm putting her ass on a plane so she can go down south with her mama, hell maybe I'll put her on a bus. It'll give her more time to think.

Once I reached Bia's block I slowed down as I walked to her house. Case definitely wasn't lying about it being crazy around here, it was police and everything out this bitch. Was all of this really necessary for a fucking domestic violence call? JCPD is always stretching some shit.

Before I could get to the house like I wanted to, I heard my name being called so I looked over to see Toi walking over to me dressed in a sweat suit and her hair tied up. From the expression on her face she looked tired as fuck, I guess being out this early was fucking with her too.

"You heard about this bullshit too huh? She must've left my house and came back here. I swear to God I'm slapping the both of them for this shit, I'm tired as hell."

"Mickey," Toi said in a low tone.

"What? I'm serious, this shit is enough. I'm tired of this bullshit, but you don't want to hear this, so where is Bia so I can let her know while it's still fresh in my mind." I started to walk towards the house, but Toi grabbed my arm.

"Mickey wait, she's not in there."

"She's not? So, what happened, they locked her up to? Please tell me it was her who beat ass time, finally," I laughed.

"No, they took her out already, Mickey you need to sit down. Come with me."

"Come with you where? I'm good Toi, where is she? Where did they put her?"

"Mickey please, just come with me alright." She tried to pull me again, but I wouldn't move.

"No, I'm not going with you, the fuck is going on. Where is my cousin?"

"I'm going to tell you, but you need to hear the whole story aight. You're right Bia left your house and came back here. Just like we thought he would Kareem jumped on her ass and that went how it always does but she got her phone and called me to come get her. The reason she called me was because she knew I would have her back just like you would, but I wouldn't go off on her like you always do. I was going to save that shit for you to do once you found out what happened. I got up, got dressed came here and when I got inside, she was on the living room floor."

"Doing what?"

"Bleeding," Toi paused then looked down at her clothes and it was like I finally paying attention. The sweat suit she had on was black but the t-shirt she had on under her hoodie was white and there you could see the blood stains on it.

"Bleeding?" I cleared m throat loudly. I felt like I had a golf ball in my throat it was so damn hard to swallow. "Bleeding where?"

"From her head, I don't know what the fuck he did but that's what I saw when I got here, and his ass was gone. I called the police and the ambulance."

"So, where is she? Is she alright?"

Looking down she shook her head no. No more had to be said after that. I already knew what she meant, my cousin was gone, and that punk ass nigga did it.

I turned around and started kicking the fuck out of somebody's car, I don't know who this shit belonged to and I really didn't give a fuck. After the third kick I saw that I put one hell of a dent in the side of it, that's when Toi grabbed me from behind and pulled me away from the car.

As much as I wanted to hold in my tears, I couldn't fight them anymore I just went ahead and let them fall down my face. Toi turned me around and hugged me tight. "Why didn't she just stay at my house?" I screamed in tears.

Toi didn't answer me she kept hugging me and walked down the opposite end of the block with me. "You know we gonna get this handled right?" Toi said and I nodded my head while I continued to cry.

If Kareem's black ass thought this shit was going to just happen and go away without him getting touched, he has shit fucked all the way up. I'll be seeing that nigga again and it's going to take God himself to stop me from killing his ass.

Tiana "Taj" Jackson

"Hey." I gave Yung a small smile before hugging him. "Thank you for coming, I know you didn't really know Bia like that."

"I remember you introduced me to shorty, she was cool. What happened to her is fucked up," he shook his head. "How is Mickey doing?"

"Not good, she's trying to keep it together, but I can tell it's fucking with her. Come on it's too many people over here, move over." I grabbed his hand and moved down from in front of the church.

Unsurprisingly Bia's funeral was super packed. It's like damn near the whole city came to pay their respects to her. Everybody knew who she was. Besides a few hating ass bitches from the block nobody ever had an issue with her, why would they? Bia was the type of person to befriend just about anybody she was that nice. It's just fucked up she had to die at twenty years old behind somebody so damn stupid and ignorant.

"So, what's up with this nigga who did it? They find him?"

"Nope, not yet, but he will be dealt with. I think he forgot who Bia is. It's a bunch of niggas that are willing to handle it on her behalf."

Kareem is the biggest fucking idiot on the planet doing what he did to Bia. Not only was it just evil, it was dumb because this nigga forgets nobody really fucked with him except the wack niggas he rolls with. Bia was the reason nobody went after his ass, they were keeping him alive off the strength of her. Nigga gotta go now, good-bye, he won't be missed.

"Good, I know what the nigga looks like. If I see him, I'll blow his fucking head off, I don't like that type of shit."

"Nobody with a heart does, it's fucked up." Looking towards the front of the church I watched as they carried Bia's baby pink casket out to the hearse with her family walking right behind the pallbearers. When Mickey came out Toi was right there next to her holding her hand.

Mickey was trying her hardest to keep calm, but I knew she wasn't good. They bickered all the damn time and anybody that didn't know them too well would think they couldn't stand each other but Mickey and Bia were close as hell. Despite the good act she was putting on right now I knew once she got alone, she was going to break down.

Breaking my eyes away from Mickey and Toi I looked at Yung who was staring at me like he had something he wanted to say. "What's up? Why are you looking at me like that?"

"No reason, I can't look at you now?" He chuckled.

"I didn't say that but you're staring, that's something different. Are you going to the repast?"

"Nah, I'm gonna let y'all handle that I just came to pay my respects. You're going right?"

"Yeah then I'm going home."

"To your man?" As soon as those words left his mouth, I rolled my eyes. Why the fuck did he have to go and bring that shit up?

"I'll talk to you later," I was about to walk off, but he grabbed my arm pulling me back. "What?"

"The attitude for what? I'm asking you a real ass question. It's not like you don't have a nigga."

"You brought him up for what though?"

"I'm not trying to be your side nigga ma, so you tell me what the fuck you want to do about this shit."

"You're not a side nigga, we're cool and that's it. I haven't even kissed you before so how are you a side anything?" I felt myself getting upset so I took a deep breath to calm down. "This is not the time or place to talk about this shit alright so just drop it. You're leaving, I need to go before I get left out here and don't know where I'm going. I'll talk to you later or something." He tried to grab my arm, but I snatched it away and kept walking. Nobody had time to deal with that shit right now.

"YOU'RE a confusing ass somebody Taj for real," Toi said while I drove. We just left the repast and I was on my way to drop her ass off at home, but my silly ass made the mistake of telling her what happened with Yung earlier.

"How am I confusing?"

"You like his ass, that much is obvious but you're still dealing with Darrell for what reason?"

"I've been with the nigga for five years, hell he's paying all my bills."

"Bitch you have a job, you can handle your own bills I know Beautii pays your ass very well."

"That's not the point."

"So, you wanna stay with a dog because he's paying bills that you can handle for yourself?"

"It's not that simple La'Toia."

Toi doesn't get it, walking away from somebody I've been with for five years is not easy. The shit is hard as fuck actually. It wasn't just about the money it's just too much work to start over with somebody else. Darrell and I have been through a lot, cheating, lies, fights, the whole fucking nine and we're still together. Do you know how long it takes to build a foundation like that with someone else? Who has time for that?

"No, it is that simple. Come on now have you not learned anything from this shit with Bia?"

"Kenneth isn't beating my ass so I'm not getting the connection."

"If Bia left the nigga, she would be alive but it's too late now. What

I'm saying is you're trying to hold on to Darrell and keep Yung too. That nigga is not about to deal with that shit. You keep playing he's going to find somebody else and you're going to be stuck on stupid being jealous as fuck. What I'm saying is go after who you really want and what's best for you. It's not Kenneth trust me."

Before I could say anything else my phone ringing caught my attention, so I answered it. I didn't have shit to go against what she said anyway.

"Hello?"

"Taj, it's Qua," she said.

"Oh, what's up?"

"Nothing much, let me ask you something. Are you and Darrell still together?"

"Yeah we're still together why?"

"Oh well does this nigga know that because I just saw him go in his apartment with that big bitch Naja."

"The fuck? Are you serious?"

"I'm dead ass you know he lives right across the street from me and you know how that broad works. She's not in someone's apartment unless she's on her hands and knees."

"Oh, hell no, thanks for telling me." I hung up my phone then looked at Toi. "I'm going to take you home but let me handle something right quick."

"Handle what? Who was that?"

"Qua, she said she just saw Kenneth go in his house with that thot ass bitch Naja."

"Didn't he cheat on you with her before?"

"Yeah and I told him to stay away from her ass."

"I know you're not about to go fight this bitch."

"Fuck that, I've beaten her ass too many fucking times. I was just defending the damn relationship, and this is the bullshit he's doing. You know what Toi? You're right. This shit must stop and it's ending today. I'm done with this nigga." I made a U-Turn then drove to Darrell's house. As soon as I parked my car I hopped out and went straight to my trunk.

"Taj what are you doing?" Toi got out of the car and asked me.

"I'm handling it," I grabbed the metal bat I kept in the back and walked over to his car.

"Didn't he just buy this shit?"

"He sure did, brand new 2016 Porsche," I swung the back and smashed in his back window setting the alarm off.

"Oh shit!" Toi yelled while I went to the side of the car and smashed the driver's window in too. Walking around to the front I climbed on the hood of his car just as he came running outside with no shirt on just some basketball shorts.

"THE FUCK IS YOU DOING TAJ! HAVE YOU LOST YO FUCKING MIND?" He shouted with a crazed look in his eyes.

"FUCK YOU! YOU WANNA HAVE A HOE IN YOUR HOUSE LIKE I'M NOT GOING TO FIND THE FUCK OUT!" I swung the bat a good three times at his windshield before it finally broke like I wanted it to.

"YOU ON SOME FUCKING BULLSHIT!" He screamed at me. Laughing I got off his car and walked over to him before slapping the complete shit out of him.

"No, I'm done is what I am! I'm done with the bullshit for real, the lying the cheating the fucking heartbreak it's over. Fuck you, fuck your life fuck everything you stand for! I'm burying my friend and you're trying to get your dick wet! That's what the fuck we do now?" He tried to grab my arms, but I just snatched away and slapped him again.

"Don't fucking touch me!" I dropped the bat then walked back over to my car.

"You stupid as fuck if you think you not paying for this shit Taj!" he shouted at me.

"I'm not paying for a fucking thing, you balling right? You can pay for another one. Call the cops, go right ahead I dare you. I'll tell them muthafuckas where every single one of your stashes are, don't fuck with me. Toi let's go." We both got in my car and I sped off.

"Well that was intense," Toi said.

"It felt good so it's whatever. I'm not even shocked that he was still fucking with that bitch I'm just disgusted. I'm at a funeral for one of my friends and this nigga takes that as an opportunity to cheat on me. Who the fuck does that?"

"Fuckboys."

"I see that now," I shook my head. "Fuck him man, I'm done with that nigga."

"Alright, it's official. After five long years Miss Taj is single again. Turn up bitch."

"Oh, I definitely plan on doing just that."

Toi

*P*ulling up in front of my grandmother's house I saw Kayla sitting on the front porch with a group of boys her age. Now I don't know what the fuck she thought this was, but she obviously lost her damn mind having these little niggas in front of my grandmother's house.

After parking my car, I got out of the car and walked up to the house. "Kayla," I said her name getting her attention.

"What's up Toi?"

"What the hell is all of this? Why are they over here with you?"

"We just chillin' Toi it's nothing." She looked up at me and I immediately noticed she was higher than hell.

"I know you're not in front of my grandmother's house smoking." I shook my head then looked at all four boys. "Y'all gotta go, get the fuck off this porch and don't come back over here. I'm dead ass serious, now move!" They all sucked their teeth and whispered little shit under their breath, but they knew to fucking move off the porch like I said. "Let's go," I pulled Kayla up by her arm and pulled her in the house. "The fuck is wrong with you?"

"Nothing is wrong with me, you're doing too much right now. I was just chillin' you act like you don't smoke."

"I'm grown, how many times do I have to tell your little ass that you're not?"

"Get off me!" She snatched away from my grip. "You don't even live here anymore so I don't know why the fuck you're trying to come back over here like somebody is supposed to listen to you."

"You know what, I'm not going to punch the fuck out of you like I really want to do. I'm not because I didn't come over here for that, but you better remember this shit when your ass needs something. Don't ask me for a fucking thing, get one of those little bastards to buy your clothes and shit because I'm not fucking doing it." I mushed her in the head then walked towards the kitchen where I knew my grandmother was. That's where she always is.

When I got into the kitchen, I saw my grandmother at the stove stirring something while my mother sat at the table snapping green beans. "Hey Grandma," I kissed her cheek.

"Hey Toi, what are you doing here baby?"

"Just came by to see how you were doing. Where's Jayla?"

"Upstairs on that phone like she always is. I heard about Bia, I can't believe that boy killed that girl and left her like that. You went to the funeral?" My Grandmother shook her head.

"Yeah, I went, I rode with Taj. I changed clothes and came over here after she dropped me off at home. How can things go from being good to being so bad so fast? We were just with her that night."

"Well she's in a better place now, to be absent from the body is to be present with the lord. It's sad she didn't get to live her life all the way through but that just shows you, you never know what can happen."

"You're right. It looks like I came here on the perfect day, you're cooking. Who went food shopping? I told you to call me when you needed to go to the store."

"I went," my mother said. "I rode with Arlene from next door."

"That doesn't say who paid for it."

"I have food stamps La'Toia."

"Oh, okay. Well that's good I guess."

"It is good, your mother has been making a lot of good choices since she's been back. She's coming to church with me, she has a job down at the daycare down the street," my grandmother told me.

96

"They let you work with kids? You didn't even raise your own how did that happen?"

Chuckling she shook her head. "I work in the kitchen as a cook, not that you care."

"You're right I don't."

"La'Toia," my grandmother said my name in a tone that meant shut the hell up. "Come on in the living room you have some mail in here." Sighing I followed her into the living room and sat across from her. "I should pop you in your mouth for talking like that to your mother."

"Grandma, she's been gone for how many years?"

"That doesn't matter. Your mother was sick."

"No, she was a feen, she walked all over the city looking for a hit instead of being a parent. I can't respect that."

"You may not respect it, but you need to let it go. She was young and she made some bad decisions, I understand you're angry. That doesn't give you the right to be rude and disrespectful. You're acting as if you've never made some mistakes."

"None like that."

"A mistake is a mistake. You smoke that weed stuff, that's a drug."

"It's not the same thing grandma."

"Why not? It's not the same because it's not as addictive? Your mother was fifteen when she had you and seventeen when she got strung out. She started out just like you, smoking weed thinking it's nothing but a quick high then somebody she thought she could trust laced a blunt with cocaine in it and she didn't know. Do you think your mother wanted to leave you all these years? She missed you growing up. She missed your prom, graduation, and she regrets all of it. What I'm not going to let you do is kick her while she's trying to build herself back up alright?"

Not saying anything I just nodded my head to let her know that I understood.

"Um," I cleared my throat. "What mail came for me?"

"Oh yeah." She got up and walked over to the mantle then grabbed a stack on envelopes then gave it to me. "Here you go."

"Thank you."

"No problem, now you're welcomed to stay and eat dinner but only on two conditions."

"Okay, and those are?"

"Well one, you're going to mind your manners and stop being so disrespectful, you were raised better than that. Number two, you're going to go wash your hands and help her snap those green beans." Laughing I stood up and hugged her before stuffing the mail she gave me in my purse. "I love you grandma."

"I know I love you too. Now come in here and help us."

Mickey

*C*oming out of Extra Supermarket I was about to walk towards my car when I bumped into a hard chest. Looking up I sucked my teeth when I saw Case standing there. Can this nigga leave me the fuck alone already? His ass just won't stop popping up.

It's been a week since Bia's funeral, and I've been on edge since then. Everything irritates the shit out of me, especially niggas. Call it not really dealing with my emotions or grieving properly, I don't give a shit. I just know I'm tired of niggas getting on my damn nerves and Case was the main one not getting off.

"Chill with the attitude Mickey," he said.

"I don't have an attitude now excuse me I need to get to my car." I was about to walk past him, but this nigga would not move. "Bruh, you're really working my nerves right now and I am not in the mood. Move!"

"Why the fuck is you acting like a bitch with me? We were all good not too long ago."

"You're right, we were good before your bitch fucked it up. You think I need all that messy shit in my life? Fuck no I have enough going on, I don't need your bullshit added to it."

"So, you wanna act like a stuck-up little bitch? You weren't worried about my girl when you were fucking me!" He shouted as if I was supposed to get offended.

"Let me let you in on something bruh, yeah I fucked with you. I was cool even knowing you had a girlfriend but guess what, I don't give a fuck about that bitch. I don't give a fuck about you, or your relationship. Muthafucka I don't even give a fuck about your life. Keep trying me and you'll really see a side of me you will grow to hate. I'm not even playing with you."

"Man, fuck you Mickey."

"Fuck you too bitch. Go about your business Case for real. You're irking the hell out of my nerves I'm tired of seeing you. Leave me the hell alone or I swear to God." I walked over to my and put my bags in the trunk.

"Damn, you really don't play, do you?" A voice behind me said. Turning around I chuckled when I saw Tone standing there.

"You damn right I don't, I thought you figured that out already."

"I did but that just confirmed it." He came closer to me and I gave him a small hug. "How you been?"

"Not too good but I've been through worse, so I guess I'll be alright."

"I heard about your cousin, that shit was fucked up. I'm sorry you had to deal with that shit."

I nodded my head. "Me too, but you know what they say; what doesn't kill you will make you stronger. Expect me to turn into Hercules round this bitch," I joked.

"That nigga still missing?"

"I haven't heard anything, he just better hope somebody gets to him before I do. If I get my hands on that nigga it's going to be pretty."

"You coming like that?"

"Definitely, that's my cousin he did that bullshit to. I plan on fucking him the fuck up. Matter of fact, I think I might need your help."

"Talk to me."

"Alright so I know you work with Legend, y'all have to have eyes all over this damn state."

"Mhm, what are you getting at? You want us to handle him for you?"

"Nah, just keep an eye open for him. If you find him let me know, I'll handle the rest from there."

Chuckling he nodded his head yes. "Aight you got it, I'll put the word out. If your cousin is as well-known as you make it seem, the nigga probably got the fuck out of Jersey."

"Well if and when he comes back, I need to know about it."

"I got you, don't worry about it. Enough about that though, what's good with you?"

"What do you mean what's good? Nigga what are you even doing here?" I asked with a laugh.

"I gotta eat too, I needed to pick up a few things. Come on ma, I know you can tell I'm feelin' you."

"Oh really?" I laughed. "That's crazy."

"How is it crazy?"

"Most niggas don't come right out with it. They like walking around like they're too good to let somebody know if they feelin' them or not."

"That's little nigga shit, I'm a grown ass man I don't have time to play."

"So, what exactly are you trying to make happen here Tone? I'm not into relationships too much."

"I'm trying to figure out why. I want to know why you are the way you are. I just need you to not be shy when it comes to me."

"Shy? Oh, you definitely have so much to learn about me," I laughed.

"Give me the chance then, I'm willing to do that."

"Mhm, I'm sure you are. You don't have a girlfriend, baby mama, or anything do you?"

"I have none of the above, I'm free and in the clear. You just make sure you tie up any loose strings you have hanging around. Once I get involved all that shit is going to be a wrap."

"You sound so confident about this."

"I have no reason not to be," he came close to me then kissed me on the cheek. "I gotta go but I will be seeing you later." Smirking he walked past me and into the store.

I couldn't help but laugh while I got inside of my car. Tone is on some other shit, I would be lying if I said I wasn't a little bit interested to see where shit can go but that was just a small part of me. The bigger part of my brain was telling me to not even waste my time. Nine times out of ten it would be the same thing I went through with Bryson and I'm not trying to deal with that bullshit again.

Toi

*L*ooking around the empty space I was trying to figure out if this was the right spot to have my spa in. The location was perfect since it wouldn't be too far from my neighborhood so everybody who knows me can get to it easily. Seventy-five thousand square feet, and it had four stories. The only thing I was worried about was could I afford to even think about opening anything in this space.

"Yo Toi, these people don't have all day. What are you thinking? You like it or not?" Dutch asked me.

I had her here with me since Que had some business to handle so he couldn't come look with me plus he said he trust her opinion about it, so he wanted her to come too. I was a little apprehensive when he first brought her up talking about, she's his sister. Usually when niggas say that it means it's a *friends with benefits* situation but upon meeting Dutch, I knew that wasn't the case. She was a little taller than me, light skin, with tattoos covering her arms, hands, and neck. Her hair was braided back into long cornrows and her clothes were baggier than Que's. There was no way in hell she wanted him and he damn sure didn't want her either.

"I like it, but do you think this is the right space?" I looked her way.

"I think so, remember everything we talked about. You're going to have a floor for each service you're offering."

"Right and this does have four floors."

"Even better this has five so the first floor could be the lobby, you'll make it work. To be honest I think this is perfect. It has enough space, all you need is people to come in and fix it up. If you're really on it like you're supposed to you could be done by next fall."

"It's August now, do you think a year is good enough?"

"It should be perfect, let them work through the winter, spring and next summer. While they're doing that you can handle all the licensing and permits you would need to get everything goin. You'll be good. What are you worried about?"

"Whether or not I can afford it. How much do they want for this?"

"Well we buy shit over here ma ain't no renting and they want four point five."

"Four point five what?"

"Four point five million dollars," when she said that my mouth dropped, how in the fucking world?

"What the fuck? I can't afford that, maybe I should lease another space because nobody is going to approve me for that much. The only way I could probably do that is if I use my grandmother's house as collateral. I'm not doing that and if I did it still wouldn't be enough."

"Approved for what?"

"The loan I'm going to take out. Remember that's why you helped me with a business plan," I said, and she started laughing. "What the hell is so funny?"

"He didn't tell you?"

"Who didn't tell me what?"

"Legend didn't tell you he was going to be your investor?"

"Wait what?"

"Let me tell you something. He wanted me to help you with a business plan so he would know if it was worth putting money into. I gave him the green light for that weeks ago, he's going to help you with all of this. You really don't have anything to worry about."

"Are you serious? I thought when he got you to help me with my business plan it was going to be so that I can get a loan. I didn't think he was going to really give me the money." I was so confused right now it's not even funny.

"Yeah go ahead and call him if you don't believe me. Just be quick about it, you can't keep people waiting." As soon as she walked out, I pulled my phone out and called Que who picked up on the second ring.

"What's up ma?"

"Hey, um why didn't you tell me you were going to invest in my spa?"

"I did tell you, I told you I was going to help you. That's why I hooked you up with Dutch."

"I thought it was to help me set me up for my loan. Quentin this is too much."

"How you figure that?"

"Do you know how much they're asking for? It's four point five million dollars. I can't let you spend millions of dollars on me."

"Do you trust me?"

"Huh?"

"La'Toia, do you trust me?"

"Yes, I trust you, what does that have to do with anything?"

"Alright then so just trust me on this and stop worrying. I told you I wanted to help you and that's what I'm going to do."

"It's too much money Que."

"Too much money for who? I'm cool, you're the one over there buggin' out."

"I'm buggin' out because we're talking about millions of dollars. That's a big deal."

"You just said you trusted me, right?"

"I do bu-"

"But nothing, let me do my job as your man."

"My man? When did that happen?"

"Oh, so you're not claiming me now?" He chuckled.

"I didn't know you wanted to be claimed," I smiled to myself.

"Well now you do, I got you aight. Just stop worrying and get the building if that's the one you want."

"Are you sure?"

"Yes, I'm sure, I gave Dutch a blank check before she met up with you. All you got to do is sign the papers ma." For some reason I can't even tell you why I started tearing up. This is the first time anybody has done anything so special for me.

"Thank you," I sniffled.

"Are you crying? What's wrong?"

"Nothing," I laughed. "I'm just happy, thank you Quentin for real you don't even get it."

"You're welcome baby, just go handle your business I'll see you later aight."

"Alright, later." I hung up the phone then wiped the tears that ran down my face away before going to where Dutch was with the real estate agent.

"You alright?" Dutch asked me.

"Yeah," I nodded with a smile on my face. "I'm great, we're good to go. I definitely want this building."

"Great, all we need you to do is sign the papers and this will be yours. Can you come by the office tomorrow?"

"Yeah, is ten a.m., alright?'"

"That's perfect. It was nice meeting you Ms. Henderson. Dutch we'll be in touch okay." The agent smiled at the both of us then walked out with us. As soon as she walked off, I screamed jumping up and down while Dutch stood there laughing at me.

"I can't believe I'm officially about to be a business owner. Oh my God. This shit is crazy. Thank you for helping me." I hugged Dutch around her neck.

"No problem ma, you just make sure I get free shit when I need it."

"I got you," I laughed. "Now that this is over I wanna eat. Come on, I'll treat you to lunch."

"You already know I'm not turning down free food. Let's go." Still laughing we walked up the block so we could get to my car. I can't believe I'm about to really do this spa shit. I can't wait to tell my grandmother.

Anthony "Yung" Barnes

"Four million dollars? Nigga what the fuck? The pussy must be marvelous because that's way too much money to spend on somebody you just like." I shook my head at this nigga Legend.

We were in the car waiting to go handle some shit with somebody who came up short when this nigga decided it was a good time to let the cat out of the bag about him giving a grip of money to Toi. Don't get me wrong, Toi cool as hell she's like my little big sister if you get what I'm saying but that's too much money to be shelling out when you just met some damn body. I personally wouldn't do the shit but hey if he wants to do that for her, it's on him.

"I'm making it back, you act like I just gave it to her."

"Oh, so you're like a silent partner in her shit? Alright that makes more sense I thought you was just giving it to her. Never mind."

"Stupid ass nigga," he shook his head while laughing. "You talking about me at least I know she's mine, you the one chasing a girl with a nigga already."

"First off she's not with that nigga anymore she left his ass."

"Oh word? So, what are you going to about that shit then?"

"Well after we handle this shit, I'm going to see her. I'm trying to lock that shit down but I gotta make sure she's not stuck on that fool ass nigga."

"How long was she with him?"

"Five years."

"Five years? Who gets over somebody that quick?"

"When you got a nigga like me in your life, you'll forget every-body," I chuckled.

"You can quit feelin' yourself. Real shit though she is not going to be over that nigga unless she didn't love his ass period."

"I don't give a fuck to be honest, as long as she's not on the bullshit with me we're good." I looked out the window and saw the person we were waiting for coming out of the barbershop. "Aye man, there he goes right there."

"Pussy ass looking around and shit, come on." We both hopped out the car and walked over to ole dude. When we got close enough Legend tapped him on the shoulder and he turned around. As soon as he saw us his eyes got big as quarters. This nigga looked like he was about to piss himself.

"What are y'all doing here?" He asked us.

"We just came by to have a little talk real fast. Let's go inside and chat," I told him. My guess is he knew I wasn't even about to talk to his ass, so this nigga tried to run off screaming. I almost wanted to laugh but this wasn't the time for that shit.

"Get yo ass back here," Legend snatched this nigga up by his shirt and pulled him inside of his barbershop while I went inside behind them and locked the door before pulling the shade over the window down.

This was about to get a little messy.

⬥

"PLEASE TELL me that is not blood on your shirt." Taj looked at me with her face scrunched up. "Eww give it here so I can wash it. That is so nasty." I pulled my shirt off and gave it to her. "What the hell did you do?"

"Had a little accident with some clippers," was all I said before I started laughing. Just thinking back on that shit was funny. If you ever wondered what pressing a pair of clippers on someone's face could do, don't try to test it out unless you're ready to deal with a lot of blood.

"I don't even want to know keep the rest of that story to yourself." She went and put my shirt in the washing machine then came back in the living room and sat on the couch away from me like she was nervous or something.

"The fuck is you acting scary for? Come here."

"I'm not scary and I'm good right here." Sucking my teeth, I grabbed her leg and pulled her close to me then lifted her up before sitting her on my lap.

"Why are you playing?"

"I'm not playing, I'm dead ass serious."

"Yeah aight." I looked around her living room for a brief second then back at her. "This is a nice spot, how long been living here?"

"My whole life, my parents owned this house."

"Really? So, what happened? They retired to Florida or some shit?"

"No," she chuckled. "They died in a car accident when I was thirteen."

"Oh shit, I'm sorry."

"It's okay. After they passed insurance paid for the house and my grandmother came and lived with me so I wouldn't have to move away. She handled the other bills until I was old enough to get money for myself then she passed two years ago so it's just been me in here ever since."

"That nigga wasn't living with you?"

"No, he paid the bills or whatever, but he never lived here."

"Y'all were together for five years and you never lived here but was paying the bills? Damn, that's what you call a stunt dummy ass nigga."

"How was that a stunt dummy? A man is supposed to take care of his girl."

"True but a woman can take care of herself too. Don't tell me you're one of those kept women."

"No, I'm not, I'm good on my own. Between my job and the money

I get from my parents' estate I'll always be good, but he just wanted to do it so that's on him. I never needed him too."

"Oh alright, I just needed to make sure of that. So, what were your folks like?"

"They were like normal parents what do you mean?"

"I mean what they did for a living that type of thing."

"My father was a pediatrician my mother was a lawyer."

"Real life Huxtable shit, I'm going to call you Rudy from now on."

"Fuck out of here no you're not," she laughed.

"I'm dead ass serious." I laughed along with her. "So, you were the rich kid on the block. Why were y'all still living in the hood if they had it like that?"

"They were born and raised on this block. My father said it's what made them who they were, so he didn't want to leave."

"Damn, your pops sounds cool as hell. Most people would have gotten the fuck out of here as soon as possible."

"I know but that's just how he was. What about your parents? What do they do?"

"My father doesn't do shit but dodge child support. My mother worked at a hospital as a nurse, now she doesn't do anything but chill out since I pay all of her bills."

"That's nice of you."

"Nah, it's my responsibility. She took care of me all my life. it's her turn to be taken care of now," I shrugged.

"True but you don't have to do it. Do you know how many people would let their parents struggle while they ball out? Some people are just fucked up like that."

"True but it ain't me so I don't give a fuck. Let's change the subject. What's up with you?"

"What about me?"

"How many tattoos do you have?" I looked at her arms. Another thing Taj had that l liked was a lot of tattoos. She had more than a couple and I was feeling that, it showed me she didn't give a fuck, she could take pain and by the one on her chest she wasn't a punk.

"I don't know after the fifth one I stopped counting. Why?"

"I'm just wondering. I like the fact that you're tatted though."

"You've told me that a couple of times already. I think I know," she smiled. "How many do you have?"

"I have no fucking idea," we both laughed. "Let me ask you something."

"You always want to ask me something. Forever got a question ass nigga."

"That's how you get the information you need, you're supposed to ask questions. For real though I have a question."

"Alright, what is it?"

"What's up with your old nigga? You still stuck on him or nah?"

"Hell no, ew. I'm good on that nigga, trust me."

"You saying eww like you weren't with him for five years. You had to love the nigga or something."

"I did love him, at first. Then the more he fucked up the more I started to hate his ass. The only reason I was with him that long was because he was paying my bills and I didn't even want to deal with the trouble of getting a new nigga."

"What trouble?"

"Getting to know somebody else, that shit takes a lot of time and the niggas that were coming at me were full of shit."

"So, I'm different how?"

"You tell me the truth, I don't have to worry about you lying. Well at least not right now because niggas get slick the more, they get to know people."

"I don't have a reason to lie to you so don't expect that shit from me anytime soon."

"Mhm we'll see. Oh, and by the way I'm calling you Anthony, I'm not one of your hoes or your homeboys. I'm using your government name."

"Go right ahead I'm using yours too Tiana."

"Eww," she covered her ears laughing. "I hate that name."

"Why?"

"I just do, I'm used to Taj so let's stick to that."

"Man, hell nah," I laughed at her. "Why do you hate your name?"

"I just do," she shrugged.

"Where did Taj even come from?"

"My full name is Tiana Ann-Marie Jackson. My initials are TAJ, so I just started calling myself Taj."

"That's weird but I get it I guess."

"I'm glad you do. Now that you're done with your questions, I'm about to order food for myself. I'm hungry."

"You see me sitting here and you're talking about for yourself, the fuck?"

"What nigga? You hungry too?"

"Hell yeah, what are you getting?"

"Chinese food, so what do you want and don't be greedy with it." She got off my lap and grabbed her phone from the coffee table.

"Get your ass out my face first of all." I slapped her ass hard as hell then laughed when she tried to hit me.

"Muthafucka that hurt, you get on my damn nerves."

"You know you love me girl!"

"Lies you tell, I don't know where you got that shit from." She laughed hard as hell while walking into her kitchen.

She can find that shit funny right now all she wants to but give me a couple of months. I'll have her ass loving me.

Legend

"Shit that feels good," I groaned louder than I intended. I didn't even want to make noises but the way she was doing this shit had me sounding like a bitch.

"I told you I'm gifted." Toi giggled before she hopped off my back. "Are you good now?"

"Hell yeah, I hope you plan on giving the massages at your spa. I'll be your number one customer because that shit felt better than a muthafucka." I sat up on the bed stretching my arms out.

Laughing she went into the bathroom and came out with a small hand towel to wipe the oil off her fingers. "I wasn't planning on doing them, but I got you. You'll be a VIP client." She came over to me and pressed her lips against mine. The kiss started off small at first, but then it grew bigger and more intense when I lifted her body on top of mine.

Smiling, Toi released herself from the kiss then licked her lips before pushing me down on the bed and kissing me again. Our breathing got heavier as we explored each other's mouths, sucking and licking each other's lips. I moved my hands down her body and gripped her ass in the black lace boy shorts she was wearing under the big t-shirt she obviously took out of my closet.

"Mmm shit, don't grip my ass like that," she moaned.

Chuckling I flipped us over so that she was not laying on her back.

I slowly peeled the clothes she had on, off then stood back looking at her. I don't think Toi knows how pretty she really is, I know she's confident and sure she thinks she's cute, but baby girl is absolutely beautiful.

Climbing back on the bed I began to kiss her legs, leading to her inner being. I tantalized her insides with his tongue making her moan in pleasure. Just by the way her body was reacting I could tell I was taking her places she had never been before. With her back arched away from the bed, she screamed begging me to stop so she wouldn't cum yet. Smiling I obliged and lifted my head up and licked her stomach. Circling my tongue all around, I traced my tongue along each of her nipples, biting and sucking them at the same time.

Not being able to take any more, she pleaded, "Que baby please put it in."

"Are you sure?" I asked wanting her to beg.

"Yes, I'm sure, please, please, please," she whined.

"Take my boxers off for me," I told her. Sitting up she pulled my boxers down exposing me. The look on her face was a mixture of shock, and intrigue.

"Damn."

"Lay back ma." I kissed her again while teasing her opening.

"Baby," she whined again making a smile come across my face. She led him to her open field of sin. As I entered her, I felt her body tense up.

"Relax baby," I whispered in her ear before attaching my lips to her neck.

"You're so big Que shit," she groaned as I pushed more of myself inside of her. I stroked her slowly at first, then I began to speed up when I saw the pain leave her face.

"How deep do you want it?"

"As deep as you can go," Toi answered. I gripped her waist going as deep as possible making her scream louder.

"Ooh fuck! Don't stop baby please don't!"

"Damn your pussy tight as fuck!" A loud grunt left my lips. "You know this my pussy, now right?" I asked and instead of answering me a long cry left her lips while I hit her spot.

I pulled out and flipped her on her stomach. "Put that ass in the air ma."

I saw a smirk grace her face while she obliged my command. Grabbing her hair, I wrapped it around my fist before slamming myself into her from the back. "Ahh shit Que!" She moaned out while immediately arching her back.

"I know you heard what the fuck I said to you!" I questioned while I pounded inside of her.

"Yes! Yes, baby I heard you fuck!" She screamed, as I stroked her harder.

Crying out from gratification, she moaned mine and God's name begging me to keep going. "That's who you better call. Yo ass stuck with me now," I went deeper and harder into her pussy while she continued to scream in pleasure.

"Oh God I'm about to cum!" Toi yelled as her body started to shake. When I felt her juice run down my dick, I bit my lips and came deep inside of her. Catching my breath, I pulled out and laid down next to her pulling her body closer to mine.

"I'm tired now," Toi said while lying her head on my chest.

"Go to sleep then."

"I am, I know one thing though. You better be here when I wake up."

"What you think I'm going to get up and leave? The fuck, am I? The coochie crook."

Laughing she shook her head. "No, that's not what I'm saying. I just don't want you to leave tonight."

"I'm not and if I do need to go somewhere, I'll wake you up and let you know, but for right now go to sleep." I kissed her forehead then laid my head back. I don't know what the fuck this girl is doing to me but I'm not complaining. I'm here for it.

Toi

"Where the fuck you been? You were M.I.A all damn week," Mickey asked me as soon as I sat down. Today I was meeting her and Taj out for lunch so they could pry into my damn life. I knew that's what they really wanted to do, they were not trying to give me free food for no reason.

"I've been living my life. Good God damn can I live?" I lifted the Gucci sunglasses of my eyes, placing them on the top of my head.

"Fuck no, and I know you did not just walk your ass in here with a Birkin bag!" Taj exclaimed pointing to the HERMES Togo Birkin rose colored bag I carried in with me.

"No that is a Birkin bag, matter of fact that whole damn outfit is new. This bitch walked in here looking like a whole new person. Don't think I didn't clock those brand-new Gucci glasses either. I had my eye on those last week, but I said I was going to wait. What's up Toi? Give up the damn goods," Mickey said with a smile on her face.

"You two are so annoying it's not even funny," I laughed at them.

"I'm completely fine with being annoying. I'm trying to figure out how the hell you get that bag and where you been? By the hickies on your neck I'm guessing Legend has something to do with it."

Hearing his name immediately put a bigger smile on my face. That has been happening a lot lately. "He might have a little something to do with it."

"Or a lot, I see you bitch. Those bags are nowhere near cheap so how you get it?" Taj asked me.

"Alright fine damn. Que bought me the bag, and the glasses. The clothes I've been had I just didn't wear them yet," I answered not telling them everything. I don't feel like they need to know Que took me shopping and dropped damn near fifty thousand dollars on my ass. I'll keep that piece of information to myself.

"Aww that's so sweet, he must really like you ma that's a lot of money. So, you been getting your ass cracked huh?"

"Shut the hell up Mickey," I laughed again. She is always in my business, but she was right at the same time. I hate that this bitch knows me so well.

"Yeah that's what it is he's been beating them walls down. Well it's about time you got laid. So, are you two officially a couple or are y'all still trying to figure out what it is?"

"I know what it is, that's mine," I said with confidence. Que and I had a long talk and we decided to make our relationship an official thing. We're not just talking and seeing how it goes, that's my man.

"He's yours?"

"Yeah," I smiled.

"Okay, Toi got a man!" Mickey shouted in excitement. When people started looking over at us, I hit her arm.

"Girl relax, you got people staring at us and shit."

"What you want me to say? My bad? Nah I'm good. You and Legend though, that's cute. Y'all would have some pretty ass babies."

"Again, relax. The nigga has been my man for a week, nobody is thinking about babies right now. Besides, we both have too much going on."

"Yes, being the woman of Legend fuckin' Santana is a job, a lucrative one at that," Mickey laughed.

"Money isn't everything," I told her.

"Says the woman rocking a twenty-thousand-dollar purse, I know he didn't buy only that. Let's not forget he bought you a diamond bracelet the day he met you."

"I'm not off the nigga dropping four million dollars on her." Taj decided to add her input.

"He didn't drop it on me, he dropped it on an investment. This is damn near a partnership, he's just a silent partner and before you even ask, yes everything is in my name. I am not stupid." I trust Que, I don't think he would ever snatch my business away from me, but I'm not dumb either. Everything will be in my name, of course he's going to get his share in whatever, but my business will be MINE.

"All I'm saying is you found a fine ass, rich ass, boss nigga. Bitches have been after that man for years and come up with nothing but a wet ass and maybe a few dollars. He's claiming you, basically taking care of you and he's just now getting the ass. You're a bad bitch," Mickey held up drink up like she was giving me a toast.

"Don't I know it," I flipped my hair dramatically before laughing. "Nah for real, his money doesn't mean anything to me. I'm not saying it's not a nice add-on, but I don't care about that."

"We can tell. Just have your fun, enjoy your man, and keep getting fucked," Taj shrugged.

"The fucking part is not an issue. He's been keeping me busy all week with that shit. I'm tired as hell."

"Girl you better get your damn strength up, with him being your nigga you have to be on point," Mickey said in a warning tone.

"What do you mean?" I looked at her confused.

"You know it's hoes on top of hoes after that. Have you not been to the club with him?"

"I've never been in the club with him like that so I wouldn't know. Well except at the Mansion and I really wasn't paying attention I was too busy having fun."

"Well the nigga is a hot commodity, bitches are on him heavy. Now that y'all are together it's going to be times ten. People know y'all are together. You've been around his ass so much it's going to get out there and they will be on him so you might have to stab a bitch or two."

"She's right, bitches are all over Anthony's ass and he's not even the head nigga in charge. He has stain but he's not Legend, you have that nigga you better be prepared to keep him," Taj added in.

WALKING into the barbershop I looked around for Que but didn't see him. I was about to turn around and walk out because I started to feel uncomfortable. It was a couple of guys that I've never seen before sitting around and they were looking at me like they never seen a woman before.

Before I turned to leave, I spotted Tone and he got up from the chair he was in coming over to me.

"What's up T?" He said before hugging me.

"Hey, where is Que?"

"He went to get something to eat, he told you to come here?"

"Yeah, when did he open a barbershop?"

"When the owner signed it over to him," Tone laughed.

"Why would the owner just sign his business over?"

"Let's just say he couldn't handle the upkeep. You can sit down and wait for him though." He looked around at the dudes who were looking at me. "Quit fucking staring!"

"Yo Tone, who she belong to? A bitch like that needs to be on my roster," some nigga said, and I got pissed immediately.

"I don't belong to anybody. I'm not a fucking dog or a pet so watch who the fuck your ugly ass is calling a bitch!" I snapped at him making Tone laugh.

"Calm down shorty, go sit down. I'm about to go call this nigga for you."

"Thank you Tone," I went and sat down in an empty chair in the front pulling my phone out.

A good ten minutes went by before Que finally walked in with bags of food in his hands and he came right over to me. "You good?" He asked before kissing me on the lips.

"Yeah, I'm fine, what took you so long?"

"I got hungry, so I had to get something to eat. So, what do you think?"

"About what?"

"The shop, it's mine now. I'm going to call it Legendary Cutz."

"Of course you would," I chuckled. "It's cool for what it is. You should paint and change the vibe. Oh, and make sure rude ass niggas don't get in." I rolled my eyes.

"What was that?" He looked at me suspiciously.

"What was what?

"Why did you roll your eyes and say what you just said."

"What do you mean?"

"You know what I mean. Come outside with me real fast." I got up and he put the bag on my seat. I walked outside of the shop with Que coming right behind me. "Did somebody say something to you in here?" He asked me as his jaw clenched.

"I was speaking in general."

"You're lying, that shit all in your eyes. What did they say?"

"Que it's no- "

"Tell me what the fuck they said Toi, right now!" Looking up at him I could see the anger in his eyes. I knew if I didn't say something, he was going to blow shit up, so fuck it.

Sucking my teeth, I folded my arms over my chest. "He was talking to Tone but talking about me."

"What did he say?"

"He said who does shorty belong to, a bitch like that needs to be on my roster."

"Which one?"

"The dark skin nigga with the braids, but don't do anything, Que. It's not deep just let it go." Not saying anything to me Que turned around and walked inside of the shop with me right behind him.

He stayed quiet as he walked over to the guy who said something about me and out of nowhere and he pulled a gun from his waistband and started smacking the hell out of him with the butt of the gun repeatedly.

"Yo what the fuck are you doing?" Tone tried to make him stop but he kept going so I walked over and grabbed his arm.

"Que!" I pulled him back some, but it was like he wasn't trying to hear me.

"QUE STOP!" I shouted louder pushing him back. He tried to push past me, but I grabbed the bottom of his jaw making him look at me. "Stop and calm the hell down!"

Que snatched his face from my hands then looked down at the man on the floor whose face was covered in blood. "Get this nigga the fuck outta here and clean this shit up! Let this be a lesson to all you muthafuckas. Don't disrespect what's mine!" He grabbed his food then my hand. "Let's go."

Not even bothering to hesitate I walked with him out the door not even bothering to look back. "Can you calm down please?"

"I'm calm Toi. I didn't want you to see me like that bitch fuck it. I can't let niggas disrespect you. If they disrespect you it's disrespecting me, and I don't tolerate that bullshit alright."

I nodded my head then looked up at him. "I understand."

"Good." He leaned down and kissed me on the cheek. "I'm sorry you had to see that shit."

"Whatever don't lose your temper like that around me again. It's too much, you could've killed him, Que."

"That was the point. You have a lot to learn about me baby."

"I see." He couldn't be more right saying that.

Geneva Henderson

*S*inging His Eye is On the Sparrow I swept the living room trying to get it at least looking decent since the twins act like they're allergic to cleaning up. They don't listen to me, they don't listen to mama they just do whatever the hell it is that they want. I can understand why they would look at me crazy when I tell them to do something but the disrespect, they give my mother has me almost at my breaking point. I'm trying to stay in a positive lane but I'm going to choke one of these little heifers out in a minute.

Once I swept the trash into the hallway, I was about to get it up when Kayla came walking right through it like she didn't see the pile there. Do you see what I mean? Disrespectful asses.

"Kayla, you didn't see that it was trash right there?" I asked her and she shrugged her shoulders.

"I saw it but who cares?"

"I care, you saw the trash there and your little ass just thinks it's okay to step on it? You know what, you and your sister are really trying my patience."

"We're trying your patience? You said that as if you're about to do something to me. Hit me and I'll hit you back, I'm not scared to fight an old woman."

"Little girl, I will smack the hell out of you. Don't disrespect me

122

like that." Before she could open her mouth, the front door opened, and Toi came walking in.

"Before either one of you say anything to me, I heard it outside since the both of you are louder than hell. Kayla, I don't know what the fuck your problem is or if you bumped your damn head, but you don't talk to an adult like that," Toi told her making her roll her eyes. "Don't roll your damn eyes at me I will slap the life out of you. The fuck do you even think you're going?"

"I'm just going outside."

"Uh huh, stay your ass on this block. Don't go in nobody's house, if I don't see you when I come back out this house, you're going to have a problem on your hands. You understand?"

"Yeah I got it," Kayla said to her.

"Alright then, apologize to her then get the hell out of here."

Kayla looked up at me and sighed. "I'm sorry for disrespecting you Aunt Geneva."

"Thank you, Kayla," I told her then she went rushing out the front door. I looked up at Toi and nodded. "Thank you for doing that."

"You're welcome, you just have to let them know you are serious. They'll get it after the first slap. Where's grandma?"

"She went to bible study."

"Oh yeah today is Wednesday I forgot. Well when she gets back, can you tell her I was looking for her."

"I will," I grabbed the dust pan and got the trash up while she stood right there.

"Question, was that you singing when I came in?"

"Yes, I didn't think anybody heard me."

"Oh, I definitely heard you. You sounded great."

"Thank you, your grandmother wants me to join the church choir, but I don't think I am."

"Why not?"

"Toi, I haven't sung in front of anybody since I was at least sixteen. I don't think I'm ready for that. Hell, I'm lucky that my voice is still intact." I don't feel like I have much to offer anybody, but one gift God did give me was my singing voice. I started singing before I could really talk, the fact that my voice hasn't gone anywhere after the years of hard drugs and chaos is amazing to me.

"Maybe that's for a reason. You have a gift use it, if I had a voice like that I would never shut up. I can barely hold a note."

I laughed. "That's not shocking, your father couldn't sing worth a damn either."

"My father?"

"Yeah, he used to try and keep up with me, but it really didn't work out too well." Looking at her I could tell she was a little bit confused. " What's wrong?"

"Nothing, can we sit down and talk for a minute?"

"Sure, come on." We went into the living room and sat on the couch. "What's going on Toi?"

"It threw me off when you said something about my father. I've never heard anybody speak about him. Grandma mentioned him here and there, but she never gave details."

"That's for a reason."

"Well what's the reason? Where is he?"

"As far as I know, your father is in Atlanta living his life. Hopefully, he's still sober."

"He was on drugs too?"

"Unfortunately," I shook my head. "Stay here I'll be right back." I got off the couch and went up to my bedroom and got my old photo album then came back downstairs and sat next to her.

"What is that?"

"These are pictures from a long time ago. Some of you when you were a baby, and some before you were even born."

"Is that Auntie Grace?" She pointed to a picture of my older sister.

"Yeah that's her," I took the picture out and looked at it. Grace was too beautiful for words. We shared the same light complexion, inherited from our father. At the time, the picture was taken Grace had platinum blonde hair, the dark eyebrows, dark lip liner and the mole right above her lips. Lord the picture is like ninety's hell.

"Wow, she looked so pretty here. What year was this?"

"Ninety-five I think I'm not too sure. That's not what I wanted to show you though," I put the picture back in then went to what I wanted her to see. "This is your father." I took the picture out and gave it to her.

"Really? Wow, he was a pretty boy."

Laughing I nodded my head. "Yeah he was."

"Wow, why does he look like Raheem from Juice though?" she asked, and I busted out laughing again.

"He does but he was fine just like him, that's what I liked about him though," but he wasn't a joke either."

"Alright so what happened because from what I was told he used to sell drugs?"

"He did, not all the time but he felt like he had to after I got pregnant."

"He started after you got pregnant."

"Yes, he felt like that was the only option. He was only sixteen, it's not like he could run out and get a good job at that age so that's what he chose. First everything was going great you had everything you needed, we were both good but then we decided to start smoking."

"Smoking what?"

"Weed first, that was cool until one of his friends if you can call them that gave him a laced blunt."

"Laced with?"

"Cocaine, he did that for a while then he got me to do it, I was young dumb and in love, so I went along with anything he told me. By the time I was eighteen I was strung out, and so was he. Mama and daddy sent me into this program to get better and when I got sent away his parents sent him down to Atlanta to live with his grandparents to sober up. I haven't spoken to him since the day he left to go down there."

"Wow," Toi shook her head. "So, if they put you in a program why didn't it work?"

"It did, for a little while. I got out and stayed clean for about four months until I went to a party and relapsed. After that it was like I couldn't gain control of it. I kept using, making myself and the addiction worse. At that point I just decided to stay away from here because I didn't want my parents or you to see me like that."

"You don't think I deserved a mother? It killed me that you were never around."

"I know and I understand that but what kind of parent would I have been? I was broke and strung out on cocaine, being around me wasn't what you deserved. You needed better than me and that was my parents. Same thing with the twins."

"So, you never did Heroin? Auntie Grace died from a heroin overdose."

"She did, that was Grace's drug of choice. I never went that far." Grace doing Heroin was definitely a shocker to me. I'm not saying that being addicted to cocaine is a better route, but I wasn't willing to try Heroin. I stayed away from that shit.

"So, what makes this time different? You've done this before."

"I'm tired Toi, I can't be out there anymore, and I know you think its bullshit but I'm serious. I've been clean for a year not a couple of weeks. I go to my NA meetings, I talk to my sponsor all the time, I'm putting the work in to be a better person. The only thing I can say is give me the chance to show you."

She sat there for a good moment as if she was thinking it through then looked at me. "I'm willing to give it and you a chance. I just don't want to look or feel stupid for doing it."

"You'll be proud of me I promise you." We both stood up and hugged each other.

"Okay enough of this stuff I can't get emotional right now. I really don't want to," she laughed.

"That's fine, are you hungry? Your grandmother cooked last night."

"What did she cook?"

"Pork roast, mashed potatoes, corn and cornbread."

"Oh yeah I definitely want some."

"Go in the kitchen then." We made our way to kitchen.

"I have another question."

"What is it?"

"Can you teach me to sing like that?"

"I can teach you to hold a note, but you have to born with a voice like mine. I can't help you with that," we both laughed.

I know this doesn't mean our relationship is about to be perfect, but I was happy to even get this far. We're finally getting somewhere.

Mickey

I started to get off my bed, but a strong pair of arms gripped around my waist pulled me back making me laugh. "Where are you going?" Tone asked me with his eyes still closed.

"I'm going to the bathroom, stop sweating me nigga," I laughed again.

"Yeah aight." He kissed the back of my neck then let me go. Reaching down on the floor I grabbed his shirt off the floor and put it on then went to the bathroom. After peeing I brushed my teeth then hopped in the shower coming out in a towel twenty minutes later.

"See now, I was about to get dressed but god damn let me take that towel off of you," Tone smirked at me.

"Yeah right, hell no," I smiled. "You had enough last night and this morning. It's almost one in the afternoon bruh, you're done for now."

"Scary ass."

"Nobody is scared of you Antonio," I called him by his government name earning a laugh from him.

"Oh, you went there? I got you Michelle," he countered back. "What are you doing today?"

"Going to get my hair done then after that nothing, why what's up?" I went to my dresser and pulled out a panty and bra set then put it on. I didn't give a fuck if he was standing there or not, nigga already saw me naked, why be shy now?

"Alright, so you heard about that Tyrese show?"

"What Tyrese show?"

"In Newark, it's New Edition, Tyrese, Monica and Jahiem performing."

"Where at? The Prudential Center?"

"Yeah, we got tickets."

"Who are we?"

"Me, Yung and Legend, I'm surprised your girls didn't tell you about the shit."

"Wait, are you asking me out? Like a date?" I turned and looked at him confused.

"Yeah, I got tickets with those niggas, but I got them for me and you. You thought I was playing about locking you down? Come on now ma."

"I'm not saying that, but niggas don't date anymore."

"I'm not your average nigga, you already know that much. Listen, I'm taking you to the show. The doors open up at seven, so I'll be here to get you at six. Cool?"

Raising an eyebrow, I looked at him then smiled. "Alright that's fine, should I get dressed up?"

"Yeah, we're going out to eat afterwards. So, make me look good you get what I'm saying?"

"I got you," I laughed again while he continued to get dressed.

"You know what? I wasn't expecting your bedroom to look like this. All white?"

"What's wrong with white?"

"Nothing, you're just a real colorful type of person. Your living room looks like you, but this is different."

"I know, when I was little, I would watch Cribs and it seemed like most of them always had an all-white room that nobody could go into. So, when I moved in here, I wanted it to be my bedroom because nobody is allowed in here."

"What do you mean nobody is allowed in here?"

"Put it like this, I've been living here for three years and nobody has ever seen my bedroom except you and Toi. The only reason you've seen it is because you just made yourself a little bit too comfortable and came straight in this bitch."

"I didn't know the shit was off limits, but you could've kicked me out." He reached into his pockets and pulled out a stack of money. "Here." He peeled off a couple of hundred-dollar bills then handed it to me. I counted it then looked at him.

"This is two thousand dollars."

"I know I want you in some new shit tonight. I know you go to Taj for your hair, tell her to make your shit extra fancy aight. You're going to be on my arm I'm going to make sure you're straight."

"Nah you keep this I don't need your money." I gave him his money back almost shocking myself. Its two things I don't give to people. Apologies and their money back, once it's in my hand it's mine.

"Take it Mickey, I want you to take that and do what you need to do. I know you don't need my money, but I want you to have that."

"Are you sure?" The fuck is going on with me?

"Yeah I'm sure." He came over to me and kissed me on the lips. "Ready by six ma." He smiled at me.

"I will," I smiled back. "Oh, and just for future reference, I like everybody on this little line up, I fuck with New Edition heavy don't get me wrong but next time I would much rather see Beyoncé or Chris Brown. Just saying."

"Yeah aight," he laughed. "I'll see you later ma." He walked out

"WHAT THE FUCK?" Toi shouted after I told her everything that went down causing everybody in the damn nail salon to look at us like we were crazy.

"Will you shut your silly ass up? Yelling and shit."

"I'm sorry," she laughed. "That's crazy though, how did y'all end up hooking up?"

"I had a stunt last night."

"Oh lord Mickey, when are you going to stop?"

"When I choose too, hell the way this nigga is making me feel it might be soon. Anyway, after I got rid of the car or whatever I picked my car up then went to the after hour on Orient to get something to drink and he was in there getting something too. We blew down a bag and talked for a minute. Then he came to my house and boom it went down."

"Ooh, was it good?"

"Good? Toi the nigga slept over, in my room. That's self-explanatory."

"Damn, so he asked you about the concert before he left?"

"Yeah, so now after this we have to go shopping. Hair done, nails done, clothes are next."

"I'm with you, Taj is meeting us at Nordstrom's."

"Cool with me."

"So, what made you change your mind about Tone? When we talked you didn't want to deal with him because of whatever feelings you have for Bryson's stupid ass."

"I'm still on that I mean it's only one date but he's different Toi. It's like his whole demeanor is different. He's not walking around trying to be hard. Like think about it, I know this nigga is in the streets, how many dudes like him are taking a woman to an R&B concert. A classic R&B concert, not this new shit that's damn near sounding like rap, he's taking me to see New Edition bitch."

"I know I'm going too nigga," Toi laughed. "I told Que about the show and asked him to get tickets, he said he didn't want to go at first, but he convinced his friends to come too. I guess he would feel less corny with this homies there, I don't fuckin' know."

"Well that's what I mean about Tone. He's comfortable with who he is, and he doesn't play. I like him, I'm just...being careful."

"That's the smart thing to do, but I think you two would be good together. Go on and let somebody love your mean ass."

"Shut up," I laughed.

Antonio "Tone" Montega

I knocked on Mickey's door waiting for her to answer. "COME IN!" She yelled from inside, so I opened the door and walked in closing the it behind me. "I'm coming down in a minute!"

"Aight!" I sat down on the couch and sparked up a blunt after I pulled it out of my pocket. I was damn near done with my shit when Mickey finally came down.

"Alright I'm ready," she said as she entered the living room. "How do I look?"

"You look good, damn!" I told her while I admired her frame in the electric blue long sleeve bodycon dress she had on. Mickey is bad as fuck and she knows it, she tries to play it off around me, but I know she knows what she's dealing with.

"Thank you," she smiled. "You look nice. I want to know why I'm in heels and a dress and you're all casual. I'm not mad, I can tell you're wearing Balenciaga down to your feet but damn, you couldn't wear a button up or something?" I was wearing a black Balenciaga t-shirt, jeans, and sneakers. It was causal but what the fuck was I supposed to have on? A suit? Nah, I looked damn good, yeah it wasn't dressy, but I made it look close enough to it so fuck it.

"This is how I dress up. You want the rest of this?" I gave her the blunt and she took it smoking the rest of it down. "You ready now?"

"Yeah come on." After she locked her house up, we went over to my car and got in. The ride to Newark was cool, there was no weird awkward silence plus she kept me laughing so that's a plus too.

When we got to The Prudential Center, I got a park after waiting a good twenty minutes. When we got out of the car, we walked hand in hand to the big ass hockey statue that was in front so we could meet up with everybody else.

"Do you see them?" I asked her while she looked around.

"Yup, I see Toi and Legend right there." She pointed behind me. "I see Taj right behind them, they're walking over here."

I turned around and saw them walking over so we went to meet them halfway. "Nigga we've been walking around for ten minutes looking for your ass," Legend told me once we met up.

"We said meet by that big ass statue why you ain't take your ass over there?"

"This nigga wanted to walk off. Simple ass nigga." He pointed to Yung. Of course, it would be him that get niggas lost and shit.

"Fuck both of y'all man."

"Whatever, what's up Taj," I hugged her then did the same to Toi.

"Hey big head, can we go inside now? I'm trying to hear Jahiem not you niggas go back and forth," Toi said.

"That's fucked up, come on man." Legend grabbed her hand again and turned towards to the entrance, so we all walked that way.

LAUGHING we walked through my front door. "That was so good, those niggas are like fifty and still have all the moves down pact."

"I'm surprised your young ass knew every word." The concert was just what I expected it to be, what I didn't expect was for Mickey knowing every word to every damn song by each person who performed. You would think she was the one on the stage she was singing so damn much.

"Just because I'm young doesn't mean I don't know good music. I got my entire being tonight, thank you for inviting me."

"You're welcome. Come on," I pulled her into the living room before turning the light on.

"Your view is crazy from up here," she said as she walked over to the window.

"This is really nice."

"Thank you, that's the reason why I got it."

"Good choice, it doesn't freak you out a little bit? There's nothing blocking you, it's just glass."

"Nah I'm good here, why? You would be scared?"

"I wouldn't say scared, but it would be something I would need to get used to."

"Stick with me and you'll get used to it in no time. You want something to drink?"

"Yes please, what do you have?" I led her into the kitchen and got a glass for her.

"Water, juice, I don't drink soda so that shit ain't in here and I have wine. I got some liquor too but I'm sure you don't want that."

"You're right, not about to have me in here trying to jump out windows. I'll have a glass of wine though."'

"Red or white?"

"White."

"You drink Chardonnay?"

"Yeah that's perfect." I poured her a glass then fixed myself a drink before going right back into the living room and sitting down on the couch with her.

"So, Ms. Michelle."

"Oh God," she laughed. "What do you want Antonio?"

"Don't do that ma," I laughed along with her. "So now that I've taken you out and shit, do you realize how much I'm feelin' you yet?"

"I've been realized it, I'm just apprehensive."

"About what? Come on ma you gotta talk to me if you want me to understand."

"I've been through a lot. I've put my trust into niggas only for them to turn around and treat me like shit. I don't want to go through that again. You're a good guy and I can tell you are, but it's freaking me out because this is how it always starts."

"What?"

"You start off nice then as soon as you get me where you want me the evil in you comes out. I've seen it happen before."

"I don't know what your ex did to you but it's obvious whoever that nigga was did some type of damage to you. You're closed off like a muthafucka."

"I don't like getting close to men, they just fuck up afterwards. It happened with my ex, hell it happened with my father. He was the nicest man at times then out of nowhere he's snapping on me and my mother. Next thing you know, I'm stuck crying in the corner with a mouthful of my own blood while he's beating the shit out of her." She put the glass down on the table then stood up and walked over to the window. "Do you know what it's like to sit there and watch your mother get beat and you can't do anything about it?

"I don't," I shook my head. My pops never laid a hand on my mother. He's actually the reason I'm not on the stupid shit out here with a bunch of bitches on my arm. I saw the way my father loved my mother and I hope to have that one day. It can't happen if I'm fucking a different bitch every night.

"Of course not, you should consider yourself lucky," she chuckled. "Then I turn around and get with a man who's exactly like him. I cooked, I cleaned, and I did everything he ever wanted me to do. I would still end up with a black eye or a busted lip every other day."

Putting my glass down next to hers I walked over to her and made her turn around to look at me. "I know it's not as easy as saying it, but that's some shit you have to let go."

"I have let it go."

"No, you haven't. If you're looking at every man like he's about to dog you out because some punk ass nigga couldn't treat you the way you should've been treated, then you haven't let it go."

"I'm good, I just don't want to waste my time."

"I'm not going to waste your time because I don't have time of my own to waste. I'm not about to shit on you, I'm for damn sure not going to put my hands on you."

"How am I supposed to know that's true?"

"What reason do I have to lie to you? Picking up a girl ain't hard Mickey, you've seen how these bitches out here are. If I wanted somebody to dog out, I would go pick a bitch with low self-esteem and no self-worth to do that to. I'm feelin you and I want to show you how a real man treats a woman you just have to let me."

"It's not that simple," she shook her head. It's crazy how tough Mickey likes to come off but she's clearly low-key sensitive as shit.

"With me it is, all I'm asking you to do is let me show you. If I fuck up, I'll let you slap the shit out of me no questions."

Laughing she shook her head like she didn't believe me. "Why Tone? For real, you barely know me."

"I'm interested in knowing more of you that's why. I see you behind the attitude and all that other shit you be on."

Mickey's whole get up was a defense mechanism. Not saying she's not true to herself creatively, but the way her attitude is set up is because of the shit her ex and father put her through. She's guarded, she doesn't trust men so she's blocking niggas off. That's probably why she was out here fuckin' niggas she knew weren't fully available. It was a way of not having to get close enough to anybody to get hurt.

Most people would see it as a red flag and get the fuck away from her, but I like her. Yeah, she got a crazy attitude but she's chill when she's left alone. Shorty can definitely handle herself and I appreciate that shit.

"I'm not really into the relationship thing, but I'm willing to at least see where it can go with you. Just don't make me look or feel stupid."

"That's fine with me, you're on the same page as me just so you know. Females aren't too innocent either."

"Oh, I'm far from innocent but I won't bullshit you."

"You better not. Give a kiss." Grabbing her waist, I pulled her close to me and kissed her then she hugged me around my neck.

Toi

*L*ifting one of my grandmother's pots I started to poke a finger a in just to get a quick taste, but she popped the fuck out of my hand. "Ow, grandma was that necessary?"

"Yes, it was, get out of my pots. Go work on what you need to, so people can eat on time please."

"What time are we eating again?" I asked just for clarification. This wasn't my only stop of the night and I needed to manage my time well.

"If you do what you're supposed to do, we'll be eating at seven o'clock. Your friends know that time, right?"

"They will as soon as I send this text message." I sent everybody a mass text just to let them know what time.

"Good, where is Mickey she's usually here helping us."

"I know but she said she had some running around to do. She's coming with Tone."

"Is my baby coming?" My grandmother asked, talking about Yung's silly ass.

"Yes, he's coming grandma," I said while rolling my eyes.

The relationship my grandmother has with Yung is weird. It's like she's the one who gave birth to him or something. For whatever reason when they met, they just clicked. She likes him, Tone and Que but Yung is her baby, and nobody can tell her any different. I think it's because the nigga is low-key a baby, so she treats him like one.

I'm jealous to be honest, it's like my ass doesn't even exist when he comes around. It's been like that since they met at the cookout we had right before school for the twins started back up.

"Quentin?"

"Grandma," I laughed. "Everybody is coming okay. That's the reason I bought the bigger dining table."

Usually it would just be me, my grandma the twins and Mickey for thanksgiving dinner so a big table wasn't needed. My grandmother insisted on everybody coming to here this year so I bought her a new dining room set so everybody would fit and be comfortable.

"I know that, but I just want to make sure everything is perfect. You know how I am."

"You're a perfectionist, yes I know. Everything is going to be fine trust me." I kissed her cheek then sat down at the table and went back to peeling sweet potatoes.

"Mama, taste this." My mother held the spoon with some of her string beans on it and my grandmother ate some.

"More pepper Neva," she told her.

"Ma," I called out to my mother when she walked back to her pot. She either didn't hear me or she ignored my ass, so I picked up a sweet potato peel and threw it at her. When it hit the back of her head, she turned around looking at me like I was dumb.

"What Toi?"

"Let me get a neck bone, you have a lot of them. I know how much I bought."

"Girl if you don't leave me the hell alone, you've been begging me for food all damn day," she waved me off.

"I've been hungry all day. Once these sweet potatoes are done, I need to get dressed."

"Dinner isn't until seven it's only two."

"I know but I have to go by Que's uncle's house first. I'll be back on time trust me and if I'm not Taj and them will be here. Just give them dinner rolls until I get back," I said making all of us laugh. "I'm for real grandma don't start eating without me."

"Toi I already know okay, you just better get to moving." I nodded my head and kept peeling the potatoes.

I was so damn excited about today. Thanksgiving is my favorite holiday next to Christmas. I get to be around my family and be a complete fat ass eating whatever the hell it is that I want. This thanksgiving was special to me for a couple of reasons.

One of them being Quentin, this is our first major holiday together. The other reason is my girls are in happy and healthy relationships for once, and I know they were excited to be with their boo's just like I was. Especially Mickey, she's a completely different person because of Tone and it's refreshing to see. Don't get me wrong she's still her sarcastic tough self but she's happier and it's written all over her face every day.

The main reason I'm happy for today is because this is the first thanksgiving I'll be spending with my mother in years. I don't even remember the last time I was with her for a holiday, so I was praying everything went well today at least as far as my family is concerned.

After finishing my sweet potatoes completely, I covered them and put them on the counter with the rest of the food that wasn't done. Looking at the clock I saw that it was almost four o'clock. Que would be here to get me in thirty minutes, so I had to hurry up and get ready.

I ran upstairs to the bathroom and took a quick shower before putting my clothes on quickly so I could spend the rest of the time doing my hair. Being that I was meeting Que's mother today I was very mindful of how I dressed, Of course I'm not about to dress like a nun but I can't meet someone's mama with my ass out.

I decided to wear a cream Ralph & Russo off the shoulder cashmere sweater, dark skinny jeans, and rose gold Giuseppe Zanotti open toe ankle boots on my feet. My hair was brushed back into a sleek low ponytail, thin gold hoops were hanging from my ears while a gold watch sat on my wrist. Just as I was putting my lipstick on, I heard Que calling my name being called from downstairs.

Why did he come inside? Now they're about to talk like niggas have time to waste. I thought to myself while grabbing my purse.

"I'm coming!" I yelled back then made my way downstairs and going straight to the kitchen because I know Que's fat ass went in there as soon as he came in. "Why didn't you wait outside?" I asked before kissing him on the cheek.

"I was going to then I thought that would be rude, so I came in to speak." He looked me up and down with a smirk on his face. "You look good baby."

"You do too, nigga you look like me what the hell?" Que was wearing a cream Ralph Lauren cable-knit sweater, some jeans, and light brown Common Projects boots. We were matching and it was not cute, I find shit like that corny.

"I didn't know what you were wearing, don't come at me like this was on purpose," he laughed. "Are you ready?"

"Yeah." I looked at my grandmother then went over and kissed her on the cheek. "I'll be back grandma."

"Be on time Toi."

"I'll have her back on time Grams," he said, calling her by the nickname he, Yung and Tone gave her. "Don't even worry about it." He kissed both my mom and grandmother on the cheek then grabbed my hand and we left the house.

"You think your mother is going to like me?" I asked him once we were settled in his car.

"She'll like you just fine, my mother isn't stuck up or anything. You'll be fine besides, my uncle and Beautii will be there and if Beautii likes you're already in."

"Alright we'll see."

"Stop being so scary you'll be alright." He picked my hand up and kissed it then pulled off.

It took us almost an hour to get to Saint and Beautii's house and just from that drive alone I knew we were going to be late going back to my grandmother's house. Just great, she's going to kill me.

When we pulled up to a modern Georgian style mansion, my mouth literally dropped. I knew they had money, but I've never seen a

QUENTIN & TOI: A LEGENDARY HOOD TALE

house this big in person in all of my life. Talk about life goals, this is definitely it.

"Is this their house?" I asked, there is no way only two people live in this house.

"Yeah, my mother lives around the corner," Quentin laughed. "Why do you look so shocked?"

"Look at this shit Oh my God. This is a damn mansion Que."

"It's not that serious."

"Like hell it ain't," I chuckled. My grandmother has a nice size home, six bedrooms, four bathrooms, nice backyard that we don't even use. It's pretty big, but Beautii and Saint's house is on another damn level.

Que got out of the car then came around on my side and helped me out. We walked up to the front door and instead of knocking he just walked right in leading me inside. Just looking around this big ass house had me shocked, if this is the type of lifestyle her salon bought her, I couldn't wait until my spa opened so I can upgrade.

"This is so crazy."

"I take it you like the house," he smiled.

"I love it, wow."

"Come on," he pulled me down the hall and the more we walked the louder the music got. I take it everybody was back here chillin. The first room we went in looked like a living room just with a strong masculine feel to it. When I saw the group of niggas occupying the room, I was given the impression that this was Saint's little hangout.

"The fuck you niggas doing?" Que shouted getting all of their attention.

"I told you his big head ass was going to walk through the door in a minute." Saint stood up from his seat and hugged Que then looked at me. "Toi, what's up with you?" He hugged me.

"Hey Saint," I smiled hugging him back.

"You're looking good girl. Is my nephew treating you right?"

"Yeah he's being a good guy so far," I laughed.

"He better." Saint looked at Que. "You my nephew and I love you but she's my niece too, I'll fuck you up if you do some bullshit."

"Well damn, I thought it would be her family members threatening my ass not my own. What the fuck?" Que shit back with a laugh.

"Just letting you know nigga."

"Mhm yeah aight." Que introduced me to everybody that was in the room with Sin and it turns out they were all his cousins. Come to find out, Saint wasn't only the youngest child he was the only boy out of five kids.

"So, your mom and aunts are in the kitchen?"

"Yeah come on." Que pulled me out of the room then further down the hall to the kitchen. "This is what I like to see, women at work!" He announced when we walked in the kitchen earning a dirty look from every single one of them.

"Boy, are you trying to get slapped the fuck up? Don't play with us." Beautii came over and mushed him in the face then hugged him. "You bought my baby, hi Toi!" She squealed when she saw me then pulled me in for a tight hug.

"You already know I had too. Y'all this is my girl Toi," Que told them. "Toi these are my big head aunties. That's my Auntie Lilianna, we just call her Lily, Auntie Anita, Aunt Elena, she's the baby and that beautiful woman right there is my mother Maria," I said hi and gave a hug to each one of them.

To be honest I was stuck looking at them. They were all so damn beautiful and didn't look a day over thirty. It's obvious they have some good genes in their family because these women were flawless.

"So, this is who has my son's nose wide open," his mother smiled at me. "You did good son, she's beautiful."

"I know she is." Que kissed me on the cheek. "Y'all done cooking yet?"

"Do you see us eating yet?" His Aunt Elena said, and I couldn't help but laugh.

"Don't ask dumb questions Quentin. You and your uncle are annoying. Go sit down with them and get out of my kitchen before I burn you," Beautii told him.

"Burn me? Aight it's time for me to go," he laughed then looked at me. "You good in here with them?"

"Yeah I think I'm fine. You can take my coat and hold my purse for me though. Thank you." I gave him my stuff and he walked out after sucking his teeth. He'll be alright. "Do you guys need help with anything?"

"You can take the stuff out of the oven, things are pretty much done. We're just adding the final touches on everything," said Lily and I happily obliged.

After getting the food out of the oven I went in the dining room with Anita and helped her set the table while they put the final changes on everything. While were in there she basically let me in on a little bit of information about their family.

I learned that they're half Dominican because of their father, hence their last name. Anita herself had two boys, Dante, and Bryan. Elena has one son, Noel. Lily had three sons, Carnell, Zyair, and Nate. And of course, Que's mother has him and a daughter named Mia who was a year younger than me. I knew Que had a sister, but he doesn't really talk about her too much, I'll ask him about that later.

When we were done, they sent down to the living room to get everybody and I went in the bathroom that was downstairs and washed my hands before joining everybody at the table. Just as everybody was sitting down the front door closing got everyone's attention.

"That's probably Mia," Que's mother got up and walked out into the hallway. Next thing you know we heard a bunch of squealing.

"Yup, that's her," Saint shook his head. It was a few more seconds before they both came walking in the room. When my eyes laid eyes on his sister they went wide a little bit.

"Hey y'all," Mia waved at everybody and hugged a few of them. "My bad I'm late I had to pick my friend up."

"What friend baby?" Her mother asked her.

"Just an old friend, she'll come inside in a minute." Mia looked around then stopped when her eyes landed on me. "La'Toia?"

Sighing I gave her a head nod. "What's up?"

"Y'all know each other?" Que looked at me and asked.

"Something like that," I answered, keeping it simple.

"Oh, I know her, Que please tell me you're not claiming this hoe," Mia laughed. I turned my head looking at her like she was an idiot.

"Who are you calling a hoe?" I was about to get up from my chair, but Que pulled me back down.

"Wait a minute, what the hell is going on right now?" Their mother looked back and forth between me and Mia.

"It's something very old and stupid," I answered her.

"She's right ma, it's old but the fact that she's a hoe is not. Just ask about her if you don't believe me."

"They can go right on ahead and do all of that. I bet they don't hear one grimy thing about me. Don't even go there with me Mia I will let all your shit bare. Do you really want me announcing the moves you making out here?" I looked straight at her, I wanted her to keep running her mouth so I could embarrass her dumb ass.

I know she would hate for me to open my mouth and tell her family about all her hoeish activities. This bitch is out here busting it open to anybody that'll give her a second look. If she wanted to talk about reputations and whose really out here hoeing, we could go there.

Rolling her eyes, Mia waved me off. "Whatever let me go see what's taking my friend so long," she said before walking out of the room.

"What the hell was all of that about?" Que questioned.

"I'll tell you about it later. I don't feel like talking about it right now."

"Aight." It was a minute or two before Mia came back in the room with some tall Hispanic looking girl behind her.

"Y'all remember Isyss right?" Mia said with a big smile on her face.

"Oh shit," Noel tried to mumble but he was right next to me so I

"We're going back to your grandmother's house. Let's go."

"Quentin, don't leave," his mother told him, but he shook his head.

"No man I'm out, I'm not about to sit here like she didn't just walk in here with this bitch. Toi let's go." I stood up from the table and waved at everybody before walking out with Que. I don't know what the fuck that was but I'm about to find out.

Legend

"So, what the fuck was that about?" I asked Toi while I drove. I don't know what the fuck the issue between them is but clearly there is one.

"I was about to ask you the same damn thing, who the hell is Isyss?"

"She's a bitch but fuck her, how do you know my sister?"

"Remember I was telling you about the chick basically stalking my ass because of my ex?"

"Yeah."

"Well your sister was that bitch. Don't feel a way about me saying this but, your sister is a ho."

"A ho?"

"Yes, a ho, a big ho. I don't know if niggas know y'all related so maybe you don't hear her about her too much, but I've heard some shit and it's never good.

I shook my head, that's sounds like Mia. I know my sister and I know she's thirsty for male attention with her daddy issues having ass. "I'm not even surprised by that shit."

"You're not?"

"Hell no, Mia is a fucking trouble maker. She lives for drama which is why she went and bought Isyss with her over there."

"What do you mean? Who is she?"

"My ex, we broke up four years ago. She was really close with Mia, so I'm not surprised she still talks to her, but she was on some bullshit bringing her to the house."

"So, she brought your ex over there for you basically? For what? I don't understand why people are so fucking sneaky."

"It's whatever, I'm not dealing with that bitch. I don't even fuck with Mia like that."

"Why not?"

"You see how she is and you're asking me that question? I don't have time for the sneaky bullshit. That's all she's about so I don't deal with her ass."

"That's sad, I don't think you should have left like that. You should've just ignored the both of them."

"Oh, please there is no ignoring my sister, she'll annoy the fuck out of you until you speak to her. It's whatever though. At least I know there will be no drama at your grandmother's house."

"You have a point." She shrugged her shoulders.

I don't know what the fuck Mia was trying to prove or accomplish by bringing Isyss to my uncle's house, but I don't even care enough to find out. I hope my mother slaps her ignorant ass, it's always her that has to fuck shit up when things are going well. Sister or not I'm not about to be surrounded by stupid shit so she's barely around me and it ain't changing no time soon.

<hr>

"So how many barbers do you need?" Tone asked me while we sat in the barbershop. I was one week away from opening this shit and I still needed one more barber in here.

"One more, I'm opening this shit whether we have one or not though," I shrugged.

"Do you, you got it looking good in here." The last owner had this shop looking old school as fuck. I did a complete remodel and updated everything. I can't have my name on some bullshit.

"I know, I wasn't about to have my name on the shit with it

looking the way it did. This shit was wack, I had to change it up. Now it looks like something muthafuckas wanna sit in."

"True, what's going on with Toi's spa?"

"She got them working on it. She's in that shit everyday making sure everything goes right. I told her anything that's going to have your name on it can't be fucked up. She's been on top of it so she's good. When she's not there she's running around trying to get all her permits together. Shorty on her shit," I answered him.

"That's what's up, Mickey talking about going back to college or whatever."

"What does she do for a living?" I asked him and he shrugged.

"I don't even know. I asked but she said I didn't need to worry about it because she was done with it. I been asking around and I know she wasn't selling ass or something, so it really doesn't matter to me."

"Toi said the same thing, I don't know what the fuck they were doing but I can bet money they were in on it together. Whatever it was, it had to be something crazy because they were making stacks from it." Toi has yet to tell me what she used to do for money. She makes it perfectly clear that she wasn't prostituting herself, and she wasn't involved with drugs. I wanna know what the fuck the big secret was but I'll let her tell me when she's ready. I'm not going to sweat her about it.

"I know, you don't think they were low key moving weight, do you?" he raised his eyebrow.

"She said it wasn't drugs, hell I don't know. As long as she stopped the shit, I'm good now she's about to be legit."

"I feel you," I said before taking a seat in one of the chairs. I started going through my phone when the bell signaling someone just walked in made a noise. Looking up I raised my eyebrow when I saw Isyss standing there.

"The fuck you doing here?" I asked her.

She rolled her hazel eyes then placed one of her hands on her hip. "I heard about the open barber position, so I came to see about it, what are you doing in here?"

"I own this shit and there is no way in the highest fuck you're working here so you might as well turn right back around ma."

Isyss is my bum ass ex of five years. I used to be in love with her ass something crazy, we had that hood love shit going on. I honestly thought I was going to marry her one day until I found out she was cheating on my ass with a nigga that worked for me. I couldn't swallow it and move on, so I left her alone.

"What the fuck? You can't do that!" She snapped at me.

"Why can't I?"

"That's not right, you know I'm good at cutting hair so don't even act like I'm not. Just because you got a new bitch doesn't mean you can be an asshole," she ranted while rolling that damn neck of hers.

"My bitch doesn't have shit to do with you not working in here. I'm trying to have a thot free business. Last time I let you in a place of mine you started fucking one of my employees. Or did you forget?"

"You know what, I am so sick of you being on that. I cheated on you, okay alright fine whatever, you cheated on me too so stop acting like I broke your nonexistent heart."

"I really don't give a fuck about the shit you spitting right now. How the fuck did I go from not seeing you in four years to seeing you twice within a week? My sister put you up to this shit?"

"No, Mia did not put me up to this. I saw that this place was hiring on the internet and I came in for a job. You don't have to like me Que I really don't like your ass too much either but damnit I need this. I have a fucking child to feed and I don't need your pettiness to stand in the way of that."

"Why the fuck should I help you do anything? Your kid doesn't have shit to do with me," I told her, and she laughed.

"Listen, I just need this job alright. You don't have to talk to me or anything, you don't have to pay me any type of attention. You know I'm good, and if you forgot just look through my portfolio and see for yourself." She walked over to where I was and handed me the binder.

I looked through the pictures and she was right, she's good at cutting hair. I used to let her cut my shit back when we were together but I'm still on the fence about this bitch working here. I looked at Tone and he shrugged his shoulders.

"Aight," I sighed giving her, her binder back. "You can work here, you have to wear black every day and you need to be here at nine every single day. You start Monday."

Smiling she took her book back. "Thank you, I won't let you down I promise." When she walked out, I shook my head while Tone stupid ass laughed.

"The fuck is so funny?"

"You nigga, how the fuck are you going to explain to Toi you're about to have your ex bitch working for you?"

"Man, Toi ain't like that, she's not a jealous broad she won't care."

"Yeah aight that's what you think. All women are jealous, I don't know who the fuck told you different."

I waved this nigga off he doesn't know what the fuck he's talking about. Toi isn't going to care; besides, she's working in a barbershop it's not like she's right up under me or something.

Mickey

"'m going to be so damn bomb tonight. Just to prepare you Mickey I'm getting white girl wasted. Y'all are going to have to carry my ass out of the club," Toi said while I drove down the street.

We just got finished shopping for our girls' night out and she was a little too hyped up about it. I understand her excitement just because we haven't been out partying since the night Bia was murdered but she was a little bit too happy.

"You better not be in there losing your mind Toi. Don't forget your ass has a man now."

"How the hell can I forget that when damn near everybody is scared of his ass. Trust me, I'm not going to do anything stupid I just want to have a good time with no fucking drama."

"It'll be that, but you need to chill a little bit. I just want to know how you plan to go out with the outfit you bought. Que is going to be like hell the fuck no."

"He doesn't even know I'm going out so he's not going to say anything."

"Wait," I looked at her. "He doesn't know your ass is going out tonight? Why not?"

"I don't have to tell him everywhere I'm going. Did you tell Tone?"

"No, but we're in two different situations."

"How do you figure that?"

"Maybe because Tone ass isn't going around pistol whipping niggas for saying something to me like Que. Toi tell that nigga you're going out before somebody tells on your ass. Do you feel like arguing with him?"

"No, we're not going to argue. Que will be fine trust me, we're good. Now please change the subject I don't want to talk about tonight until tonight comes."

"Fine, have you started Christmas shopping yet?"

"I've got my grandmother's gift already. I just have to get something for my mother, and the twins."

"What are you getting Que?"

"I have no fucking idea, he already has everything. The fuck do you get somebody that has so much?"

"I bought Tone a watch, I went through his shit, so I know he doesn't already have it. Be nosey to figure out your gift, it's what I did."

"What's been up with you and Tone anyway? Every time I see you, you have this big ass smile on your face."

"We're good, and I'm happy. I don't know what else to say," I laughed. Tone and I have been really good these last few months. Yeah, we argue and here and there just because I'm a bitch at times an argument is bound to take place. It's never been over anything serious so we're good.

"That is so cute, when y'all get married make sure your wedding colors involve the color red."

"Whoa there, nobody is getting married anytime soon. It hasn't even been long enough for that discussion to come up."

"Oh please, Tone ass is going to marry you. He's damn near forty, I bet he proposes to you."

"How is thirty damn near forty Toi?"

"I'm just saying."

"Nah I'm good on that," I chuckled. "Leave my relationship alone, how about you and Que. Not even six months and y'all have family drama. I can't believe that bitch is his sister," I shook my head.

I remember Mia, I remember all the drama involved that little bitch. I also remember Toi beating her ass not once, not twice, but four damn times. I didn't know she was a Santana though; the way she acts I wouldn't believe she came from money. The bitch is a bird if I ever saw one.

"I know right! This is one small world, who the fuck would ever think Bless's side bitch would be the sister of my new man. When that nigga moved to Atlanta, I thought I was done with his bullshit. But nope, one of his bitches is related to Que and we don't fuckin' like each other. That's some Love and Hip-Hop shit. I thought I was done with that bitch but nope here she goes, popping up again."

"You're a calm ass person because I would've flipped the fuck out. Beautii would've forgiven me later. Then she walked in there with his ex? Nope, it would've been fight night."

"That's because you have some fucking anger problems. It wasn't enough for me to wanna fight but it did piss me off. I don't have to be around the bitch so we're good on that, as long as he doesn't be around his ex, I'll be fine."

"And if he does? You know when shit like this happens it starts being a reoccurring theme. It's like that one situation will cause a domino effect, bitch will start popping up all over the place."

"Then I'll have to kill the bitch and fuck him up. That's not okay with me, exes don't need to be anywhere around."

"We're on the same page with that one." Just as I was stopping at a red light my phone began to ring so I answered then put it on speaker. "Hello?"

"Where you at Mick?" Tone's voice came through the speakers.

"I'm about to go to McDonalds, why?"

"Good I caught you then. Get me some food and bring it to this fuckin' shop."

"The barbershop? Why are you there?"

"I'm waiting for somebody. Yo, I haven't eaten shit all fucking day and I'm starving."

"Why didn't you eat?"

"Too much running around and I didn't have time to stop before I came here. Just come through for me."

"Alright I got you, I'll be there in like twenty minutes."

"Aight I'll see you when you get here." After we hung up, I looked at Toi.

"We have to go by that damn barbershop so I can bring that nigga something to eat."

"Ugh, I hate going there man," Toi shook her head. I don't blame her for being uncomfortable, walking in there is annoying. Niggas act like they've never seen a fucking female before.

"I know but it'll be quick, and you know what just for him making me drive down that way we're going to Buffalo Wild Wings on him before we hit the club."

"That's what the fuck I'm talking about I haven't had their wings in a minute. I'm cool with that shit."

"Good," I got the food from McDonald's then made my way to the barbershop and parked right in front. "I'll be right back you don't have to come in if you don't want to."

"I wasn't planning on it, I'm good. Go ahead." I grabbed Tone's stuff then got out of the car and made my way inside. Of course, as soon as I stepped foot in the bitch these niggas started gawking.

"Where Tone at?" I asked while they stared at me.

"He's in the back," a girl who was sitting in one of the chairs said and I raised my eyebrow.

"Can you go tell him Mickey is here?" I asked her but she didn't move. I stood there looking at her for another couple of seconds waiting for her stupid ass to get up, but she just sat there so I decided to ask again. "Can you go get him please?"

"Oh, you were talking to me?" She looked at me with a fake, shocked expression on her face. The bitch knew I was talking to her but she's trying to be funny.

"Bitch don't you work here?" I spat.

"Bitch?" Laughing she shook her head. "You have a bad attitude, if you want somebody to do something for you, you need to ask nicely."

"I asked you nicely."

"You just called me a fucking bitch, bitch."

"Before that, I wasn't rude to you at all but you wanna still sit there like a fucking idiot so I'm going to speak to you like you're one. Get the fuck up and go get him!"

"I'm not going to get shit, you better watch who the fuck you talking to!"

"Or I can bust you in your muthafuckin face, don't fu-"

"Aye, aye!" Tone came running from the back with Que right behind him cutting me off. "The fuck is going on?"

"Ask this rude ass bitch, she came in here on some disrespectful shit."

"I got your bitch, keep on fucking with me," I countered back at her only for Tone to put his hand over my mouth.

"Isyss you're on some bullshit," Que said to her.

"I didn't even do shit. You weren't out here why the fuck are you speaking on something you weren't in this bitch to witness?" She snapped at him. Walking over to her Que grabbed her arm and snatched her out of the chair she was in then pulled her outside. I hope he slaps that bitch.

"You out here about to fuck somebody up," Tone said after he lowered his hand from my mouth.

"She got smart with me. I asked her to go tell you that I was here, but the bitch wanted to act simple. Raggedy ass slut bucket ass bitch."

"Whoa damn, calm down," he told me before laughing.

"She pissed me off man. Here, I'm never coming to this bitch again." I gave him his bag of food just as we heard shouting coming from outside. We both looked out the window to see Que and Toi arguing while the bitch I was going at it with stood there with a smile on her face.

I don't know what the fuck this bitch found funny but if Toi catches that smile on her face, she might get punched in it.

Toi

Sitting in Mickey's car I was going down my Facebook newsfeed and eating the French fries I got when we went to McDonalds, when yelling from outside caught a little bit of my attention. I glanced out the window briefly then turned my head back to my phone until I realized it was Que standing out there arguing with some girl.

She had her back facing the car so I couldn't tell who she was. I rolled down the window so I could hear what the hell they were saying.

"You weren't even in there so how are you going to call me wrong? That big bitch came at me first the fuck did you expect me to do?" The girl snapped at Que. What bitch was she talking about?

"I don't give a fuck you're a fucking employee, you don't go running off at the mouth. You're lucky we came from the back and she didn't fuck you up, that would've been your ass on everything." Right then I figured he was talking about Mickey. She would go somewhere and end up in an argument.

"Whatever Que go right on ahead and take her side. You just want a fucking reason to come at my neck."

"You lucky you even got this job the fuck do you mean? I didn't have to hire you, I was trying to be fucking nice. You think I want you around anything that belongs to me."

"Oh please, what's wrong? Your new bitch is going to have a problem with me working here? If she's intimidated by me just because I'm your ex, that's not my fault." Did this bitch just say ex? What the fuck?

"Don't give yourself so much fucking credit, nobody is thinking about your stupid ass," he countered back just as I was rolling the window down completely.

"Yeah right, can I go the fuck back inside now?"

"Nah stay out here," I said loud enough for both of them to hear me. When Que looked at me, I could tell he was shocked. Smiling I opened the door and got out of the car and got directly in front of him. "So, what the fuck is this?"

"Let me tell you what's going on," Que said while he looked at me.

"No, I can see what's going on just fine, the fuck is your ex here for?"

"It's nothing, it's just business I'm serious."

"Then why the fuck didn't I know about it? You come telling me about this shop every other day, but you couldn't open your mouth and mention the fact that you got your ex in this bitch?"

"You act like I'm fucking her or something! All she is doing is working here you are overreacting right now!" He shouted at me.

"I don't give a fuck what she's doing I should've known about it!"

"Excuse me, why does where I work affect you? Last I checked I don't even know you so why you worried about me?" This bitch said while looking at me. I couldn't help but look at her like she was stupid, I knew this bitch was not about to test her luck and try me right now.

"First of all, I'm not worried about you. I don't give a fuck about you and I wasn't even talking to you so you can get the fuck out of my face," I snapped at her real quick.

"You were talking about me, that's close enough. Don't worry about what the fuck it is I'm doing. He hired me so what, why are you so mad?"

"Mad? Bitch if you don't get the fuck outta here with that shit," I was about to get in her face, but Que stepped in front of me and made me back up after he wrapped his arms around my waist.

"Chill Toi, it's not deep for real," Que said, in effort to calm me down but fuck that shit.

"I don't give a fuck, she on disrespectful bullshit. I'll slap the shit out of her out here, you better let her stupid ass know."

"Slap me then bitch! Go ahead and slap me I'll have all types of hittas at your door!" Was that a fucking threat?

"GO GET WHOEVER THE FUCK YOU WANT BITCH DO I LOOK WORRIED?" I shouted at her while unzipping my Dawn Levy coat. By this time people were standing around watching us go back and forth. Even Mickey and Tone both came out of the barbershop.

"You really need to chill the fuck out!" Que grabbed both of my arms and shook me like he lost his fucking mind. I snatched my arms out of his grip and mushed him away from me.

"Tell that bitch to chill out! Don't come at me because you wanted to keep something a secret and you got fucking caught!" I mushed him again then looked at Mickey. "Let's go before I snap a bitch neck around here."

"Aight come on," Mickey walked over to her car and got in while I looked at this basic bitch.

"I'll see you around, just wait on that shit," I warned her before getting in the car and slamming the door. As soon as I did Mickey pulled off.

"Okay what the fuck just happened?"

"Remember I told you his sister bought his ex to Saint's house? That was the bitch she had with her."

"Wait, what?"

"That's his fucking ex and he got the bitch working in his shop like that shit is okay. He's talking about its just business and it's nothing but come on bruh if it's nothing why the fuck would you not tell me about it?"

"Damn, you really mad huh?"

"Yes, I'm mad. He's at that shop all the time that means he's seeing that bitch every other day. That's too fucking much, you shouldn't be seeing her at all."

"Toi come on now you act like he's fucking the bitch."

"I don't care Mickey! I really give no fucks about whether he's fucking her or not. I should've known the bitch was working there. He flips the fuck out if he sees another nigga even looking at me, but he can work with his ex? Fuck out of here with that bullshit."

"We were just talking about that shit though, that's crazy."

"Spoke the shit up." I shook my head and looked at my phone when it started ringing. Of course, it was Que, but I ignored the shit then turned my phone off and put it in my purse. We don't have a muthafuckin' thing to talk about, he can kiss my whole ass.

"Are we still going out or are you not feeling it anymore?" I had completely forgot about tonight in the midst of the drama. A part of me didn't even want to go anymore but after giving it a second thought I shrugged that shit off. I'm not about to be bored and in the house because he pissed me off. I'm going the fuck out. Fuck that.

"We're still going, I need to go blow off some steam. Matter of fact do you have some weed?"

"I thought Que made you stop smoking," she laughed.

"Fuck him, where the weed at?"

"Glove compartment. He's going to kick your ass."

"Like I said, fuck him. He's not doing shit." I went in her glove compartment and pulled out the bag of weed she had sitting right next to a cigarillo pack and proceeded to roll up. Tonight, is about to be real.

Legend

"I told you she was going to flip the fuck out on you but nah, you didn't want to listen to me." Tone shook his head at me.

"She's not usually jealous of anybody man," I've never seen Toi act like that, bitches are after my ass all day every day and she's never said anything mainly because she has no reason to. I'm not about to do anything and she knows that so why the fuck she's flipping out now is confusing me.

"You got history with Isyss you fuckin' idiot. What woman you know is alright with their nigga hanging around their ex?"

"I'm not hanging around her."

"Her working there is good enough."

"Aight man, I gotta talk to her ass later when I get to her place."

"Oh, she's not going to be there, so you'll be going for no reason."

"The fuck you mean she won't be there," I looked at him confused. How the hell would he know Toi isn't going to be home?

"She won't be there, Mickey told me they were going out. I'm guessing she didn't tell you."

"Hell no," I should've known her ass was going to make it out to the club tonight. That's what bitches do, get into an argument and the first thing they do is go shaking their ass in a fucking club. "Do you know where they're going?"

159

"Some spot in Hoboken, I think Mickey said they play old shit or whatever."

"They're going to Mason's, that was Toi's idea," as soon as he said old shit, I knew he was talking about Mason's and knew it was Toi who came up with that fucking idea. Mason's is a spot that caters to anybody who's into old school type music. All they do is play shit from the ninety's and early two thousands. I'm talking about Ja Rule, R. Kelly, Ashanti, Aaliyah type of shit. That's all Toi ass listens too, she rarely listened to anybody that's out now. If it ain't Beyoncé, Cardi B, or Chris Brown she ain't really fuckin' with it.

"I know, so what are you going to do? Talk to her tomorrow?"

"Fuck no, I know where she's going to be. I'm heading there right after we make this drop tonight."

"You like pissing your girl off I see."

Chuckling I shrugged my shoulders. "She'll be alright," I know showing up tonight while she's out is going to blow her shit, but I really don't give a fuck.

WALKING into Mason's I looked around at everybody who were in attendance. Mason's really isn't my kind of spot, but it was poppin' in here tonight, I guess they're starting to step it up.

"You seem them anywhere?" I asked Tone and he shook his head no. "They're probably on the dance floor." After I made arrangements for a VIP table, I sat down then ordered a bottle of Ace for myself.

"Damn she got a fat ass!" Tone exclaimed when a bitch went walking past our table. He wasn't lying, her ass was on some dumb shit in the dress she had on.

"You lucky Mickey wasn't here to hear you say that shit nigga, she would've slapped the fuck out your neck," I laughed. Mickey doesn't play with Tone's ass and he knows it. She doesn't do the extra bitches around for no reason shit, I've seen her threaten bitches over his ass. It's funny as hell to me.

"That's why her ass ain't right here right now, ain't nothing wrong with looking. It's not like I'm dumb enough to go for it."

"She'll kill yo ass," I laughed again before drinking from the bottle the bottle waitress bought me. I sat there drinking and bobbing my head to the music for a couple of minutes before Tone tapped me and pointed to the bar.

"Aye bruh there goes your girl." Looking over I raised my eyebrow when I saw her. Not only did she have on some other shit, she had some pussy ass nigga smiling all in her face. She wasn't really paying any attention to him from what I could see but I didn't like how close that nigga was. I took one more swig then made my way down to where she was.

"No thank you, I have a man already!" I heard her yell to him over the music.

"He's not too good of a nigga if he's got you here by yourself!" He shouted back. I tapped him on his shoulder and waited for him to turn around. When he faced me, his smile dropped. "Oh shit, Legend what's up?" He said nervously.

"Nothing, I'm just trying to figure out why you all over what's mine." I looked at Toi so he would get the point.

"O-oh I didn't know she was your girl man, no disrespect."

"Uh huh yeah right, move the fuck on before I take it as such." With that he scurried off. Toi looked up at me then rolled her eyes as she got up off the stool she was sitting on. She was about to walk off, but I grabbed her arm and pulled her back.

"Let me go Que, what the fuck?"

"Nah come here, we need to talk ma." I pulled her towards to the hallway that led to where the bathrooms were so I could speak to her without shouting over the fucking music.

"What are you pulling on me for?"

"The fuck you got on," I questioned looking at the low cut, black spaghetti strap mini dress, and Versace, leopard over the knee boots she had on.

My Balenciaga graffiti printed distressed denim jacket hung off her shoulders, her hair was braided in the front and half of it was up while the back cascaded down the back in curls. She was rocking the large diamond hoop earrings that matched the diamond eternity necklace around her neck. I looked over her again and noticed she was wearing the silver Rolex and charm bracelet I bought her too. She has the nerve to have an attitude while rocking my shit and everything else I gave her.

I haven't known Toi for long, but I've dropped a lot of money on her already. She doesn't ask me for shit but anytime I see something I feel she needs or would like I buy it. Jewelry, clothes, shoes, anything she wants she can have. That says a lot because I don't like giving people shit, I feel like if you're not my mother why the fuck should I go out of my way for you?

Toi is different though, I like the seeing the smile on her face when I give her something. I even make it a point to deposit a few thousand dollars into her account every other week. She gets on me about it but until she opens her spa, she has no money coming in so I'm going to do for her.

"I see you out her shining, you funny as fuck," I chuckled at her. "What the fuck was that nigga all in your face for?"

"He wasn't in my face and I wasn't paying attention to him, the fuck you spying on me for?"

"Nobody is spying on your ass," I looked her up and down before clenching my jaw. "You in here on some bullshit got your titties out and shit."

"My titties aren't out."

"You don't have a fucking bra on Toi! I can see your nipples through that fucking dress. It ain't even hot outside, I know you were freezing yo ass off when you got the car." Chuckling she waved me off then looked to the side, so I grabbed her face and made her look at me. "I know your ass ain't fucking high."

"So, what if I am? I'm grown I can do whatever the fuck I want, just like you. Now if you'll excuse me." She tried to walk off, but I pulled her back and pushed her up against the wall.

"Listen to me aight, I'm not trying to disrespect your ass or hurt you but right now you're trying my fucking patience."

"I didn't even do anything to you so you're mad for no reason. You're the one around your ex but I'm getting chastised like a fucking child? How does that make any sense?"

"She works at the barbershop that's it you act like I'm fucking her or something. No bitch has my fucking attention but you, this insecure shit needs to be cut down."

"I'm not insecure. Don't even fucking go there."

"I can't tell you so fucking worried about her being around when I'm not even stunting her ass! I don't even speak to that bitch unless I'm checking her ass for something."

"I don't want her at the shop Que!"

"I can't fire her for no reason Toi! That bitch is beat enough to sue me."

"Then kill the bitch! The point is I don't want you around the bitch and as long as you got her working for you, I don't want you nowhere around me so get the fuck out of my face." Toi snatched away pushed me then walked off.

"Stubborn ass," I shook my head.

Toi

"*W*ho the fuck told Que I was here?" I asked Mickey and Giselle while I fixed my makeup in the bathroom mirror. After I left Que standing there I went and made both of them come with me to the bathroom

"I didn't, Dutch doesn't even know my ass is here," Giselle said. Giselle is Dutch's girlfriend, I met her the second time I was around Dutch, and we clicked immediately. We invited her out with us since Taj couldn't come due to her boo loving on Yung's ass, I need to talk to her about that when I see her too.

"I told Tone we were coming here earlier," Mickey said, and I sucked my teeth,

"Mickey! Damn why you tell him?"

"He asked me, and I wasn't about to lie just because you're mad over a bitch. You're being petty as hell by the way."

"The fuck? So, if Tone was working with his ex you wouldn't be mad?"

"Que isn't working with his ex, he just owns the shop. I know you don't think the nigga is going to cheat on you or something."

"No, I trust him, it's that bitch I don't trust. All the shops in the city and she has to work in his? Come on bruh. I don't give a damn what anybody says the bitch is up to something. Let her ass make the wrong move just one time and I'm pouncing on that hoe."

164

"Well you know I got your back if and when some shit goes down," Mickey told me.

"I know, but enough about that. Can we go finish turning up? I need to get as drunk as possible, I already know he's going to follow my ass home so I'm going to have to deal with him."

"Yeah just let me pee first," Mickey went into one the of the stalls while Giselle and I waited. While we were talking three women came in the bathroom and I wanted to laugh because I could tell just by what they had on they were thots.

"Girl, did you see Legend's fine ass in there? Oh my God, that nigga is just too much to look at," one of them said catching my attention.

"Yeah, I saw him, he's fine as hell. Let me tell you right now I'm getting his ass tonight," another one added in.

"You are so nasty," their friend laughed. "What are you going to do?"

"What do you think? Call me nasty all you want to, that dick will be all mine tonight. Just wait on it," I looked at Giselle who was laughing. Truthfully, I couldn't help but laugh at these bitches too, these hoes are something else.

"Are you laughing at us?" The main hoe said.

"Actually, I was, let me ask you a question. This Legend guy you're talking about, is he tall, brown skin, tattoos?"

"Yeah that's him, you know him?"

"Oh, I know very well, I just wanted to know if were talking about the same person." When Mickey came out the stall she went over to the sink and washed her hands then came to where I was.

"What are you going to do? We can slide these hoes right now."

"Nah I'm good," I laughed. "Come on, let's go finish turning up." We walked out of the bathroom and back over to the table were sitting at.

"I'm surprised you didn't jump on one of those bitches."

"For talking? Nah I'm good, they're not going to get him so I'm not worried about it. I'm worried about these drinks though." I called the waitress over and ordered another bottle and shots for us.

Once our drinks came, I wasted no time in drinking all of my shots down.

Standing up I moved my body to the beat of R. Kelly's Ignition remix while the liquor I've been consuming all night finally started doing its job and this song was helping buzz. This is the reason I love Jordan's so much, they played the right music. I couldn't groove to anything that's out now; the fuck is a Young Thug?

When the song went off, I was about to sit down until I heard them put on Feelin' on your booty. I almost lost my mind when I heard that song come on. Before I could really get into it, Mickey tapped my shoulder then came close to me and spoke in my ear. "Those broads from the bathroom are making their move on Que."

"What?"

"Look over there," she moved my head to the right where Que and Tone were sitting down with those bitches right there in the section. Tone I wasn't really concerned about, he's not dumb enough to try Mickey. My eyes went right to Que who had a bottle of champagne in his hands while he bobbed his head to the music. Nothing really stuck out to me until the thottiest bitch in that little crew sat her fat ass right next to Que and started to whisper in his ear.

"These bitches," I chuckled. "I'll be right back," I told her then I made my way to their section. I was feeling way too good to even be mad about this broad and her hoe goals. With every step I took to get where they were my buzz was getting stronger.

When I got to them, I stood directly in front of Que and Tone. Tone noticed me but Que wasn't even paying attention until I tapped on his shoulder making him and the bitch next to him looking up. When she saw me, she looked confused.

Que sat back in his seat and smirked while looking up at me. "What's up ma?"

"Nothing, I just came over to see what's up with you. Was I interrupting something?"

"As a matter of fact, you were, so you can go and move on while we finish talking," the girl snapped at me.

"Talking?" I laughed then looked at Que. "All you want is conversation? I can give you more than that."

"Word?" He smiled at me. He knew exactly what I was doing, and I could tell he was amused, I was too. I was about to get this hoe heated. "Show me what you mean ma."

I sat down next to him and pulled his face closer to mine then kissed him. Que lifted me onto his lap deepening the kiss. I was so wrapped into the kiss I didn't even notice this bitch stood up to do something until I heard Tone yell the word chill. Pulling away from Que's lips I looked at her and smiled when I see that she was really upset and standing behind Tone who I'm guess was blocking her.

"Oh my, baby girl are you mad?" I turned my body to face her without leaving Que's lap.

"You saw me talking to him and you want to come over here and do some bullshit, cock blocking ass hoe!" She screamed and a big smile came across my face.

"Let me let you in on something sweetheart just in case you didn't know or didn't catch the fuck on. This is my nigga, I'm the only one he's going to be fucking so move you thirst bucket head ass on somewhere."

"Oh please, he was going to fuck me if you weren't here. Niggas like him don't settle down bitch," she countered back. I was about to get up, but Que tightened the grip he had around my waist.

"I wasn't even thinking about fucking you so don't get shit twisted. It's only one bitch getting this dick and she's on my lap right now. Get the fuck over it and get out before I let her loose on your ass. I promise she'll fuck you up," Legend warned them.

"Fuck who up?" The girl said just as her friends stood up with her making Que and I both laugh. I looked back at him and smiled.

"Baby, can I?" I asked him and he kissed me on the lips.

"Go ahead ma." As soon as he let me go and I got up I snatched that bitch by her dry ass weave, pulled her down since the bitch had some height over me and started landing blows to the side of her face. I wasn't even worried about her little bitch buddies because I knew

Tone and Que weren't about to let these broads jump me. Besides, if I know Mickey the way I think I know her ass will be over here in about two point five seconds.

Legend

I don't know where the fuck Mickey's ass came from but while Toi was fucking this tall bitch up one of her friends came flying across me. When I looked over to see what the fuck was going on it was Mickey dragging the fuck out of the girl, she was actually dog walking this bitch.

When she got her where she wanted Mickey started fucking the girl up, let me tell you Toi has hands and I like that my bitch can fight but I'm hoping her, and Mickey never fall out. Mickey hits like a fucking nigga. She only got the girl three times and the bitch mouth and nose were bloody.

The third girl that was with them didn't even bother to help either one of her friends, I guess she was smart enough to know that she didn't want to get her ass beat too. It's a punk ass move, but I don't blame her.

Security came over and was about to break the fight up, but I made them back the fuck up, I'll be damned if they yoke my girl up on some strong man shit. Tone and I both were laughing at this shit, it was funny as hell.

"Aight that's enough for real let me get Mickey before she kills this bitch." Tone went over to where Mickey was still beating the hell out of the girl. He snatched her ass up off the bitch then walked out of the section with her. After I was done getting my laughs off, I grabbed Toi and threw her ass over my shoulder and walked out of the section. Once were good and they calmed down I let Toi down so she could get her stuff from Giselle.

"Y'all are crazy as hell," Giselle told them while laughing.

"She tried me man, but I'm good," Toi told her then looked at Mickey. "Good lookin' out."

"You already know what it is. Fuck with one of us you gotta deal with both of us," Mickey shrugged. "Can we go now?"

"Hell yeah, aye bruh Mickey drove here so I'm riding with her. Giselle you need a ride?" Tone said.

"Yeah, I'll see you later Toi." Giselle hugged Toi then waved at me before walking out with Tone and Mickey.

"You good?" I looked at Toi and asked.

"Yeah, I'm fine, can we go please?"

"Let's go," I made sure the both bills were good then grabbed Toi's hand and we left the club.

While we were in the car, I told Toi everything that thirsty ass bitch said to me when she came over to me and were cracking up.

"Oh my God! Ew she wanted to suck your dick?"

"Yeah, she said she wanted to suck the nut out my shit. Hoes are crazy man." I shook my head still laughing. "You fucked her up though, I liked that."

"Liked what? Me fighting? That shit ain't sexy."

"I know that, I mean you fighting for your man."

"I had to, the bitch was getting out of pocket. I can't believe she wanted to suck your dick, you should've told her that was my job."

"Bitch face would've been on the floor with that shit, I was laughing at shorty though. I wasn't even thinking about doing shit with her, I have better sense than that. I told you I wasn't giving the dick to anybody but you."

"I know," she smiled. "Baby, I'm sorry for flipping about that barbershop shit."

"Toi I'm not about to fuck us up aight, I told you that shit from day one. If I ever feel like I'm going to do some shit I would break up with you before I just cheated on you. Nobody has time to be on that sneaky shit. You're not all the way wrong though I should've told you about it so I'm sorry too."

Smiling she leaned over and kissed me on the cheek. "Thank you for apologizing. Now hurry up and get me home so I can get some dick please."

"Oh, you want some?" I chuckled.

"Hell yeah, I know you want me too." Toi moved her hand up my thigh.

"Of course, baby," I grabbed her hand and put it on my dick, which was harder than a fucking rock right about now.

"Damn," she mumbled while she gripped it. "Pull over Que."

"Why?"

"Just pull over." Nodding my head, I drove up a little more until I found a park. As I was turning the car off, she undid my jeans then pulled my dick out of my boxers.

I saw that freaky gleam in her eye as she smirked at me. I leaned my back as she tossed her hair back over her shoulders, leaned down, and wrapped those soft luscious lips around the head of my dick and began teasing it with her tongue.

"Unnngh," I groaned, sensations shooting all the way down to my toes. I grabbed a fistful of her hair, watching my dick disappear down her throat. "Fuck, girl suck that shit." I bit down on my bottom lip while Toi allowed me to fuck her throat.

I felt myself on the verge of a nut I reclined my seat all the way back. "Come here ma." Lifting her up I brought over onto my lap. I snatched the thong she was wearing off then her down on my dick slowly.

"Sh-shit," Toi groaned. With her hips in my hands I moved her up and down slowly so she could get used to my size. Once I was sure she was good to go I let her bounce on my dick like she was riding a horse.

I grabbed a handful of her hair and wrapped it in my hand. I hit that pussy with skill. I wanted to make sure she was feeling every inch when she came back down.

"What the fuck!" She whined loudly, she sounded like she was near tears the way her voice cracked.

"Shit," I grunted when I looked down and saw her sweet juices covering my dick when it slid out of her. Gripping her waist tighter I rolled my hips into her spot. "Oh... my... God! Que! Yes! Right there!"

"Here?" I started hitting her wall repeatedly. Pushing her face towards mine I pulled her into a sloppy kiss. Our tongues wrestled together until she started screaming even louder than before.

"Fuck I wanna cum baby! I wanna cu-cum!"

"Cum for daddy, soak this dick baby," I said with my lips pressed against her neck.

"O-Ooh shit!" I continued to fuck her like crazy until I felt her juices running down both of our legs and my nut was shooting full force into her.

"Damn girl," I said once I got my breath and body under control. I lifted Toi off me and placed her back in her seat. I put my dick away then drove off while Toi handled her own business. I was trying to get to the apartment as fast as possible. If she thought this was over, she got me fucked up. I'm just getting started on her ass.

Mickey

"So, did you get the money?" I asked my mother while we spoke on the phone. She was talking about one of her church members and all their messy shit, but I didn't care to hear that. All I wanted to know was how my son was doing and if she got the money, I sent her. Everything else is irrelevant.

"Yes, I got it, I paid the mortgage this morning," she answered me.

"Okay good, how is Myles doing?"

"He's doing great Michelle, of course you would know that if you came down here and saw it for yourself."

"Mama, please don't start this alright. I just called to make sure that you two were alright and didn't need anything."

"Well he does need something, he needs you. Are you going to give him that?" Without saying anything else I hung the phone up and sat back on the couch. That's exactly why I don't like calling my mother all she does is bitch at me like she doesn't know what the fuck is going on. I can't stand her ass sometimes.

Getting up I went into my stash and rolled myself a nice thick ass blunt. Before I could light it, my doorbell ringing stopped me.

"Ugh what the fuck?" I got up and went to answer the door. I was ready to go off until I saw Tone standing there.

"What's up ma?"

"Hey," I said dryly going back into the living room.

"What's wrong with you?" He asked while closing the door.

"Nothing I just have a lot on my mind right now."

"What's going on with you?"

"My mother just pissed me off that's all. Every time I speak to her, she starts the bullshit."

"What kind of bullshit?"

"Throwing shit in my face or just being sarcastic for no fucking reason. You ever have somebody do something for you then they throw it in your face afterwards?"

"Yeah I get that shit sometimes."

"Well that's what she does it's annoying as fuck to be honest."

"What does she do for you?"

"She takes care of someone for me."

He looked at me confused. "Takes care of who?" When I didn't answer he sucked his teeth. "Mickey don't do this shutting down shit."

"What are you talking about?"

"Every time I ask about your past you start getting all quiet and shit like you got something you need to hide."

"I'm not hiding shit I just don't feel like talking about it."

"You don't feel like talking about a lot. Look, I know you been through a lot of shit, aight? I get that but if you don't let me in, how the fuck are we supposed to make it work. I gotta know who I'm dealing with."

"What do you want me to do then Tone?"

"Open your mouth and speak, holding that shit in isn't going to do anything."

"Alright," I sighed then looked at him. "What do you want to know?"

"Who does your mother take care of?"

"She takes care of my son."

"Your son? You have a son?"

"Yes, I have a son."

"You told me your mother lives down in North Carolina."

"She does live down there. I pay all her bills and she has my son."

"Why don't you have your son? You don't seem like the type to not take care of yours."

"I do take care of mine; did you not just hear me say I pay all the bills? My son has everything he wants because I provide it for him so don't do that," I snapped at him.

"Alright I'm not trying to start an argument. I can tell you're about to get all in your feelings, but I need to understand this shit. What type of mother doesn't take care of her son?"

"The kind that can't give him what he needs outside of material things. I couldn't be a good mother to him so to make sure he was always good and not put in the system I gave my mother custody of him."

"I'm asking you why though, what you just said sounded convincing, but I can tell when you're lying so what happened ma?"

Shaking my head, I decided to just tell him the whole situation, just because I know he's never going to leave me alone if I don't.

"I got pregnant when I was sixteen. I had Myles when I was seventeen. Everything was going well, I graduated high school, I was taking college classes, had my own place, his father was bringing in the money, Myles was taken care of, I was on the right track."

"What changed that?"

"Bryson," I chuckled. "His father switched up on me, when I say this nigga changed overnight, I mean it. We were good, yeah, we argued but that's not anything big. One day after I picked my son up from day care, and Myles had to be about two years old at this point, I get home and this nigga has a bitch in my bed."

"Oh shit."

"Oh, shit is right and to make it worse, it was a bitch I was friends with or at least I thought the hoe was my friend. I put my son in the play pen, and I went off, I beat that bitch's ass like she just stole something from me. Now most niggas in that situation would beg for forgiveness and try and tell me sorry. That muthafucka took that bitches side and slapped me across my face after I kicked the bitch out of my house."

"Are you fucking serious?"

175

"I'm dead ass serious and you know me I'm not a punk I hit his ass back but his big ass," I laughed. "I couldn't beat him, so he whooped my ass that day. He apologized and like a fucking dummy I accepted the apology and took him back. It went on from there."

"That's crazy, so what happened with your son? Why did you give him up?"

"I'm getting to that. I stayed with Bryson after that dealt with all the bullshit for three years. The day I decided shit was going too far was when he hit my son. Myles was about to turn five years old, and he was a mama's boy. He couldn't stand to be away from me, and Bryson hated it. I think he was jealous because my son didn't want him like he wanted me. What he didn't understand was this is a four-year-old boy who sees you yelling and screaming all the fucking time he's scared of you but of course he's an idiot so he wouldn't get it."

"Not to cut you off but that nigga is a bitch. Continue."

I laughed a little bit then kept going. "I was home with Myles watching a movie or something I don't know what was on TV, but Bryson came home, and he was high as hell and drunk as usual. That's not a good combination with this nigga and I already know he was going to try and start a fucking problem. I sent Myles to his room and told him to stay in there. Not even five minutes into this nigga being home we started fighting I don't know what triggered my son but all I know is while we're going at it, I hear him screaming and crying." I paused swallowing the lump that was forming in my throat.

"It's alright ma," Tone pulled me closer to him and rubbed my back.

"He was screaming, 'stop hitting my mommy, get off my mommy leave her alone.' Well Bryson didn't like that, so he pushed me so hard into the wall it felt like my back broke and he smacked my son clear across the room." I wiped the tears that fell down my face. "The sound of my son screaming set me the fuck off. I got up and I picked up this glass lamp that was in the living room and yanked it so hard I broke the damn plug from the wall. I hit that nigga over the head with that lamp, picked my baby up off the floor and with just the clothes we had on I left, and we went to Toi grandmother's house."

"Wow, at least you got his ass. So that's how y'all broke up?"

"Yeah, he kept coming to her grandmother's house on some bull-shit. Trying to fight me talking about he's going to kill me and my son, just some crazy ass nigga stuff. So, my mother was leaving to move to North Carolina with her sister and I sent Myles down there with her. I love my mother but she's a selfish greedy ass bitch. She said the only way she would take him is if I gave her custody of him so that not only would she get a check from the state she would try and get child support from me too. This bitch took me to court and everything, the judge didn't put me on child support, but he still gave her custody. The reason I pay for everything is because I know Myles is still my responsibility and I know she wouldn't keep him if I didn't."

"Why not get him back? You're good now."

"I don't have a legit income; my mother doesn't know what I did for money but she knew it wasn't legal and her ass will tell the judge just so I can still take care of her ass. So, until I'm legit and I have a steady income I can't get him back."

"Alright that I understand, so what happened to that nigga you used to fuck with?"

"He got locked up a couple of months after my son went down south. I don't speak to him, I don't do shit for or about that nigga, but he won't let it go."

"What do you mean?"

"If you asked around some niggas who I am they would say oh Brick's baby mama or they'll say Brick's girl. He would tell these niggas he's still with me and all that bullshit. As you know I moved on, I guess some of his homies told him I was dealing with whatever nigga I had at that point and he's pissed off. He's convinced himself that we never broke up, so he feels like I should be there holding him down through his bid and I'm not so word is when he gets out, he's supposed to be coming to see."

"The fuck?"

"That's what I was I told, and I told them to tell his ass when he comes to see I hope he's ready to die that day because I'm blowing his fucking head off. He's fucked up so much in my life now he wants to throw threats out there? I missed two years of my son's life because of his ass."

"First of all, let's start with this. That nigga is not touching you, I'll be damned if I let that happen. Don't even worry about that, trust me. Second, how old is your son now?"

"He's turning seven in February. I talk to him when I speak to my mother, that's if she's not being a complete bitch. She acts like she's doing this big favor to me by keeping him, but she just has him because I can't get him back right now and she's getting paid for it. Bitch does not have to lift a fucking finger."

"Do you want your son back?"

"Yes, I want my son back more than anything but it's nothing I can do about it right now, so I don't talk about it or let it consume my mind too much. I just make sure my son is taken care of and I make sure he knows I love him. As long as I know he's safe that's all that matters to me at this point."

Tone nodded his head then kissed my forehead. "You're a strong person Mick, and you're a good person. As tough as you try to act your ass is a big softy and you know it," we both laughed. "You keep doing what you're doing, it'll work out for the better. Don't even worry about it."

Taj

"So, miss Taj," Toi said after sitting down in my chair. "Where have you been these last couple of days? It's like you're never around anymore."

"I know, I've been busy. I heard about you whooping ass at Mason's the other night. The fuck happened?"

"Bitches running their mouths, you know how that goes. We wanted you to come with us, but you were M.IA."

"I was with Anthony, I don't think I need to go into detail about that do I?"

"No," she laughed. "I get it, trust me I do. I miss your big-headed ass though."

"Aww boo I miss you too I'll be around more I'm just getting used to being back in a relationship."

"How is it going anyway?"

"It's going good, I met his mother. It was over FaceTime but we talked," I chuckled. "I met his daughter too."

"Aww, is she good or is she one of those bad ass little girls?"

"Well she's only one so I really don't know too much yet. She's been sweet around me and that's all that counts in my book. That mother of hers though," I shook my head. "Girl, she's the baby mama from hell."

"She's that bad? I thought he was just trippin'."

"He wasn't, all she does is call and text him all fuckin' day and night talking about some bullshit."

"Like what?"

"I guess when she got pregnant, she thought they were supposed to be together or some shit and he was like fuck no. He doesn't want to be with her ass, so now she's miserable about it."

"Have you met her?"

"No but guess who she is."

"We know her? Oh lord, who?"

"Do you remember Keyana from high school? She was a sophomore when we were juniors."

"The bitch who was fucking Rah and Sean from the football team and made them get in a fucking fight?"

"Yup that's her! That's his baby mama, when I saw that girl's picture, I almost hit the fucking floor."

"She's always been a bitch. You were about to fight her that one time, right?"

"Yeah, she came at my neck about some nigga she was fucking with. I'm coming in the classroom to say what's up and this bitch said something smart. I laughed at her though, until she threw a fucking punch. Bitch lucky she missed me."

"You pushed the fuck out of Ms. Watson," Toi laughed. "Her old ass went flying into the damn desk."

"She was in the way, but yes that's who this nigga decided to get pregnant."

"That's crazy, damn good luck with that. It's going to be some type of drama with that hoe."

"I know but I'll be fine. The bitch can't beat me, he doesn't want shit to do with her so I'm not worried about a damn thing. Enough about that girl, what the fuck do you want done to your hair though?"

"Well I need you to wash my shit and all that good stuff, but I just want it straight after that."

"Why do you always want me to straighten it? I'm giving you some body wave curls."

"Fine do what you do just get started on my shit. I don't even know why I'm paying you, it's going to get fucked up dealing with Que anyway."

"I know what you mean, I told Anthony's ass I pay too much money for my hair just for you to go and fuck it up. These bundles are nowhere near cheap. Bella dream is a luxury boo," we both laughed.

I PUT my coat on and picked my work case up before waving at everybody and making my way outside where Anthony was in his car waiting for me. When I got in the front seat he leaned over and kissed me on the cheek.

"Hey baby," I said before he kissed me on the lips.

"What's up shorty. You stacked that bread today?"

"Let's see, I had six clients, five of them were full sew-ins so I made a couple of bucks."

"That's what I'm talking about. Get that money," he boasted, making me laugh.

"Toi came in for me to tame her mane and got on me for going M.I.A."

"What do you mean?" He asked while pulling off down the street.

"I've been wrapped up in you, and not around them. They miss my ass, you're keeping me busy."

"I'm just helping you stay in a good mood baby." A smile came on his face causing another one to break out on mine too. Anthony always earns a smile from me. He's just that good to look at, baby is tall, caramel, tatted and built like a damn basketball player. He's a fine ass nigga for real.

"I know but you do your business all day while I'm doing mine. Then when I get off, I'm with you the rest of the night. I need some girl time, just like you need a break from me. If we're around each other too much, we'll get sick of each other."

"I get what you're saying, but fuck all of that for tonight. It's me, you and lil mama tonight."

"Wait what?" I looked at him confused.

"KeKe called me earlier about taking Naima for tonight."

"I thought you only take her every other week?"

"I do but she said her grandmother was in the hospital and she doesn't want to Nai up there with her so I'm about to go pick her up. You're not mad about this right?"

"No," I shook my head. "That's your daughter you have to be a parent. I was just trying to understand what was going on. So, are we going to your place after?"

"Yeah, it'll be alright she won't be up long anyway." Instead of saying anything I just nodded my head and pulled my phone out.

To be honest, I don't mind that he's going to get his daughter, she's a sweet little girl but I just feel like his baby mama is on some bullshit. Now, I know I shouldn't be jumping to conclusions. Her grandmother could be in the hospital for real, but I think the bitch is lying. She's either lying to get him to come over there so she can try some shit, or she's lying to get a Naima free night.

"Yo you good?" He asked me after a couple of minutes.

"I'm fine."

"Nah, you're lying, what's going on? What's the problem?"

I sucked my teeth then looked at him. "Aight, are you sure she's telling the truth?"

"What you mean?"

"Is she telling the truth about her grandmother being in the hospital?"

"Why would she lie about that Taj?"

"So, you can take Naima while she has her free time. What time did she call you?"

"Earlier like around one or something."

"Okay why didn't you go to get her then?"

"She said she didn't need me to come get her until tonight."

"Baby, it's almost 7:30 hospital visiting hours at most hospitals are over 8:00. She had all day to see her grandmother and she waits until now to go see her? Come on now, you really don't believe that do you?"

"You really think she's lying?"

"Yeah, it doesn't make sense."

Clenching his jaw, he nodded his head. "Aight."

"Are you alright?"

"Yeah, I'm good, I'm dropping you off. I'll be back."

"Anthony, what are you going to do?"

"I have to handle something, that's all you need to know don't ask me again." He drove to his place and dropped me off. As soon as I got out of the car he pulled off. I don't know what the hell he's about to do but I know it's not well.

Yung

*N*ot even ten minutes after dropping Taj off, I was Keyani's house banging on the damn door. I can't believe I was about to all for the bullshit story she told me. When she answered the door, she looked at me like I was stupid.

"What the fuck are you banging on my door like that for?" She snapped at me. I pushed past her and looked around at all her thot ass friends in the living room.

"I thought you had to go to the hospital?"

"I am going to the hospital, what the hell are you even doing here? You were supposed to call me when you were downstairs so I can bring her outside." KeKe moved her hands to her slender hips. I looked at the dark chocolate beauty in front of me. Keyani is 5'6", dark skin with a petite frame. She had a pretty ass face and always wore her hair in a short pixie cut. If she wasn't so damn simple, I probably could've made it work with her, but the bitch acts slow.

"Yeah well I decided to come up here and get her myself. I find it fucking funny that you got these bitches in here, but you're supposed to be going to the fucking hospital. The fuck you need to get drunk on some cheap ass Amsterdam for if you're doing that?"

"Hold up," Keyani put her hand up. "First of all, who are you to come in here questioning me about what I'm doing? I'm grown so I can do whatever the hell it is I want to do."

"You don't fucking lie to me about it though! I almost believed your dumb ass. I'm glad my girl told me your ass was lying."

"Whoa, whoa, wait a minute," she laughed. "Your girl told you I was lying? Why is she even talking about me?"

"She wasn't talking about you, she told me what time the visiting hours at the hospital were over. So why the fuck would you just now go over there?"

"I don't give a fuck she needs to mind her fucking business."

"No, you need to quit fucking lying."

"Yeah aight, you wanna be in here all hyphy over that bitch word, does she know you still fucking me?" KeKe folded her arms across her chest while smirking.

I chuckled darkly, this is the type of shit that makes me want to ring her neck. "Let's not act like fucking you mean anything. The only time you get the dick is when she can't."

"Let's see how she feels about that when I tell her ass."

"She ain't gone feel shit because you're not opening your mouth to say shit!" I snapped at her. "See if I give you this dick again since you wanna run your fuckin' mouth." I walked away from her and went down to my daughter's bedroom and went inside where she was asleep in her crib. I put her coat on her and picked her up then went back out.

"You better not have my baby around that bitch," KeKe snapped at me but I waved her off and left the apartment with her running her mouth in the hallway like she was fucking stupid. If I didn't have my daughter in my arms, I would've fucked her up, but nobody had time to deal with her ignorant shit right now.

Isyss Perez

"*H*ow is it going with my big head ass brother?" Mia asked me while we ate lunch together.

"It was fine until his girlfriend started losing her mind one day. The bitch was going off about some bullshit and I had to that her I will have this whole fucking city at her door."

"I can't stand that bitch," she rolled her eyes. "Wait until you meet her big ass friend, you'll really be sick to your stomach."

"I think I know who you're talking about. Her name is Mickey, right?"

"Yeah that's her, she's too fucking much. All she does is fight that girl's battles, Toi is a punk ass bitch who wouldn't be shit without that big bitch in her corner."

"Oh yeah I met her, she came in the shop looking for Tone me and her got into it too. Then Que came at me like I started it, he gets on my damn nerves for real."

"Que is just an asshole, that's never going to change. What he needs to do is get rid of that whore he's trying to sport. She probably told him to fire you and everything."

"She doesn't want me working there but it's not up to her. I wish he would fire my ass I will hurt him, and he knows it."

Que knows not to fuck with me like that. I will go off on his ass just like I did the day his bitch wanted to act she wasn't on her leash. I was really looking at him like he was stupid for not controlling that hoe, she was about to get fucked up something stupid if she didn't get her ass back in that car.

"She probably thinks y'all are going to start fucking around again, which you will. Whenever y'all are around each other it happens."

Mia made a really good point. I've known Que for more than ten years and the whole time I've known him I've been the one thing he can't resist. We would break up and get right back together all the time because he can't keep his hands off me. He can front for his new girl he wants too but I know how that nigga works, it's only a matter of time before I'm getting the dick again. She should be lucky I don't love his ass anymore or I would take him, but she can have that headache I for damn sure don't want it.

"All I have to do is say one fucking thing and that relationship is done."

"Oh boy, are you going to tell him?"

"A part of me wants to, but then again your brother is a fucking maniac and he will act a damn fool."

"True, but I think you should tell him, and I know just how you should do it."

"I see the wheels turning in your head girl, I need to brace myself," I laughed.

Mia always came up with some crazy shit to do. I know she is about to make shit blow all the way up.

"Mommy!" My daughter Diamond came running up to me when I walked into my mother's apartment.

"Hi baby," I kissed her cheek after picking her up. "Where's your abuela?"

"Watching TV."

"Alright come on," I went into the living room where my mother was and sat on the couch. "Was she good today?"

"She was alright, you know you need to get her into an after-school program or something. I'm getting too old to baby sit every damn day."

"I know but I can't afford it right now so until I can, I need you to help me."

"Don't go there with me Isyss I've been helping you. I helped you when you first got pregnant and didn't want to tell her father. I even went and raised her without for a couple of years because you were too self-involved."

"You're always throwing that in my face, what the hell do you help me for if you're so fed up?"

I don't understand my mother at all. She agrees to watch Diamond for me but wants to complain about it. Just say no if you're going to bitch so damn much.

"I'm fed up with you being ungrateful and selfish, you live here rent and bill free. I watch your daughter for free and you're just now getting a job. Grow the fuck up Isyss."

"What do you want me to do? Tell me so you can get off my back."

"Didn't I just say grow up? That's what you can do, grow the hell up and appreciate what I do for you. I've been the only one helping you all these years."

"Well you know what ma, you don't have to help me anymore. I'll get off your back. Diamond, go put your coat and hat on we're going somewhere."

"Where mommy?" She looked up at me and asked.

"We're going to see your father. Hurry up."

Legend

I was coming out of the corner store with a bottle of water when I heard my name being screamed from up the street. Turning around I looked at Isyss like she was dumb when she came stomping up the block holding the hand of a little girl who looked like her twin. She looked like a complete maniac storming over to me. I don't even get how this bitch is running up on me right now.

"The fuck is the matter with you?" I asked her once she got close to me.

"Listen I need to tell you something and it can't wait."

"You don't have to tell me shit, what part of I don't fuck with you don't you get?"

"This isn't about me and you…Well it is, but not really."

"I don't have time for this bullshit, I gotta go." I turned and started to walk to my car.

"This is your daughter!" I heard her yell making me stop dead in my tracks. I turned back around to face her.

"The fuck did you just say?" This bitch didn't just say what I think she did. She has officially lost her whole mind.

"I said this is your daughter," she looked down at the little girl she had with her.

"I don't have time for these fucking games right now Isyss."

"This isn't a game Que, she's yours the fuck do I need to lie for?"

189

"How the fuck is she mine? She looks like she's at least six years old, how the fuck would I not know you had a baby."

"Remember I went to Puerto Rico with my mother for a couple of months?" She said and I raised my eyebrow at her.

"What about it?"

"I was four months pregnant when I left, and I didn't really go to Puerto Rico. I was in Florida at my grandmother's house. After I gave birth to her, I came back while she stayed with my mom down there. She's yours Que." I looked down at the little girl then back at her.

Before I could stop myself, I slapped the shit out of Isyss sending her into the corner store wall. "Are you fuckin' serious! How could you do this to me? How could you not tell me I had a fuckin' daughter Isyss, after six mothafuckin' years! Six birthdays, six Christmas', six Thanksgivings, six years, and I never knew about her! Why?!"

"Que stop, just let me explain, please. It's not what you think!" She screamed out with tears rolling down her face.

"Oh, now you wanna explain? Six fuckin' years later you wanna explain? Nah, ma, you can save your explanations. This is some bull-shit!" She had me out here looking like a mad man. I grabbed her by the throat and slammed her against the wall still screaming in her face. We were like that up until the fucking cops pulled up and pulled me off of her.

"You need to calm down!" One of the officers said to me but I was too mad to listen to that shit right now. I was going so fucking crazy they had no choice but to slap handcuffs on my ass and put me in the back of their car.

When they closed the door, I looked at the little girl who was standing there with tears in her eyes. I immediately started feeling like shit. I shouldn't have done all of that in front of her but fuck it, Isyss had that shit coming.

I WALKED out of the police station with Toi right behind me. As soon as they let me use the phone, I called her down to get me out and she came as soon as she could. She didn't ask me what happened when we were inside the station, but I know they told her ass what the situation was. Knowing Toi, as soon as we got in the car, she's going to grill my ass.

We walked over to her car and got in. As soon as she pulled off, she started the questioning. "So, do you care to tell me why you're on the corner yoking bitches up?"

"She pissed me off what else is there to say?"

"There's a lot to say I want to know what happened. The fuck did she do that made you act that way?"

"Just talking out the side of her neck," I lied. I wasn't about to tell Toi this bitch claims to have my child and make her go crazy too. I need to figure out if she is telling the truth before I tell anybody anything about this shit.

"Saying what Que? You have a temper but it's not bad enough for you to go acting like that with a female, on a street corner no less."

"She came at me about some bullshit, it's nothing. I only reacted like that because she caught me at a bad time."

"Are you sure that's it?"

"Yes, I'm sure. Drop me off at my car I have to go handle some shit."

"Alright," Toi drove me to where my car was then I got out and got in my shit. She honked her horn at me before she pulled off down the street.

I sat in my car for a good couple of minutes before I finally decided to pull off and drove to Isyss' house. The only reason I know where the bitch lives is because she had to give me her information so she could work at the shop.

When I pulled up in front of her house, she was sitting on the steps smoking a cigarette.

When she saw me getting out, she rolled her eyes. "Look you got away with that shit before. If you put your hands on me again, I'm fucking you up and pressing charges!" she snapped at me.

"Shut the fuck up I'm not going to touch you even though I should be knocking your head off your shoulders. Why the fuck would you not tell me you were pregnant?"

When this bird bitch left, she told me she was going to Puerto Rico with her mother to check on her sick grandma. All that shit was a lie, she was hiding a damn pregnancy like a fuckin' dummy. I wasn't a perfect boyfriend to Isyss but that doesn't have shit to do with what type of father I would've been. If I could shoot this bitch and get away with it right now I would.

"Tell you and what? Let's not act like you didn't get two bitches pregnant before me and what did you do? You made both of them have a fucking abortion and I didn't want to do that, so I hid it."

"Those bitches were birds you think I wanted a baby by some quick ass nut busters? I wouldn't have made you have an abortion you were my girl."

"So, you weren't going to make me get rid of her?"

"No, I wouldn't have, I would've stepped up. It's fucked up you kept that shit from then you came back up here and acted like she didn't even fucking exist. The fuck does that?"

"I made sure she was good; every single time you gave me money I sent some down there to my mother for her. I'm not a dead beat I don't give a fuck what you or anybody else says."

"But you let me be one?" I chuckled bitterly. "What's her name?"

"Diamond."

"Alright, and how old is she?"

"She's six years old, anymore questions?"

"Not right now, but I do want a DNA test. I know some people over at the clinic, so you need to take your ass down there tomorrow and get her swabbed. If she's mine I'll take care of her, if she's not, stay the fuck away from me. You understand that shit?"

"Oh, trust me I got it. Can you go away now?"

"I'm not playing, tomorrow Isyss," I told her again before hopping back in my car and pulling off. All of this is some fuckery, who the fuck feels like dealing with reality show bullshit?

Toi

"*A*lright I'm done, can we open them now?" Jayla said with a mouth full of food. For her to be a whole damn teenager she was way too excited about gifts up under the Christmas tree.

"Ew, you need to chew your food and swallow before you speak," Kayla said to her.

"Whatever, grandma can we open our gifts now? Please?" Jayla looked at my grandmother and asked.

"Go ahead girl," she laughed at them and they both went running in the living room.

"Don't open anything until I get in there!" I shouted at them. I grabbed all the plates and loaded the dishwasher then went in the living room with everybody.

"Alright I'm here now go ahead," I smiled.

It was Christmas day and here I was at my grandmother's house celebrating with my family. I decided to come over here yesterday and spend the night so I could be here this morning. I didn't want to wake up in an empty apartment by myself since Que did the same thing as me and went to his mother's house. I would be seeing him later.

Sitting next to my mother and grandmother I watched Jayla and Kayla go crazy over the stuff I bought them. They each got three outfits a piece, a pair of Giuseppe sneakers, and a Chanel bookbag. When they saw those bags, they both jumped on me.

"Thank you, Toi!"

"You're welcome," I laughed grabbing the other two boxes that were under the tree. I gave one to my grandmother and the other one to my mother.

"You really didn't have to get me anything," my mother said, and I shrugged.

"I wouldn't leave you out like that, besides I have no problem bearing gifts," I chuckled. "Go ahead and open it."

When she opened it and saw the heart pendant necklace, I bought her, her mouth dropped. "Oh my God, this is so beautiful. Thank you so much," she hugged me.

"You're welcome." After we hugged, I looked at my grandmother so she could open hers. My grandmother wasn't too big on designer things and she had enough jewelry from me to last her a lifetime. This year I decided to have a friend of mine design and make a church hat for her. Of course, she loved it, she spent most of her time in church anyway so why wouldn't she?

After the gifts were opened and done, I got up to go take a shower. I wasn't bothered about not getting gift under the tree, I've grown out of that. Besides, my grandmother makes me a chocolate cheesecake every Christmas. That's her gift to me and I was perfectly fine with that.

⁂

I SLAMMED my phone down and sat back on the couch crossing my arms over my chest. This nigga was pissing me the fuck off. To feel like I wanna kill somebody on Jesus's birthday, isn't right and I'm mad as shit Que is the cause of it. I literally felt like I was about to explode until I heard the doorbell ring.

"This better be him bruh," I said to myself while I walked to the door. When I opened the door and saw Mickey, Tone, Taj, Yung, and his daughter on the other side I rolled my eyes.

"Eww, merry Christmas to you too bitch," Mickey said, and I shook my head.

"My bad I'm just irritated, y'all can come in." They all walked in with me closing the door behind. "Hi baby bop," I kissed Naima's cheek. Yung's daughter is the sweetest little girl ever, granted I've only seen her one other time but still.

I hugged the rest of the bunch then we all went in the living room. "Is your grandmother done cooking?" Tone asked me.

"No not yet, be patient greedy." Just like Thanksgiving these fools were here to eat all of my grandmother's food. "So, you two," I pointed to Mickey and Toi. "What did y'all get me?" I cheesed. All three of us exchanged gifts with each other like we do every single year.

"So, what did you and Que get each other?" Mickey asked me.

"I got him some stuff from Tom Ford," I answered with a roll of my eyes. I bought Que a Tom Ford jacket, cologne, and some nice ass cufflinks. "I paid for it with my money. Not the money he puts in my account, I spent my actual money on that nigga."

"Well I'm sure he'll like it Toi. What did he get you?"

"You know what? I wouldn't know because I haven't seen him all fucking day and he's not answering my calls. Bruh I'm about five seconds away from going outside and giving his jacket and cologne to a homeless nigga. I'm returning those damn cufflinks too."

"Damn," Yung laughed. "Well I spoke to him earlier and he sounded alright. Maybe he got caught up with the fam."

"Fuck that he could still answer my phone calls. I swear to God if his ass is not here or calls in the next ten minutes some random nigga is about to hit it big."

"Don't do that ma," Tone said but I waved him off.

"Fuck what you talking about I'm dead ass serious." I sat there while the rest of them talked about whatever until I heard her Jayla calling my name from the hallway. I got up and walked out to see what she wanted.

"What's up?" I asked her.

"Where's Que? He's coming today right?"

"Yeah, he's supposed to be, I don't know where he is though. Why?"

"Do y'all know someone named Mia?"

"Mia? Yes, that's his sister's name," I said, and she smiled as if she was relieved.

"Oh okay, I thought something else was going on."

"What do you mean?"

"I follow a girl named Mia on Instagram and she posted a picture of him with some lady and a little girl. I thought it was sketchy but it's just his sister so oh well."

"He was at his family's house so it's probably his mother or one of his aunts," I smiled a little bit knowing he was still with his family. That made me less mad knowing it wasn't some bullshit going on. "Let me see it," I took her phone and looked at the picture. As soon as my eyes landed on it the smile that I had on my face dropped. "What the fuck?"

"What's wrong?"

"That's not his fucking aunt or his mother."

"Well who is it?" I put my hand up and walked back into the living room.

"Tone, what the fuck is this?" I gave the phone to Tone and asked him. When he looked at the picture his eyes got a little wide.

"Oh shit, damn. Toi, I promise you I didn't know about that shit mam" He told me. Mickey grabbed the phone and looked at it.

"What the hell is going on?" Taj asked me.

"My nigga is in a picture with his ex bitch on Christmas," I answered.

"Wait what?"

"His bitch of a sister took a picture of him and his fucking ex and posted that shit on Instagram. He's with that bitch on Christmas, at his fucking family's house. He can't call me back, but he can be around that bitch? Man," I ran up to my room and grabbed the bag that had his jacket and cologne in it before coming back down.

I walked straight to the front door and launched everything I bought his ass outside. Whoever wants that shit can have it. "Toi," Mickey came in the hallway to get me. "Calm down ma, maybe it's an explanation to this shit."

"What type of explanation Mick? I been calling him all day and he hasn't been answering. He knows what we were supposed to do today and he's over there with his fucking ex. The bitch I told him to stay the fuck away from. Nah man, fuck him."

I sat on the stairs and put my head in my hands trying to calm myself down. "No hell nah, what you're not going to do is cry over that nigga." Mickey lifted my head and wiped away the tears that fell from my eyes. "We're better than this crying shit Toi."

"I'm not crying out of hurt Mickey, can't no nigga hurt my feelings. I'm mad as hell, I told this nigga to stay the fuck away from this bitch. I told him to fire her ass the day all that bullshit in front of the shop happened. Not only did he not do what the fuck I said he has the nerve to stand me up and chill with this bitch on Christmas like it's alright? I'm ready to fuck both of them up."

"Well then if you want to handle that bitch and him, I got you, but you need to wipe these tears away. Angry or not he has your ass crying and I'm not feelin' that shit. Come on get up." She pulled me up from the stairs and I wiped my face again. "What do you want to do right now?"

"My grandmother cooked her ass off. I'm not fucking up her dinner because of him. We're all going to sit down and eat but after that, oh I'm going clean the fuck off."

"I got sneakers in the car, so you know I got you." She put her arm around my shoulder, and we walked towards the dining room.

Whatever the fuck is going on, Que better have one hell of a reason he's around that bitch or shit is going to get real. If I don't like what the fuck he has to say, Jesus himself will have to come down on a cloud and touch me to get my hands from around that niggas neck.

Legend

*L*ooking down at my phone I sighed before answering it and putting it to my ear. "Yeah?"

"Nigga, where the fuck are you? Do you know your life is in danger?" Tone said through the phone.

"I'm at my mother's house, fuck are you talking about?"

"I'm talking about Toi killing your ass when she sees you bruh. Shorty over here fired the fuck up, why aren't you returning her calls?"

"Man, I've been caught up with Diamond and shit." I had every intention on calling Toi but every time she hit me up, I was pre-occupied with Diamond. I missed six years of her life, just getting to know her. I didn't want to walk away from her just to talk on the phone.

"I thought you were dropping gifts off then leaving how the fuck did all of y'all end up at your mother's house."

"Mia invited them over here," I shook my head. "Wait, how did you know they were here?"

"Oh yeah that's the reason you're losing your life. Apparently one of Toi's cousins follows Mia on Instagram and she posted a picture of you with Isyss in it."

"ARE YOU FUCKING SERIOUS?!" I shouted. Toi doesn't know anything about Diamond being my daughter. I should've told her as soon as I got the results back, but I had to adjust to the news myself. I wasn't even supposed to be over here all day. My plan was to drop Diamond's gifts off at Isyss' place but to my surprise she popped up over here because of Mia.

"I'm dead ass serious, Toi knows that bitch was around you all day on top of you been ignoring her calls. Nigga you're in for it. She took the shit she bought you and threw it in the fucking street."

"Fuck! Where y'all at now?"

"We're at her grandmother's house, it's your best bet to come over here and talk to you. She won't disrespect her grandmother by kicking your ass in this house. If she catches your ass on the streets nigga you're doomed."

"I'm about to come over there, keep her in that house aight."

"Aight I'll do what I can, but you might wanna tell Isyss to watch her back. They already plotting on her ass in here. It's not looking good man."

"Thanks for the heads up I'll see you later." I hung up the phone and went back into the living room and grabbed my coat.

"Where are you going?" My mother asked me.

"I have to go see Toi," as soon as I said that Mia and Isyss sucked their teeth. "The fuck is wrong with y'all?"

"Quentin, I don't think she's the right girl for you. Look how much drama she's caused between you and your sister already," my mother said, and I shook my head.

"Ma, Toi has nothing to do with me and Mia. I don't fuck with her because she's messy as shit, you know she's messy. Nothing that happened at Thanksgiving was Toi's fault, your daughter instigated that shit." My mother has been on this shit about Toi since that day. She doesn't even have a reason to dislike Toi, but Mia has a problem, so my mother is taking her side. "Now I gotta go see my girl, if y'all got a problem with that I don't know what to tell you."

"You're going to leave your daughter on Christmas to see that broad? Who the fuck is she?" Isyss snapped at me.

"My woman, you know what that is right? It's what you used to be before your thot ass fucked it up. Diamond is upstairs asleep so fuck what you talking about? Matter of fact you can fuckin leave I don't even know why you stayed. Just because you had Diamond by me, it doesn't make you fuckin' family to me. Get the fuck out."

"She's my friend," Mia added in.

"Fuck outta here with that bullshit Mia, you lucky I'm not slapping the shit out of you. I know you posted a picture of me with her ass on Instagram. You be doing shit on fucking purpose, stupid ass." I kissed my mother on the cheek then left and headed towards Toi's grandmother's house.

After I rang the doorbell it was a few seconds until the door opened with Jayla standing there with a smile on her face. "Hi Que."

"What's up baby girl, where's your cousin?"

"In the living room," she moved to the side and let me in. "I hope you know how to duck."

"What do you mean?"

"I mean, she's mad as hell and she's going to hurt you," she patted me on the shoulder. "Good luck." I shook my head at her then made my way into the living room. When she saw me come in, I let out a deep sigh. I could tell just by the look on her face she was mad as hell, this was about to be a problem.

"Toi let me speak to you for a minute," I said, and she laughed.

"Speak to me? You know that's funny, I been waiting to speak to you all day, but you wouldn't pick up the phone. So now you come over here wanting to talk, that's some funny shit man. What do we have to talk about Quentin?" Quentin? She said the government? Aww shit. "Are we going to talk about how you're so full of shit? How I've been waiting around for your ain't shit ass all day? Or how you've been around your ex bitch on Christmas? Pick a subject my nigga."

"Baby just let me talk to you please," I asked again trying to be as patient as possible. I wanted to snatch her ass up but I'm not going to do that in front of her grandmother.

"Toi, talk to that boy. You've been sitting here huffing and puffing the last couple of hours and frankly you're getting on my nerves. Now go on ahead and talk to him," her grandmother told her.

Rolling her eyes, she got up and walked over to me. "Outside," was all she said before walking past me.

"Thank you, Grams," I told her grandmother then followed her out the door.

"Look, I know you're mad aight, and it's not what you're thinking it is," I said as soon as I closed the front door.

"Oh really? So, you didn't forget about me and spend Christmas with that bitch?"

"Not exactly, she wasn't supposed to come to my mother's house that was all Mia's doing. I was supposed to go to her place and drop off presents to- "

"You were supposed to go to her house and do what? The fuck you bringing that bitch presents for Que?"

"It wasn't for her, it was for Diamond."

"Who is Diamond?"

"My daughter," when I said that, she looked at me like I was stupid.

"Wait, I have to be hearing shit because I know you did not just say your daughter. What fucking daughter? You have a baby by that bitch and didn't say anything?"

"She's not exactly a baby and I didn't know about her up until like two weeks ago."

"What the fuck? How would you not know about having a daughter?"

"She didn't tell me when she got pregnant. Her ass went out of town for a couple of months and I didn't think shit about it. When she came back, she didn't say anything to me. The little girl is six years old and I didn't know shit about her until Isyss' loud mouth ass came screaming on me that day I got arrested."

"Oh, you mean the day I picked you up from the police station?"

"Yeah."

"The day I asked you what happened, and you told me nothing. Que I asked you what the fuck went on and you said it was nothing, but this bitch came to you about having a six-year-old daughter. That's something to tell me!"

"I was confused about the shit and I didn't know whether or not the bitch was lying to me Toi! I got the DNA test done and it came back positive, I'm her father."

"So why the fuck wouldn't you tell me then? Why is it that when it involves this bitch you can't open your mouth?"

"It's not like that Toi."

"It is like that! You give the bitch a job and you say nothing to me. She says you have a daughter and you say nothing. You take a fucking DNA test and you say nothing. You find out she's really your daughter and you say nothing! What type of fucking sense does that make Que? Every time this bitch comes up it's because you're hiding something. So, tell me, if the bitch makes a move on you are you going to keep it a secret?"

"No aight! Look I didn't want to say anything until I knew for sure she was mine then when I found out I got so preoccupied with getting to know her I didn't get the chance to tell you. I was wrong and I'm sorry for not telling you about it. That was stupid of me."

"You fucking think?"

"I'm apologizing, don't be extra with your mouth ma," I told her, and she rolled her eyes. "I'm not going to keep shit from you anymore."

"Yeah right."

"I'm dead ass serious, anything that goes on with me I'll tell you about it. Now quit being a baby and stop being mad at me," I smiled at her.

"Shut up," she started laugh.

"Nah man, come here." I grabbed her arm pulling her me. "You threw my shit in the street?"

"You damn right I did, you pissed me off. Don't keep shit from me." She stared off into the street for a second then looked back at me. "So, she's really your daughter?"

"Yeah, that shit shocked me too."

"What's going to happen with that now? She's your daughter, so that means you're going to have to see that bitch which I am not okay with."

"What do you want me to do?"

"First of all, I want you to fire her ass. Let her find another job, she doesn't need to be up under you all the time. Second of all, y'all need to figure out a schedule, we'll go pick your daughter up and you keep her for however long then you take her back home and go on about your business. I don't want you hanging around that bitch, I don't want you spending time with her none of that."

"So how am I going to handle that shit without you two getting into it? I don't want you fighting her ass."

"Oh, I'm sorry, that's going to happen, I don't like that bitch."

"Why can't you ignore her?"

"I'm not ignoring shit, she's disrespectful and she's up to no good. Come on now Que, you can't sit here and tell me you don't know why she told you about your daughter."

"What you mean?"

"She told you about that little girl to cause a problem between us. The bitch knows I don't like her, so she's probably thinking that your daughter would be a reason for me to leave you alone."

"That doesn't make sense to me."

"Oh my God, think about it. She tells you about your daughter six years later out of the clear blue sky. Then your sister who doesn't like me posts a picture of you with the bitch knowing a lot of people know me, and they know we're together. She knew I would find out about that shit; do you see where I'm getting at?"

Now that she explained it, I understood what she meant and that sounds like something Mia would plot. She's a sneaky ass bitch like that.

"I get it, I'll get all this shit handled alright. I won't be around the bitch like that."

"I'm going to be there when you fire her ass and y'all figure that schedule out."

"Hell no, I'm not about to have you fighting her. I don't feel like dealing with it, I'll have Tone and Yung with me when I talk to her. How about that?"

"Fine." She shook her head. "If the bitch tries something one of them better punch her ass."

"Mean ass. I'm mad you really threw my shit in the street."

"You should've called me back. You missed out on a nice ass Tom Ford jacket. I saw some man pick it up, at least he'll be warm and stylish."

"You fucked up for that," I chuckled then kissed her on the lips.

"I did get you some cufflinks, they're nice. I didn't throw that out, it's still in the house."

"Aww shit, I want it. Don't try and hold my shit hostage."

"Yeah aight we'll see," we both laughed.

"Your gift isn't ready yet. I can show you a picture of it though."

"You do? Let me see," I pulled my phone from my pocket and pulled up the picture of the 2017 Porsche Cayenne I bought her. It was supposed to be done yesterday but niggas decided to move slow, so her custom candy red paint job and customized interior wasn't done yet.

"Here," I gave her the phone and she damn near screamed.

"Oh my God! You got me a car? Stop fuckin' playing with me Que. For real, don't play with my emotions."

"I'm not playing, those niggas are moving slow, but it should be ready this week. In the meantime, I have this for you," I went in my pocket pulling out a long box.

"What is that?"

"Open it and see," I smirked.

Toi opened the box to see the nameplate necklace that had Legend scripted in diamonds. "A necklace with your name on it is my gift?" she asked with a laugh. "This would be some stupid shit from anybody else but you. I like this though, it's nice. Thank you."

"You're welcome. Merry Christmas baby."

"Merry Christmas," she gave me a perfect smile then a kiss.

"I need one thing from you though Toi."

"That would be?"

"When you meet Diamond, don't let the shit with her mother cloud your judgement about her."

"Que she's a child, your child at that. I'm not going to treat her a way because her mother is an idiot. I'm not that person, trust me on that."

"Thank you."

That went better than I thought it would go. I was expecting the complete worse, Toi comes off nice and innocent, but I know it's a crazy bitch inside of her waiting to bust out.

Taj

"*D*amn homie has a daughter? That's crazy, what kind of bitch doesn't tell a nigga she has his child? Sneaky ass hoe," I shook my head and told Toi as we walked around the shoe store. "So, what are you going to do?"

"Trust that he handles the situation like he's supposed to. I'm just mad I have to deal with this bitch in my fucking life now. I'm going to strangle her one of these days just wait for it."

"Well you know I got your bail money so call me when you get arrested," I chuckled.

"I will, so what's up with you and Yung?"

"We were good until…"

"Until what?"

"Well, I went through his phone right," I said, and she sucked her teeth before I could continue.

"Now why the hell would you do that? Taj you're not supposed to go looking for nothing you don't want to find."

"I know that, but I went through his phone because he told me to."

"What do you mean he told you to?"

"I was texting on mine and he started in about that. Wanting to know who I was talking to and wanting to see it, so I said fuck no. If you want to go through my phone let me go through yours. He said oh really? Aight take it go through my shit."

"Oh hell, what did you find?"

"This nigga and that baby mama of his," I shook my head. "This bitch was sending naked pictures to his phone."

"Wait how did you see that? Why wouldn't he delete it before giving you his phone?"

"He thinks his ass is slick, he has one of those apps that make his text messages disappear and look like something else. I know that shit because Darrell used to have that same fucking app and I cracked his."

"Don't you have to have a code for that shit?"

"His code for everything is one of three things, his birthday, his daughter's birthday or his mother's birthday so that was easy because I remember everything."

"Damn son, so what did you do? Was he responding?"

"Yeah, he responded, the messages said some shit like damn you really miss a nigga huh? Then he sent her a picture too. The part that really fucked him up was the nigga took the picture in my bathroom."

"Oh hell no. What did you do?"

"The fuck you think I did? I went off. I broke his phone, and I mean broke it into pieces. Then when he tried to touch me and tell me that you don't understand bullshit, I slapped the shit out of him. I split his lip a little bit when I did that. I was like a fucking crazy woman and he sat there like he was shocked. I'm like nigga if I can take a bat to my ex's brand-new car, the fuck makes you think I won't go off on you?"

When I went through Anthony's phone and saw those pictures, I was ready to kill him in all honesty. I don't like feeling or looking stupid. The fact that he was on my head about leaving my ex to be with him, just so he could turn around and do the same bullshit had me heated. If I wanted a friendly dick having nigga on my arm, I could've stayed with the muthafucka I've known for five years. I didn't get in a new relationship to deal with the same old bullshit.

"This happened on Christmas?" Toi questioned, and I nodded.

"I saw the messages Christmas night when we went back to my house."

"So, it was only three days ago. Have you spoken to him?"

"Yeah he came by my house before I came here to meet up with you dropping off flowers and money with that, I'm sorry bullshit niggas give out every time they get caught."

"What are you going to do?"

"I don't want to leave him off one fuck up, but I don't know just yet. I'm going to make his ass sweat I know that much."

"I'm here for that part, what is with these ex bitches? They can't let go for a damn thing."

"I know it's annoying as fuck to be honest. You don't see me here out sweatin' Darrell's bitch ass."

"Damn why I gotta be a bitch?" I heard a familiar voice from behind me. When I turned around and saw this nigga standing there, I rolled my eyes.

"Hell no," Toi said before laughing.

"Why the fuck is you behind me like a damn creep?" I asked him.

"I was walking past, and I saw you in here, so I came to speak, damn you still mad at me?"

"Darrell, get the hell out of my face."

"What? You mad your new man might find out we talking? Word is you were seeing that fool when we were still together. Is that true?' Darrell asked and I couldn't help but laugh. He was cheating our whole relationship but has the nerve to question me about it. Fuck is up with these niggas?

"That's your business how?" I crossed my arms over my chest.

"If we were together it is my business."

"You can get the fuck out of my face with this bullshit. It's not your business don't fucking worry about what the fuck is going on in my life. Go worry about Naja's fat ass since you felt the need to fuck her so much."

"You need to quit being a bitter bitch."

"I'm not bitter I just want you out my face. Call me a bitch again and watch I slap the shit out of you. Move the fuck on Darrell, good-bye." I mushed him out of my face and turned to walk away when I heard laughing on the side of me.

"So, he left this for that? Oh my God Yung is losing his fucking eye sight. He went tried to replace me with a basic ass bitch." I knew that loud, annoying ass voice from anywhere. Looking over at KeKe I couldn't help but laugh. I don't know why God is testing me today but he's about to be pissed because I'm going to fail terribly.

"I know your hoe ass did not just call me basic," I said once I stopped laughing.

"Yes, I called you basic, you're a basic ass bitch. Don't be sticking your nose into my business. My daughter doesn't have shit to do with you!" KeKe shouted, making people turn our way.

"Watch who the fuck you yelling at first of all. Second of all, don't get mad because he didn't believe that fake ass story you told him about your grandmother being in the hospital. As far as your daughter goes, she spent the night at my house while you were too busy getting drunk with your friends, you're welcome. Don't come at me crazy because you didn't take care of your responsibilities."

"Whatever bitch have your fun with my baby daddy now. You're lucky I'm loaning him to you because once I tell his ass to come back, he'll be back."

"Yeah aight we'll see. Keep talking hoe, I promise I'll take one of these shoes and beat the shit outta you with it. Keep going, please do." I was waiting for this broad to keep running her mouth so I could put my fist in. I already don't like her bald-headed ass.

"Taj let's just go, you're trying to fuck around and get arrested in this bitch." Toi grabbed my arm and started pulling me away.

"Listen to your friend ho, fuck with me and I'll send you to meet your maker. Yo ass will be sitting in hell right next to your dumb ass parents!" KeKe yelled. Shaking my head, I snatched away from Toi and turned around.

"Taj no!" Toi shouted just as I swung on this bitch. As soon as my punch landed, we were in a full-fledged fight. I know the cops were definitely going to come get my ass, but I really don't give a flying a fuck I'm killing this bitch.

Yung

"Why the fuck you're mad at me for this shit? I didn't make you fight that bitch," I questioned Taj as we walked into her house.

I had just picked her ass up and got her out of lock down. Apparently, she got into with Keyani at some store and fucked her ass up. I don't know what the fuck happened, all I know is she called me talking about she got arrested and to come bail her out because KeKe scary ass went and pressed charges.

"How the fuck is this shit my fault?" Instead of saying anything she turned around and slapped the shit out of me.

"It's your fault because you need to control that bitch! I shouldn't have to deal with bullshit like that. Her mouth is too fucking reckless. Did you tell her about my parents dying?"

"What?"

"Did you tell her about my parents dying? I know you heard me the first fucking time I said it."

"I don't fuckin' remember damn is it a big deal if I did?"

"Yes! There is no reason why y'all should sitting back talking about me. If it's not about you picking up or dropping your daughter off, contact shouldn't fucking be made. I don't talk about that bitch with you, so why the fuck are you discussing me with her?"

"You're making a big ass deal out of this shit, it's not that serious."

210

"It is that fucking serious. First, you're getting nudes from this bitch and sending pictures back. Now this bitch is running her mouth about the shit you told her about me. Are you still fucking that bitch?"

"Man go somewhere with this bullshit."

"No answer the question, are you still fucking that bitch? Be a man about yours and tell me you're still fucking that bitch so I can fuck you up and go right back to jail for killing you. Go ahead and tell me."

Shaking I ran my hand down my face and looked at her. "You did it didn't you?" When I didn't say anything, she slapped me again, but she didn't stop there the fucking hits kept coming. Taj is small but she packs a mean ass punch, her hits actually hurt. I grabbed both of her wrists and held them over her head. "GET THE FUCK OFF ME!"

"Chill the fuck out and quit slapping me!" Once I was sure that she was calm, I let her hands go and she pushed me away from her. I wanted to kick my own ass when I saw tears running down her face. "Look I fucked up, and I'm sorry. That shit is over with, I promise you that."

"Oh, you promise me? Really? You promise me. YOU FUCKING PROMISE ME?!" She sighed then started again. "Fuck that bullshit. If I didn't say something you would be going on with shit like nothing happened so, no you're not sorry. You're only saying it because I figured it the fuck out. When the fuck did you have time to fuck her? It had to be while I was at work since that bitch doesn't have a fucking job. That's it right?"

She chuckled darkly. "You fuck with her in the daytime when I'm not even checking up or for your ass because I'm stacking my own bread, then you come and get in the fucking bed with me at night," she shook her head then started laughing. To be honest that shit made her look crazier than what I already knew was, especially since she was still crying.

"I said sorry."

"FUCK YOUR SORRY ANTHONY!" She screamed then took a deep breath. "Get out of my house."

"No, you need to talk to me, we're not about to end this shit over a fuck up."'

"Nigga get the fuck out before I stab you in the fucking throat! I'm serious GET OUT!"

"I'm not leaving until we sit down and talk Taj."

Once again, she started laughing like she was crazy and walked down the hall. I don't know what the fuck she was doing, I just assumed she was going in the living room to sit down so I walked down the hall too. Just as I was about to turn into the living room, she came out of the kitchen holding a knife up.

"Get the fuck out or I'm cutting your black ass Lorena Bobbitt style," she said in a menacing tone. I backed up away from her with my hands up. She was really on some crazy shit.

"Taj chill!"

"Chill my ass get the fuck outta my house!" When I tell you, she looked like something out of a fucking movie. Her face was stained with mascara and tears and she held the knife up like she was dead ass serious about killing my ass.

"Aight I'm leaving! Put that shit down."

"I'll put it down as soon as you get the fuck out! GO!" She screamed again so I turned and ran straight out the door. I know I fucked up, but she just pulled a knife on me. She really is fucking crazy.

Toi

"So, what do you think?" I asked Mickey after I finished showing her around what would be my spa once everything was complete. So far, they were done with the elevators, stairs, building all the necessary walls, and fixing up the hallways. The electricity and water are running of course, but they still have a long way to go.

"I think you're going to shut shit down when you open this spot. Toi, this is going to be so nice when it's done. I heard you tell them you want purple, gold and white everything. Why?"

"You know purple is my favorite color so there's that. All the spas I've been to have too much white and light blue going on, I want to be different. The walls are going to get darker each floor. So, this floor color is going to be Lavender."

"Uh huh, and the second floor is going to be what?"

"Iris, third floor is going to be violet, fourth floor is mauve, and the fifth floor is eggplant."

"What are you going to have done here? It's full service, right?"

"Yeah, I wanted the top floors to be for the body-oriented stuff. So, if you're getting a massage, body scrub, body wraps or anything that you need to take your clothes off you'll go up to the fourth and fifth floor."

"You mean like a sauna?"

"Exactly, things like that are going to be on the fifth floor. Facials, makeup, eyebrow waxing and anything to do with the face are going to be on the third floor. Second floor is manicures, and pedicures. This area we're in now is the lobby, you wait to get taken to your treatments and stuff here. Then back there I want to have a wine and juice bar."

"You're serving liquor up in here?" she asked with a smile. Mickey's eyes lit up at the mention of something that could get her faded.

"I'm working on getting a license for it but nah, no liquor. Just wine and champagne, I'm not trying to have people in here too damn drunk."

"Damn I thought I was going to be getting turnt in here."

"You can but this ain't a damn club."

"Drunk people spend money. This is a good area, though. It's not too far from downtown so you know white people are going to take advantage. Give this city three years and it's going to be a complete suburb."

"Things are changing around here," I replied. Jersey City has always been diverse but over the last few years there have been way more melanin deficient people than I'm used to. They're building condominium and luxury apartment buildings all over the city. Most of the people that look like me can barely afford the rent their being charged. We're literally watching gentrification happen right before our eyes.

"It is what it is. Back to this place, I think you need to at least serve cocktails."

I laughed shaking my head. "No liquor, niggas better get a buzz off some wine and leave me alone. I'm going to have people taking orders on each floor. So, nobody will actually be coming in and sitting at a bar I think that's tacky."

"Well I think you're going to be making some good money in here because that shit sounds bomb. So, have you thought about a name?"

"Belle Melanine, it means beautiful melanin in French. I'll gladly collect white dollars but they're going to know this bitch is black owned. I got branding ideas and everything already cooked up. My permits will be coming soon, I'm ready to get the ball rolling."

"That's what's up. You're really about to do some big shit with this spa though I'm proud of you."

"Thank you," I smiled. "So, what are you going to get into besides school this upcoming fall?" When Mickey told me, she was going to go back to school for Fashion Merchandising I was so happy she finally decided to put her love for clothes and money into her focus.

"I hit a lick last night," Mickey said, and I looked at her confused. She caught me off guard with that shit.

"Wait what?"

"I got some money last night, twenty thousand dollars in cash and once I sell the jewelry it's going to be more. The nigga had at least three hundred thousand dollars-worth."

"Are you serious? Who the fuck did you hit?"

"Who he is, isn't important. He's not even from here so I'm good."

"How the fuck do you know that?"

"I've been planning this shit for a minute Toi. Do I look dumb to you?"

"Right now, yes, I thought you were going to stop Mickey?"

"I never said that. I said I was signing up for school, that doesn't mean I was going to stop making money but that was my last one for good this time. I'm going to try and sell his jewelry for at least two hundred thousand dollars. If I get that I won't have shit to worry about."

"What about Tone?"

"What about him? He doesn't have shit to do with this why is he being brought up?"

"He's your man Mickey, and I know how you work. If you hit that nigga that means you had to at least kiss his ass and let him touch you. You feel like that's alright to do when you already have a nigga?" Mickey is too damn smart to sound so slow.

It's one thing to still be robbing niggas but she uses her sexuality to get the shit done. That doesn't sound like a good idea when you have a man especially one like Tone. If he's anything like his friend, the mere thought of Mickey being close to another man will have him ready to break someone's neck.

"Oh please, I didn't do anything with that nigga and what is a kiss? Tone does more than that at the damn strip club, I needed the money Toi. You know my mother has been down my back about Myles. Now she's bugging me about money and how she needs more."

"I get that."

Mickey's mother is dead wrong with how she handles Mickey and her son. On one hand she likes to criticize Mickey for not doing enough but she won't give up custody either. She's made it no secret that she will fight Mickey to keep Myles. Without a legit job and proof that she can care for Myles the courts aren't going to just hand him back over to her.

"Why didn't you ask Tone to help you?" I asked her. Tone could easily help Mickey out as far as proof of a job and steady income.

"I don't like depending on a nigga. I don't like depending on anybody, that gives them power. I can take care of myself."

"Alright, but that's a lot of money. The bigger the bank the more dangerous he is. So, who did you hit?"

"That's not necessary to know okay, it's not going to be a problem. Trust me it's fine."

"Alright," I shook my head. "So, Tone doesn't know. Where does he think you were?"

"He was working last night so he didn't really ask me where I was. Enough about me, have you spoken to Taj?"

I sighed knowing she was only bringing Taj up so she wouldn't have to think about how wrong her ass is. "Yeah this morning, she's alright."

"Is she done with Yung? She was ignoring the fuck out of his life on New Year's."

"I know. He fucked up big time. I don't know what she's going to do. The only reason she came to the party was because I wanted her to since Que was throwing it. She was going to stay her ass right in the house."

Que had a huge New Year's Eve party at the Mansion and Taj

ignored Yung the entire night. You would think the nigga was invisible with how bad she curved him. That's just how Taj is. It's damn near hurtful how bad she ignores people when she doesn't fuck with them.

"Did she beat the bitch that damn bad?" Mickey asked and I gave her the 'duh' face. She knows how Taj is I don't know why she's asking.

"You know Taj is crazy," I chuckled. "She picked up a boot with a spike heel and hit the bitch in the face with it."

Taj is definitely a little bit crazy when she gets pushed to a certain point. It's pretty damn scary sometimes. She's the nicest person when you meet her, and she's small so you think she's normal but go ahead and get her ass mad. I promise you will see a side that will scare the complete shit out of you.

"Was her face really fucked up?"

"The bitch has a scar going from her ear to the middle of her cheek and the heel put a fuckin' hole in her forehead. You remember that show College Hill, when that girl got her shit fucked up with that shoe?"

"Hell yeah," Mickey started laughing. "That's fuckin' crazy, she really got her ass huh?"

"She did damage, I was like well damn."

"You didn't get into the fight?"

"Now you know I don't do that jumping shit and none her friends jumped in it. I think they knew better. The bitches looked shocked. I was like see, you push people thinking you're tough you don't know who the fuck you're dealing with. Then, she pulled a fucking knife on Yung, had that nigga fearing for his fucking life," I started laughing too hard after that. I damn near died when Que told me that shit. Yung called him damn near crying he was so scared.

"Tone told me about that. He was like, I can't picture Taj doing that shit she's too sweet. Too sweet my ass, she was about to cut that nigga. He said Yung was scared as hell, he didn't know what to do after that."

"That's his own fault, he shouldn't have done that shit. Are you coming out tonight?"

"What's going on tonight?"

"Birthday party for one of their friends, Tone didn't tell you about it?"

"He told me he was going out, but I didn't ask details. I probably will, I don't have shit else to do so why not. I'm about to go get my hair done though, this shit needs to be tamed."

"What are you getting done to it?"

"Long, black Mohawk but I might just wear it to the side tonight. After this I'm going blonde, watch."

"You're going to look like a high lighter. You're already bright as hell now you want to add blonde to it?"

"Shut up, I'm going to be cute," she chuckled. "I'll see you later on tonight though ma."

"Aight." We hugged then she walked out.

Once she was gone, I shook my head letting out a deep sigh. That girl and this money shit is going to get her ass caught up. I don't know who the fuck she hit to get three hundred thousand dollars in jewelry but that's a lot of fucking money and niggas don't let shit like that go too easy. I hope it doesn't come back to bite her straight in the ass.

Tone

*L*ooking at Yung I couldn't help but crack up. We were sitting in the barbershop getting lined up for the homie's birthday later on and I couldn't help but picture Taj's little ass pulling a knife on him. I found the shit to be hilarious. First of all, I thought Taj was too nice to pull some shit like that, but I should've known better if she's friends with Mickey's crazy ass. Second of all, that's what his dumb ass gets for fuckin' his bird ass baby mother.

KeKe doesn't do shit but live off that nigga. The only things that bitch has to offer is a headache and pussy that more than half the damn hood done had a sample of. Why the hell would you choose to fuck over a good girl like a Taj for a bitch who ain't worth nothing? Baby mother or not, that shit was stupid.

"Fuck is so funny?" He asked, looking over at me.

"Your stupid ass almost lost your life all over a damn dummy," I said with a laugh. "Man, you stupid as shit for fucking up with Taj. Especially over KeKe."

"The shit wasn't on purpose, none of that was supposed to happen."

"You didn't think your messy ass baby mama was going to let it slip that y'all was fucking?" Legend began to laugh. "Yeah you're dumber than I thought. You know your BM is messy why would you think she wasn't going to snitch?"

219

"Whatever man, it doesn't matter. If you two niggas feel the need to talk about it so much, why don't you tell me how to fix this shit."

"Depends on what you mean by fix it. If you grow the fuck up and talk to her like you got some sense you can probably get her to calm down when it comes to being around you. Now, if you're talking about getting her back, the only way that's happening is if she's stupid," I told him honestly. From the outside looking in, Taj would be a fuckin' idiot to get back with this nigga. Fuck all that caring about each other shit, he was deliberately sleeping with another woman.

"Why she gotta be stupid?" Yung looked as if he was offended but oh well. If he wanted somebody to pacify his ass, he came to the wrong damn person, I'm going to keep it real with his ass.

"Nigga you were purposely cheating. It ain't like it was some shit that just happened one time, you went into the situation with Taj knowing you were still fucking your baby mama. Go fuck that bitch while Taj at work then go and get in the bed with her later that night, that's some disrespectful shit. You did all of that knowing she just got out of a situation with a nigga that was doing the very same shit. Shorty would be a fuckin' fool to get back with your ass right now and that's just real," I explained to him.

"He's right, you knew what you were doing. If you go to Taj on some that was a mistake shit, she's going to try and slice your ass again because that's bullshit. Man up, tell her the truth. You took her for granted and was being selfish, if you can't do that leave her the fuck alone," Legend added in.

"I hear y'all man. I don't know about the leaving her alone part, but I hear the rest of that shit." Yung said and I chuckled. "Let's get the fuck out my business, look who about to walk in," he motioned towards the entrance. We looked out and I sucked my teeth when I saw this nigga Bless coming towards the door.

"This muthafucka here," Legend said before chuckling. When Bless walked in he had a smirk on his face. I sat up watching this nigga every move. Bless was known to be a slick nigga and I wanted to make sure this nigga wasn't catching anybody off guard. Plus, I needed to see this exchange between he and Legend without missing anything.

"This shit lookin' real nice my nigga," Bless said while he took a look around the shop.

"I know, what I don't know is why your ass is in here," Legend replied. "I thought you was down south somewhere since you couldn't get your shit moving around this way."

"I think you got your history a little fucked up, but it doesn't even matter. I'm up here for other reasons."

"Am I supposed to give a fuck about those reasons? Nigga you came in here for a reason, spit that shit out instead of talking in circles," Legend snapped at him.

"My cousin Scrappy has been missing for a couple of months now. I get up here to figure out what the fuck is going on and the fact that he worked for you came up."

"Aight so?"

"So, I'm asking you if you know where my cousin is."

"That's what you here for?" Legend laughed. "Good luck finding your cousin man."

"Was that supposed to count as an answer nigga?"

"You can take it however you want, you heard what I said. You can walk the fuck out my spot or you can get removed. It's really up to you," Legend warned him and every nigga that was on our team stood up. Looking around Bless realized he was outnumbered, and a small smile came to his face.

"Same ole Legend, it's aight I'm out," Bless said before walking out the door.

I looked over at Legend. "You know that nigga about to try some shit, right?"

"Of course, he is. I'm not worried about his ass, he can try me and get his life cut short if he wants to. It really doesn't matter to me," Legend answered me.

I shook my head knowing this was about to be some shit. Bless and Legend have a long history, they actually grew up and came in the game together. When it came time for Legend to really be the head of this shit, Bless thought he could do whatever the fuck he wanted because they were best friends. With anybody else Bless's dumb ass would be dead because of the bullshit he tried to do. Legend decided to let the nigga live as long as he got the fuck out of Jersey. Now he's back and he's about to pull some stupid shit because of his thieving ass cousin.

"That nigga is still salty as shit obviously," Yung pointed out.

"That's his business," Legend shrugged. "Fuck him, let's just focus on the turn up tonight. I'll deal with bitch niggas tomorrow."

I WALKED into my bedroom where Mickey was standing in front of the mirror looking at her reflection. The way the black jumpsuit she was wearing hugged her curves, had me ready to bend her over and say fuck the club. "That ass though!" I shouted making her jump.

"You scared the shit out of me, don't do that," Mickey laughed.

"My bad ma, you look good though. You just bought that?"

"Yes, I just bought it."

"Where you get that? Rainbows or some shit?"

"Don't play with me," she began to laugh. "This is a Karl Lagerfeld Karl X Kaia Jersey Cat suit nigga. I don't so Rainbows get that shit straight. Now, do you like it or is my ass in it too much?"

"Nah you good, if you were doing too much, I would've told you to change."

"So, I'm good? Put me on your Instagram then."

"What is that supposed to be hard or something?"

"I've seen your comments, bitches are on you my nigga."

"I know you've seen my comments, you like commenting on that shit too. You like having your ass on there arguing with bitches like you're not the one getting this dick all the time. Come on let me take your picture."

"Take it when we're about to leave."

"Well if you're done, we can leave, you take long as fuck."

"I'm done I didn't know if you were ready. Alright come on." She grabbed her things and we headed out. When we got in the hallway, I made her stop so I could take her picture. After I was done, I posted the shit on Instagram.

"I wanna see that shit when we get in the car," she said after putting her coat on.

"That's fine with me." We went down to my car and got in. Once we were in the car, she took my phone from my hand.

"Damn can I unlock my shit first?" I took it back then put the code in before showing her the picture I took.

"Ooh I like that picture, I look good as fuck."

"Feel proud?" I laughed.

"Shut up I'm just saying."

Once we arrived at the club, I grabbed her hand as we walked across the street. It was packed as fuck out here and I knew all of that was for Case's party. This nigga knows damn near everybody in the state of New York, he's not limited to one borough. I slapped hands with the bouncer when I walked in and he moved the rope so we could go in.

The inside was crazier than outside for sure, I wasn't surprised. When this nigga throws a party it's definitely on some movie shit, that's why I already planned to be drunk as hell by the time I leave this bitch.

"I see Que and Toi over there!" Mickey shouted in my ear. I nodded and walked over to where they were and took a seat next to Legend while Mickey chopped it up with her girl.

"Bruh I care about my girl, but God damn I wish I was single for one night. Do you see these bitches walking around?" Legend said in my ear making me laugh. He was right though, It's January and cold as fuck in Jersey but bitches in here walking around damn near naked, like somehow the cold was going to stop because their thot asses wanted to party.

I grabbed a bottle of Henny and drank from that while I watched Mickey dance with Toi and have a good time. Sometimes I look at her wondering how the hell I ended up with her. Mickey is a lot to deal with, but I accept it because I'm not easy my damn self. The only thing I wanted her to do was get out of whatever the hell it is she's doing to get money. She thinks I don't know but I pay attention to everything she does.

Last night she didn't call me at all which is not like her, if she's not calling me about where I am or worrying, she's texting me. The only time she doesn't do that is when she's right there with me so the fact that I didn't hear from her at all told me all I needed to know.

I wanted to be mad at it, but everybody has to have a hustle. I know for a fact she's not selling pussy and she's not dumb enough to cheat so I'm not even too worried about it. I will find out what the fuck it is she's doing at some point.

After being in a club for an hour I was definitely feelin' myself at this point, the Henny I indulged had me feeling good. I looked at Mickey and laughed when I saw the Ace of Spades bottle in her hands, so I pulled out my phone and took another picture of her drinking from it, putting it on Instagram.

After I posted it, I grabbed her arm and pulled her close to me. I was about to drag her ass into the bathroom but the birthday boy Case, finally popping his ass up caught my attention. When he came over to me, we slapped hands and gave each other a brief hug.

"What's up nigga? You good?" He asked me after we separated.

"I'm aight, what about you?"

"Oh, you know I can't complain about shit as long as my money is getting made. So, who is this?" He asked pointing at Mickey.

"This is my girl Mickey, Mickey this is Case." They shook hands then he looked at me. "So, you and that nigga Legend both got women now? I see y'all trying to be on some other shit. I wanna be like y'all when I grow up," he joked.

"Shut up nigga, where that dumb ass partner of yours?" As soon as I said that this country ass nigga Tip walked up.

"What's up bruh?" We slapped hands then I introduced him to Mickey. He held out his hand for her to shake but she didn't shake it. All she did was smile a little bit then look off. The fuck is that about? "Damn you got a mean one. It's cool though it's too many women in here for me to be hurt," Tip said before walking off. Once he was gone, I pulled Mickey to the side.

"You good?" I asked her and she nodded.

"Yeah I'm fine, I just need to go to the bathroom really quick," Mickey answered.

"Are you sure?"

"Yeah Tone I'm good, I'll be right back." She kissed me on the cheek then walked off.

When she got to where Toi and Legend were, she grabbed Toi's arm and pulled her towards the bathroom. I don't know what the fuck that was about, but I'll find out.

Mickey

"*W*hat the hell is wrong with you? Why you just drag me in here?" Toi asked me while I paced back and forth in the bathroom.

"That's him!"

"That's who? What are you talking about?" She looked at me like I was losing my mind. I know I looked crazy as shit pacing around this bathroom, but my nerves were going crazy. Standing still wasn't an option right now.

"Tip! The nigga I hit last night, he's in here." When that nigga walked up and spoke to Tone I damn near passed out. Tip is a nigga I met long before I met Tone and I've been setting this shit up for a while now. He was supposed to be on a flight back to Atlanta this morning.

"Are you fucking serious? I thought he wasn't from here?"

"He's not he said he was supposed to be going back down to Atlanta this morning he must've changed his trip or something. That's not the worst part though Toi, he knows Tone."

"Wait what?"

"He knows Tone, are you deaf? You're not hearing me? He just introduced me to the nigga?"

"Did he recognize you?"

"If he did, he didn't say anything, I doubt if he did though. It's dark out there and I have these shades on. This shit can't be happening right now."

"I told you this shit was going to catch up with your ass, but no Mickey knows all right?" Toi shook her head laughing at me.

"This shit ain't funny," I snapped at her. Even though she was right I didn't feel like hearing that shit right now.

"It's not but this is low key entertaining. Look, you said he didn't recognize you right? Just tell Tone you're ready to go and get out of here."

"He's not ready to leave yet though and he's really having a good time." Tone was having way too much to leave now. Shit, I was having fun my damn self before Tip popped up.

"Alright listen. keep your shades on and stay away from him. What did you have on when you saw him?"

"A long blonde wig and makeup out the ass, I looked like a damn clown."

"Good then he shouldn't recognize you. Here," she handed me her drink. "Drink that and calm down. Oh, and if you pull me away from my nigga again, I'm going to hurt you."

"Whatever, go get his ass I'll be out in a minute." When she walked out, I downed the liquor that was in her cup then took a deep breath. Toi was right he's not going to recognize me, so I need to stop losing it. I'll be good.

I made sure I looked alright then walked out of the bathroom. Before I could go back out to the floor I was pulled back into the hallway by arm and pushed up against the wall. When I saw Tip standing in front of me, I wanted to suck my teeth, but I couldn't give myself a way.

"What's up baby girl?" He smirked at me.

"What's good?" I said back.

"I know you didn't think you weren't going to ever see me again."

"The fuck you talking about?"

"I'm talking about you. You think I'm fucking stupid? Your hair color is different, but I recognize that ass anywhere. You got me last night, didn't you?" *FUCK!* I thought to myself. This nigga really recognized me? I'm slippin' or something.

"Look I don't know what the fuck you're talking about but maybe you're drunk and losing your mind," I said still playing dumb. There is no way in the highest fuck I'm admitting anything, I'm not stupid. "You need to back the fuck up before Tone comes over here."

"You think I'm scared of that nigga? Think again baby girl, besides what will he say when he finds out he's with a thieving ass bitch!" He snapped getting closer to my face.

Okay I know nine times out of ten this nigga is probably strapped but if he doesn't move, I'm swinging. I watched my mother get her ass beat for years, then turned around and dealt with it too. If a man gets too close to me in an aggressive way, I automatically go into defense mode. When I get like that, I prepare myself to fight because now I feel like I have to defend myself.

"You really need to back up! I don't know what the fuck you're talking about!" I shouted back at him.

"STOP FUCKING LYING TO ME!" He grabbed my arms and slammed against the wall. On instinct I snatched my arm out of his grip and socked him right in the face. Before he could really recover and grab me, I punched him two more times, then slammed my knee into his balls and kicked him away from me.

"DON'T YOU EVER PUT YOUR FUCKING HANDS ON ME NIGGA YOU LOST YOUR FUCKING MIND!" I screamed while I kicked him in side. Usually I would take my heels off but fuck it, this nigga wanted to be tough I'm going to stomp his ass with these bitches on. I paid a grip for these Saint Laurent ankle boots, I might as well let them turn into a weapon.

I don't know how long I was kicking his ass in that hallway. All I do know is the nigga was on the floor tore the fuck up and I didn't stop until I felt myself being pulled away, but that shit didn't really do anything but make it worse. So, into the zone I turned around and swung on whoever was grabbing me the fuck up. When I realized I hit a bouncer I wanted to laugh just because he was mad as hell standing there with a bloody lip. Oh well don't fucking touch me.

He wiped some of the blood from his mouth then came to grab me again, but I grabbed a bottle off the bar since he pulled towards the shit and knocked him upside the head with it. "DON'T FUCKING TOUCH ME!" I shouted. I didn't mean for things to get that far but I don't like anybody walking up on me, especially a man.

I'm guessing Tone saw all the shit going on because next thing I know he was in front of me. "The fuck are you doing?"

"He touched me! I don't like being touched, ask that nigga in the fucking hallway and y'all will see. I'M NOT THE ONE TO FUCK WITH!" He shook his head and grabbed my arm and pulled me outside the club all the while I was yelling and shit. I was on ten at this point, both of those grown ass men touching me the way they did, had me heated. "Let me go Tone!" I yelled at him once we got outside.

Stopping in his tracks, Tone turned around facing me. "Fuck no, you in there swinging on niggas like you the same thing as them! Do you know I will kill a nigga if he put his fuckin' hands on you? You in there doing dumb shit in public like you want me to catch a fucking case!" He snapped at me.

"THEY CAME AT ME I DIDN'T EVEN DO SHIT!"

"WATCH WHO THE FUCK YOU YELLING AT MICHELLE!" He screamed in my face making me shut up instantly. If he was saying my government name like that he was definitely pissed off. "You on some bullshit! Go to the fucking car man." He grabbed my shit from Toi who came outside with my stuff in her hand after us.

"They touched me I didn't even do anything wrong!"

"Did I ask you for a fucking explanation? Get yo ass in the fucking car!" Tone shouted again. I sucked my teeth and walked across the street and got in the car.

He was really pissed the fuck off. I've never seen him that damn mad. I am not looking forward to going back to his house. I'm about to get an earful and it was going to be more than annoying.

Tone

$\mathcal{L}$ ooking at Mickey sit on the bed looking through her phone like shit didn't go left tonight was pissing me the fuck off. I know what type of woman I'm with so I'm not shocked that she would pop off on two grown ass men. I just need to know what the fuck happened and she's not telling me everything.

All she said on the way back here was that Tip grabbed her, but she didn't tell me what led up to that. I've known that nigga for a few years and I know he's not about to just grab her ass up for no reason especially knowing she's my woman. It's more to the story.

"Mickey, you're really pissing me off. You're on some bullshit right now," I said, finally getting her attention.

"What are you talking about Tone? Why are you the one with the attitude? I didn't touch you tonight and I didn't scream in your face like you did me, so I'm confused on why the fuck you're even mad."

"I'm mad because I know you lying, do I look fuckin' dumb to you? I've known that nigga for ten plus years ma, I've never seen him put his hands on a female period so for him to put hands on you after knowing you're with me you had to do something so tell me what the fuck is up."

"You need to be concerned with your boy and why the fuck he touched me, I'm getting screamed at because I can defend myself and I whooped his ass? Go handle that nigga then talk to me," she snapped at me. I had to look at her like she was fucking stupid because right now she sounded like a damn dummy.

"I don't know who the fuck you think you talking to like that, but that attitude needs to leave your fuckin' voice right now. Watch how the fuck you talk to me ma, I'm not playing with you."

Sighing, she ran her hands down her face and got off my bed. "You're really blowing my shit right now," she said while going into my closet.

"How the fuck am I blowing your shit? You're the reason my night got fucked up but I'm blowing your shit. Are you fucking stupid or something? I really think something is wrong with your fucking brain."

When she came back out, she had on one of my shirts and a pair of sweatpants. "You're blowing my shit because you coming at me over that nigga, like it's my fault."

"I know that nigga Mickey, he's not going to touch you like that for no fucking reason so what the fuck happened? Stop being a little ass girl and quit lying all the fucking time."

"I'M NOT LYING TO YOU!"

"YOU ARE FUCKING LYING! I CAN SEE THAT SHIT ALL ON YOUR FACE! WHAT THE FUCK HAPPENED?! WHY THE FUCK HE TOUCH YOU LIKE THAT?""

"GO ASK THAT NIGGA SINCE YOU WANNA KNOW SO FUCKING BAD!"

"YOU THINK THAT NIGGA IS BREATHING AFTER THAT SHIT? YOU'RE NOT THAT FUCKING SIMPLE! I HANDLED THAT SITUATION ALREADY! HIS DEATH CERTIFICATE WAS ALREADY SIGNED BEFORE WE LEFT THAT MUTHAFUCKA! NOW, I'M HANDLING MY WOMAN WHAT THE FUCK HAPPENED?!"

Shaking her head, she started laughing. It wasn't a regular laugh either, the shit sounded like an evil cackle. "You want know what the fuck happened Antonio? Alright I'm going to tell you. I robbed him, I robbed his ass last fucking night. I got ten thousand dollars in cash and three hundred thousand dollars in jewelry from his ass. He recognized me so he got in my face and I beat the fuck out of him! Is that what you wanted to fucking hear?"

I sat there with the fucking dumb face on. I know this bitch didn't just say she robbed him. The fuck? "The fuck you mean you robbed him? How the fuck did you do that?"

"It's what I do, that's how I get money. I pick a nigga and I take him for all I can when the time comes. There, you wanted to know what happened and why your boy came at me. You know now, you wanted to know how I got my money. Happy?" She rolled her eyes and grabbed her keys off my dresser then left while I just sat there thinking about what the fuck she just said.

Toi

I tightened my towel around my body as I ran out the bathroom and over to my phone that had been ringing for the last ten minutes. I couldn't even take a bath in peace without people fucking with me.

When I grabbed my phone, it has just started ringing again and of course it was Mickey calling. I wasn't even surprised just because I knew she and Tone got into it when they left.

Sucking my teeth, I answered the phone and put it to my ear. "Mickey, I was in the tub washing my ass what the hell are you calling me like you're crazy for?" I said to her as soon as we were connected.

"Tone just irritated the fuck out of me, and I needed to talk to you."

"Well, where are you?"

"I just walked into my house. I left his, he pissed me off."

"Damn son, but this couldn't wait until tomorrow?" I chuckled.

"No bitch it could not, we're probably over."

"The fuck? How are y'all over after a stupid ass fight that really didn't have much to do with him?"

"It's way more than that."

"What happened?"

"I tol-" Just as she started to talk my attention went to somebody banging on the door like they were the fucking police. "What the hell is that?" Mickey questioned.

"Somebody is banging on my door." I walked out of the bedroom and towards the door. "Who is it?"

"Que open the door!" he shouted from the other side of the door.

"Mickey let me call you back Que at the door on some stupid shit, nigga left his damn key again." Before she could say anything, I hung up and opened the door. When I did this nigga pushed past me and stormed inside.

"Well damn rudeness excuse you," I closed my door then faced him and for whatever reason this nigga had the screw face on. He was looking at me like I stole his damn cookies. "The fuck is wrong with you?"

"You got something you want to tell me?"

"No, am I supposed to have something to tell you?" I crossed my arms over my chest. When he dropped me off to go handle whatever he needed to for Tone we were fine. Now he's I here acting like I'm up to something.

"Yeah like where the fuck you were last night?"

"I was at my grandmother's house last night, remember you called me while I was over there. Why you acting so weird. What the hell is going on?"

"Don't lie to me alright, where the fuck were you?"

"I was at my grandmother's house, I'm not lying to you." I was completely confused as to why I was getting accused of lying. I was literally at my grandma's house last night. She greased my damn scalp for me and everything.

"So, you weren't with Mickey while she was robbing that nigga Tip?"

Damnit Mickey. That's what she called to tell me before this nigga came banging like the paw patrol. She must've told Tone and of course he went telling Que.

"What are you talking about?" I played dumb. I don't care what Tone told him I'm not saying shit about what she did. That's between them, Que and I don't have shit to do with it.

"Don't play dumb Toi, that's your best friend so I know you either knew about it or your stupid ass was right there with her ass."

"I'm not stupid so cut that shit out. I didn't know about it until yesterday afternoon when she was going. No, I was not there so I don't know where the fuck you got that idea from."

"So, you used to rob niggas too huh? Don't try and lie to me about this shit, you and Mickey did whatever the fuck it is y'all did together."

"Alright, you need to calm down and listen." He was getting too damn reckless with his mouth for me. I understand the anger and wanting answers, but he doesn't have to be disrespectful to get it.

"I don't need to listen to shit! What the fuck are you doing with me? Trying to figure out a way to get my money and go ghost?!"

"What? No! Que you don't get it alright, and you need to listen before you go making assumptions about shit!"

"I'm not making assumptions! I'm telling the fucking truth, is that not what you do? You pick a nigga get close to him and once you get close enough you take them for everything you can! ARE YOU TRYING TO ROB ME?!" He shouted in my face.

"NO! Would you shut the fuck up and listen to me!" I shouted back. If he wanted to get loud, I can get loud too. I'm not backing down from him. He needs to calm down and actually listen to me.

"THE FUCK IS THERE TO LISTEN TO? ALL THAT BULLSHIT YOU GAVE ME ABOUT KEEPING SHIT FROM YOU AND YOU NEVER TOLD ME YOU WERE THEIVING ASS BITCH! WERE SELLING YOUR PUSSY TOO?"

"Fuck you! You can kiss the blackest part of my ass with that. No, I don't sell my pussy I'll leave that up to your thot ass sister, that's not my style. I don't need to fuck for a damn thing. You were dropping millions before you even got a taste of this pussy let's not fuckin' forget. Yes, I took a couple of stacks and some jewelry from a couple of niggas so my bills could be paid, and my family wouldn't have to want for anything. So, the fuck what?"

"It wasn't your shit to take the fuck you mean so what?"

"Oh, so you're judging? That's real funny coming from you Que. You kill your own, you push a hell of a lot of weight into your own community and I'm the problem? I'm not hurting anybody. Niggas blow ten stacks in the strip club or on a chain but me taking it to pay my bills is such a big fucking deal? Miss me with that bullshit! You can't judge anything I fucking do when you're ten times worse than me."

"Whatever Toi, I don't give a fuck about what you talking about. The point is you're a scheming ass bitch!" He screamed and my hand went across his face so hard his lip started bleeding.

"I let all that other shit you said slide but you're not going to keep disrespecting me! You can be mad all you want to, but nigga don't do that!"

He clenched his jaw then shook his head. "Get the fuck out."

"Excuse me what?"

"You heard me, get the fuck out my spot!"

"You really lost your fucking mind," I shook my head.

"I'm dead ass serious. You can either get out or I'm putting you the fuck out. You think I'm going to let you steal from me? You really fucked up in the head if you think that."

Looking at him I couldn't help but laugh. I had to laugh because this was some funny shit. "You know what? I'll go. I never begged or needed a nigga for shit before you and I'll be good after you." I walked to the bedroom and got dressed in a sweat suit then grabbed my purse and car keys before walking back out.

"You can mail my shit to me," I said while I walked to the door. I opened it then turned back around, "Oh and Quentin fuck you." I pushed over the expensive ass vase he had on a stand right by the door then walked out as soon as it shattered against the floor.

After I got in my car I drove around for a little while trying to figure out where I was going to go. I started to go by Mickey's house, but I knew I would have to talk about this shit there and I really didn't feel like doing that. All I wanted to do right now was lay down and go to sleep so I headed over to my grandmother's house.

When I pulled up to the house I got confused when I saw the ambulance and a police car parked in front. I tried to figure out what the fuck might've been going on until I saw my mother and the twins standing on the front steps. If they were fine that means something had to be going on with my grandmother, so I hopped out of the car and ran over. A cop tried to block me, but I pushed him to the side and went over to them.

All three of them had tears going down their faces so I knew this couldn't be good. "What's going on?"

"Toi we've been trying to call you," my mother said with tears going down her face.

"I didn't even get the chance to look through my phone. I was dealing with some bullshit. What's going on what happened?"

"I was getting ready to go to bed, so I went in the room to check on mama and tell her good night. When I got in there, she was saying she couldn't breathe and I tried giving her, her medicine but it didn't work so I called 911."

"Well is she alright? Where is she?"

"They're about to bring her down," my mother answered with her voice cracking a little bit. I tried swallowing the lump that was forming in my throat while tears burned the back of my eyes.

"You're not answering my question, is she alright?"

"No," she shook her head. Just then Jayla hugged me around my waist. "She's gone Toi." Immediately after she said those words the tears, I had been fighting to hold back came falling down my face while a gut-wrenching scream left my mouth. I could probably wake the whole damn neighborhood with how loud I was screaming but I really didn't care at this point.

My mother pulled me into her just as my knees buckled. I guess I was too heavy for her because we both ended up sitting on the steps. My head was on chest while I cried my eyes out.

How could this even be going on right now? I literally just saw her last night and spoke to her this morning First the situation with Que now I get home and I find out the worst thing that could ever happen in life, is actually happening.

My grandmother literally means everything to me. She's the most important person in my life and she was gone. She was the only person keeping me going when I had nobody else. What am I supposed to do now that she's gone? Who am I living for?

Toi

Sighing, I kicked off my shoes, took the black hat off my head and shades off my eyes then sat back on the couch rethinking on the fact that I just got done burying my grandmother. Today was literally the hardest day of my damn life.

I really didn't expect much from my mother at all just because I knew for a fact it was tough on her. Imagine going through half your life being a disappointment to your mother then as soon as you get that relationship back together and you're connecting with her again you lose her.

She stepped up and helped me plan everything for the funeral, including being strong enough to sing during the service. I made it a point to send my grandmother out like the queen she was. I made sure the church was covered in white roses and purple orchids. Two huge pictures of her were placed on both sides of her all white and gold casket. I didn't want her in the back of some dingy ass hearse, so I got a horse drawn funeral coach.

As bad I as I didn't want to say goodbye to her and as much as it hurt me, I felt a weird sense a relief when they lowered her casket. I knew she wouldn't be down here stressing about anything anymore, she was finally at peace. I think that's what kept me from going insane.

I was grateful to know that my friends, were really my friends and they were here for me through everything. Mickey actually stayed here and slept in the damn bed with me every single night. Taj stayed with me a couple of nights. Even Yung and Tone came to the funeral to show their respects. The only person that didn't show up, didn't call, didn't text, this nigga couldn't even send me a Facebook message, was Que and to be honest I was disgusted by that.

I don't give a fuck how mad at me you get, it's common fucking courtesy to send your condolences. I don't wanna hear shit about him not knowing when both of his best friends not only knew, they showed up to the funeral. It'll be a cold day in hell before I'm even respectful to that nigga again.

"Are you alright?" Mickey asked me after she sat down next to me.

"Yeah, I'm fine, I'm just tired of being upset. I want to be happy and it's like it's not happening for me. It's bullshit after bullshit. The only thing I have keeping me cool right now is my spa, and that's still up in the air because of Que."

"He can't take your business from you Toi."

"Yes, he can, he wrote the check he paid for everything if he wants to knock that fucking building down, he can do it and I won't be able to do a fucking thing about it."

"Do you think he'll go that far? He can't be that damn mad over something that has nothing to do with him."

"Mickey, he put me out of the apartment. He didn't even show up to my grandmother's funeral and she treated that muthafucka like a son. He sat in her house at her table eating her food smiling in her face like he cared, and he didn't even call me to say I'm sorry about her, are you alright? Nothing, I haven't heard anything from him. I've been with him for this long and he's going to act like that shit doesn't mean anything over something I used to do? FUCK HIM! I hope his ass dies tomorrow."

"Toi really?"

"Yes really, I'm dead ass serious I hope his ass catches a fucking bullet to the brain."

"You need to relax. Where is your mother and twins?"

"They're all upstairs, my mother said she wanted to go lay down." I shrugged my shoulders just as the doorbell rang. "Can you get that?"

"Yeah I got it." She got up and went to the door to answer it. Just as I was about to lie across the couch Mickey calling my name stopped me.

"Toi!"

"What?"

"Come here, somebody is here to see you."

I sucked my teeth and walked to the front door. When I saw Que standing there, I rolled my eyes. "The fuck do you want?"

"Look I just came by here to tell you I'm sorry about your grand-mother. I know you're about to say it's too late but I really am. I wanted to give you and your mother these." He held out two bouquets of roses, one red and one white.

"Quentin get the fuck from away from my door. You can keep those flowers, matter of fact you can take them and shove them right up your ass."

"Toi," Mickey said my name in a tone that told me she wanted me to calm down but fuck that right now.

"That's how you feel? After all I did for you?" He asked.

"Oh, please do not come at me with that. I didn't ask you to do shit for me you offered it, and because I'm smart, I said yes. I turned my whole fucking life around for you. I was there for you, when your bitch ass got locked up, I bailed you out. I didn't leave you alone by your muthafuckin' self when you found out you had a daughter. I didn't beat the complete life out of your sister even though I can dead that bitch with my eyes closed. All of that was because I cared about you, but you can't reciprocate that."

"I bought you a whole fucking business, that's not telling you I care?"

"What is money to you Que? You have millions of it, you have businesses all over the fucking state. Your mother lives in a fucking mansion for God's sake. That shit was nothing but you throwing your wallet at me so that when you did something fucked up, I would just swallow it. I can't swallow this."

"Swallow what?"

"My grandmother died nine days ago! Nine days! It took you nine days to get over here to say something? You sat in this house smiling in her face telling her you loved her, and it takes you nine days. Even if you came over just on some friendly shit, I would've respected you for that. You know how much she meant to me. I buried her today and you weren't even here why? Because I was out here getting money in a way you don't approve of before I met you?"

"It's not like that, I'm sorry I never came by here. That was my fuck up and I'm trying to make it right."

"You can't make it right. Even your friends came to the funeral and you couldn't? Get out of my face before I really get mad."

"Toi just listen alright, I'm not trying to put any more stress on you. I'll do anything you want me to do."

"Fine, you know what you can do? You can go to your lawyer and tell him you want out of my spa because this whole silent partner thing is not going to work. I'm not here for it or you. Do that, and maybe I won't hate you."

"Is that what you want?"

"Yes, that's what I want."

"Fine, it's done. Just take the flowers please." He held them out to me again, so I took them." Que turned around to walk down my steps but stopped and looked at me. "I really am sorry about your grand-mother. I know you loved her more than anybody else and I'm sorry I wasn't here for you." He turned to walk again but I called his name. When he looked at me, I chuckled a little bit.

"You really need to sit down and evaluate how you treat people. You can't buy people shit and expect that to be a reason you just do whatever it is you want with their feelings. You don't care about anybody but your fucking self and excuse me while I say fuck you. Fuck your bitch ass sister, fuck your baby mama. Fuck your whole entire existence as a whole to be honest. Now, you can get the fuck off my porch." I went in the house and slammed the door. I started to go back in the living room, but Mickey grabbed my arm then hugged me.

The tears just started flowing while she held on to me. I'm so sick of the dramatics and this crying shit, I can't take any more hits after this.

Taj

"*D*amn how much are you going to eat?" Anthony asked me when I told the waiter to bring me another order of cheese fries.

I hadn't eaten all day, so I was going to go in now if I wanted to. Toi didn't want to have a repast after her grandmother's funeral and neither did her mother. They didn't feel like having a bunch of people over the house and have to hear condolences all damn day. I don't blame her for it all, she was dealing with enough.

"I'll eat whatever the hell I want to eat thank you very much," I replied. "Why are you even in here with me? My telling you where I was going wasn't an invitation for you to come."

"I just wanted to make sure you were good, I know today was stressful."

"You think?" The funeral was a lot, mostly due to the heart-breaking cries from Toi and her cousins. I was still a little bothered by everything, but I will be alright. I made it through both of my parents' funeral, so I'll make it through this one too. "I'm just worried about Toi."

"I've never seen anybody cry like that before, that shit was hard to watch."

"They were really close, and she was a good woman, it's just sad."

"True." He nodded then went back to eating his food. After a while he looked up at me. "So how are you feeling? I mean physically."

"I'm good, I told you that this morning."

"Are you going to keep giving me an attitude when I speak to you?"

"What else is there to give to you Anthony? I barely respect you, so I don't know what you expect. Stop acting like you give a fuck."

"I do, you're carrying my child why the fuck wouldn't I care?" I had to roll my eyes and bite my tongue, I was about to say something so rude.

I was pissed off I was pregnant by this fucking idiot. Having a child by Anthony was not my plan, I never wanted kids, but here I am pregnant and it's by him. I wanted this fool out of my life for good but not enough to have an abortion. I really have no reason to have one. I can take care of my child, I'm not struggling and my hate for him isn't that strong. He's lucky I'm not one of these evil bitches.

"That does not mean you have to be all up in my face, shouldn't you be laid up with your other baby mama?"

"You need to let that go."

"No, I don't, go be with the bitch. That's who you fucked up our relationship for you might as well go ahead and make that shit work."

"I'm trying to make it work with you. How many times do I have to tell you I'm sorry? I keep saying the shit and you just brush me off. I don't know what you want from me Taj," Anthony shook his head and had the nerve to sigh like he was stressed out.

"You can say sorry until you're blue in the face I really don't give a fuck. Do you want to know why?"

"Why?"

"I can't do a muthafuckin' thing with a sorry, that ain't shit. Is sorry going to make the shit hurt less? Is it going to stop me from picturing that shit in my head? I have to walk around this city while everybody knows my nigga was sleeping with another bitch once again." After the fight at the mall KeKe went running her mouth on social media so the fact that she was this nigga's side bitch was public knowledge. "I dealt with that shit before I'm not dealing with it again. You knew what the fuck you were doing, even down to sending the bitch dick pics you took in my damn bathroom. Fuck your sorry nigga. You want to throw that dick around to everybody, go ahead and do you. I'm not about to be out here looking fuckin' stupid behind you so this shit is a wrap."

"You care too much about what people think," he said, and it took everything in me to not reach over this table and slap him. I just said all that and he comes back with I care about what people think? I swear to God I can't stand this nigga.

"Did anything I said stick in your head or are you just that damn dumb? Fuck your sorry Anthony. Stop giving them to me because none of it means shit. You fucked us up by cheating on me, don't try and make it seem like I'm overreacting. Fuck you and fuck that bitch too. You're lucky I'm not evil because I would've said fuck Naima too."

"Don't stretch it."

"Nigga fuck you." I waved him off then started eating my food when the waiter brought it to me.

"So, what do you want me to do Taj?"

"Leave me alone, if something goes on with the baby, I'll let you know. Until then stay the hell out of my face. That's what you can do."

"Seriously?"

"I'm dead serious. Just so you won't have shit to text or call me about I'm six weeks so far, my next appointment is in three weeks I'll let you know the date if you want to come. Now can you please, leave me alone?"

"Alright, I'll leave you alone." He got up and put some money down on the table then kissed me on the cheek before leaving.

Mickey

I looked down at Toi to make sure she was still asleep before I got up and walked outside to the front porch where Tone was waiting. I zipped my coat up then looked at him.

"So how is she doing?" He asked me.

"She's asleep right now, but she's doing alright. Better than a couple of days ago."

"That's good, so what did you want to talk about?"

"Us, I'm not really the one to be in limbo. Either we're going to move past this and be together or we're not. Which one is it?"

"You're the one that fucked up, but you got the nerve to be trying to dictate shit? Yo, are you fuckin' serious right now Mick?"

"How did I fuck up?"

"Don't play dumb. You know how you fucked us up."

"I really don't, what I do or did has nothing to do with you. I was doing this shit years before I even knew you existed," I shrugged.

The way Que and Tone reacted to my situation is uncalled for if you ask me. It's not the best way to make money but it's not like their occupation is that simple. We don't judge them for that shit so why are we being judged?"

"That's true but I got to thinking about that shit. In order to get close to a nigga you would have to be up under his ass a little bit. So that means you were sneaking around with that nigga behind my back were you not?"

"It's not like I ever did anything with him. I don't sleep with any of the niggas I deal with"

"So what? That doesn't make it better baby girl. It was still some bullshit in my opinion."

"Well that's your opinion Tone, I can't do anything about the way you think. I'm just trying to figure out where we're going from here."

"I don't see the point in being with somebody I don't trust."

"So now you don't trust me? Have you and Que been talking and comparing notes? You think I'm going to rob you or some shit?"

"Nah, I know too much about you just like he knows too much about Toi for her to rob him. I just don't like the way you move, so it makes no sense for us to be together."

"So, you're breaking up with me is what you're saying."

"I feel like that's what's best for both of us right now."

"Alright," I nodded my head. "I don't agree with you but if this is what you want, we're over."

He nodded then grabbed my arm and pulled me into him. "You're better than what you do. You have the potential to be great. You're bigger than robbing and sticking niggas up. Use your brain and not your body ma," he said in my ear then kissed me on the cheek and let me go. "Take care of yourself." When he started walking down the stairs I went back into the house and sat on the steps for a little bit.

When I felt tears going down my face I hurried up and wiped them away. I never cried for a nigga I'm not about to start now. If he wants us to be over because of the way I make money when I don't judge his, that's on him.

My name is Mollysha Johnson and I'm from Jersey City, New Jersey. Growing up language arts/english has always been my best subject. I've always loved reading and writing. Once I got my hands on my first urban fiction novel I was hooked to the genre. I admire and look up to authors like Wahida Clark, Keisha Ervin, Danielle Santiago and many more.

Writing is how I express my creativity and I love putting my all into it.

STAY CONNECTED:

Email: mollyshaj92@gmail.com

 facebook.com/MollyshaJohnson

instagram.com/mollysha92

ALSO BY MOLLYSHA JOHNSON

Let A Real Boss Treat You Right (2 Book Series)

Royalty Publishing House is now accepting manuscripts from aspiring or experienced urban romance authors!

WHAT MAY PLACE YOU ABOVE THE REST:

Heroes who are the ultimate book bae: strong-willed, maybe a little rough around the edges but willing to risk it all for the woman he loves.

Heroines who are the ultimate match: the girl next door type, not perfect - has her faults but is still a decent person. One who is willing to risk it all for the man she loves.

The rest is up to you! Just be creative, think out of the box, keep it sexy and intriguing!

If you'd like to join the Royal family, send us the first 15K words (60 pages) of your completed manuscript to submissions@royaltypublish-inghouse.com

LIKE OUR PAGE!

Be sure to <u>LIKE</u> our Royalty Publishing House page on Facebook!

CPSIA information can be obtained
at www.ICGtesting.com
Printed in the USA
LVHW031620220219
608477LV00003B/310/P